Inside Laird of the Game

"*Send me an angel,*" he silently pleaded with the ancient Celtic Gods.

Laird Alexander G. MacKenna had a sixth sense when it came to routing out their enemy. The shrill battle cry of the MacKenna Clan echoed down the shoreline as the meanest, most despicable warriors that walked the earth descended on the Prince. Swords clanged — horses battled as the two powerful forces met in fierce combat!

"Bloody hell!" Alexander took a second look at the lovely lady stranded in the midst of the battle. His Angel had been delivered, but to the wrong army!

What would you do if Heaven put an Angel in your arms? Hang on, with everything you have!

Melissa Johnson's an American tourist. Her vacation in Scotland becomes a magical romp as she believes she has stepped through time. She suddenly must face life as it was in the eighteenth century – without speed dial to her favorite deli, or a blow dryer. Her manicure is a wreck, and her choice of clothing causes riots among the warriors. Through the mists of time he claimed her, and she surrenders her heart to the handsome Celtic Laird.

Alexander will risk it all. Hearts will break, battles will be won and lost, but only one man can claim title to...

Laird of the Game

Lori Leigh

What Reviewers Are Saying About Laird of the Game

Ms Leigh has once again held me spellbound. I loved the Highlander theme with all its lusty yet deeply emotional connections between not just the main characters, but some of the minor ones as well. Ms Leigh writes a well-crafted story that draws her reader in and manages to bring laughter to the fore, even in the midst of danger. **~Coffeetime Romance**

Lori Leigh has crafted a distinctive tale that is sure to please. LAIRD OF THE GAME will make you laugh and leave you with a twinkle in your eye. This semi-comic romp contains a warm hearted romance and is sure to make you sigh. I will certainly be reading more of Ms. Leigh's charming work. **~Romance Junkies**

Laird of the Game

Lori Leigh

Vintage Romance Publishing

Goose Creek, South Carolina

www.vrpublishing.com

Lori Leigh

Laird of the Game

ISBN: *0-9785368-4-3*

PUBLISHED BY VINTAGE ROMANCE PUBLISHING, LLC

www.vrpublishing.com

Laird of the Game

For Gerard Butler
My Liege, my Laird, my luv…
And, the Ladies of the Laird

Where the river runs under the trees
That's where you'll find me
In joy's embrace gazing, lovingly
There the rapture shines through the lace
Of summer's brow, hold me now

Where the heart runs wild and free
That's where you'll love me
In ecstasy's dance singing, happily
There the moment is ever a chance
Of lover's sigh, in the night

Where the beauty fades into the years
That's when you'll need me
To dry all your tears loving, laughter
There in splendor love is sweet surrender
Of moments bide, by your side

Where the moon fills sun and thee
That's where you'll lay me
On bended knee smiling, softly
Where the river runs under the trees
Of glory's passed
Home at last

Lori Leigh

Chapter One
A time to remember…

The Celtic Warrior Game in the Highlands of Scotland has begun.

The Bookies in London are having a heyday. The favorite again is the handsome Laird MacKenna; however, Prince George promised a startling upset and vowed to win the Celtic Warrior Game this year.

Alexander G. MacKenna is Laird of the Game. He's as cocky as ever and has assured his stockholders victory, as usual. The MacKenna boys are always a favorite with the ladies and will be sorely missed during the month long game.

On the Streets with Rosabel

The echo of a hundred mounted warriors thundered over the glens of Scotland. Long before the tourists that lined the country road on the edge of the *Balquhidder* caught sight of the magnificent warriors, they heard the rumble of hooves crossing the heat-baked earth and stone. The cheers rose as the Laird crested the hill on his black stallion.

The fearless warhorse reared up on his hind legs and then descended into the valley. The warriors followed their Laird in precise formation that dazzled the tourists in a spectacle of living history. The tourists that lined the road cheered them on to victory.

"Has anyone seen Melissa? Where has she gone off to now?" The Tourist Guide rounded up her group and they boarded the bus.

"Come along, ladies, we still have much to do and see. We can't wait any longer and must stay on schedule to see it all."

"She'll find her way back," the ladies commented. "She went looking for the site where they filmed *Reign of Fire*. There's an old castle on the map."

"Didn't they film that in Ireland?"

"Can we also fit in a stop for Ewan McGregor and Ioin Gruffund?"

"Did you see the warrior on that horse? Oh, Lord, wasn't he handsome!"

"There was a warrior on that magnificent Friesian?"

"Isn't this where Mel Gibson filmed *Braveheart*?" One of her charges sighed in awe.

"Tonight, we're going to one of Gerard Butler's favorite pubs in Glasgow, and then tomorrow we will be standing on the same hilltop that Liam Neeson filmed *Rob Roy*."

"Wonderful!" The group clapped in appreciation!

"It's a pity Melissa will miss it all." The Tour Guide shook her head, and started the engine.

***

Alexander called a halt on the ridge and surveyed the horizon along the rocky coastline for any sign of their enemy, Prince George. The powerful Laird's mouth was set in a determined line, and his eyes narrowed against brilliant morning sunshine. He breathed deeply the scents of horseflesh and leather. A fine spray of salty ocean wafted over him, and long-forgotten childhood memories flooded back to mingle with the mist. It was time to remember their heritage and set aside the modern-day world.

As a child Alex had watched his father stand on this ridge. He was a powerful man, formidable, but tenderhearted when it came to Lily, his wife and mother to his seven sons. As the eldest son, Alex had become the Laird and stood alone as the Chief for the MacKenna Clan, but the mantle of power weighed as heavily as the ancient sword sheathed at his side.

Alex was brooding again, as his younger brothers called the dark moods that would send him into a whirlwind of long days at his office and few hours of fun and pleasure. They were there to relax and enjoy their summer away from boardrooms. Alex let out a long sigh and focused his attention on the horizon.

It was 1745 once again, and he was a Celtic warrior!

Alexander fought a ferocious battle on his eighteenth birthday and claimed the title, Laird of the Celtic Warrior Game that their ancestor, Baron Girard Jolbert, had begun centuries ago. It was a heritage that put not only a vast fortune into their hands but also the problems that came from being young, wealthy, and handsome. His younger brothers had nearly driven him mad!

Every summer they revisited their Celtic heritage of ancient battles and mighty warriors. Modern day twenty-first century weapons were not allowed in battle. They fought on horseback, as their ancestors fought with their feet, hands, and their intuition. They wore the red and blue plaid tartan Kilt, white saffron shirt, and black riding boots that had become their signature. Eighteen years had passed, and Alex had yet to be defeated. Victory for Laird MacKenna was inevitable. Alexander MacKenna was Laird of the Game, and with his six brothers beside him, he was invincible.

Waves whooshed onto the rocky shore in frothy cream and liquid emeralds. Alex respected the power behind the waves that curled into a fist and smashed boulders into pebbles. He flexed his fingers instinctively, and rested on the hilt of the ancient sword at his side.

The tip of a feather disappeared into the clouds. The morning mist lingered in wispy apparitions of warriors long gone, and dewdrops glistened on the grassy slope in a fairy treasure of sparkling jewels that would soon evaporate in the heat of a July afternoon. His movements were deathly silent and graceful from years of training. The peace and quiet that surrounded him was a ruse that alarmed his instincts. A gentle breeze crackled with intensity, and he felt a tingle on the back of his neck. It was as if the ancient Celtic Gods were anxious that something mysterious was about to happen.

War had been declared on Prince George, and the enemy was within their reach. Alexander studied every move the Prince made for eighteen years. His cousin, Prince George, had promised a surprise. Alex stepped into the role of Laird of his domain. George had talked about retiring from the game and returning to his nightlife in London with Niki, his glamorous lady that he adored. Alex knew every move he would make before George gave the order. It had become almost disappointing and far too predictable. Alex wanted a challenge; there was no thrill in conquest when winning came too easily. It had come time for both Alex and George to retire and pass the honors of victory on to younger challengers.

As if reading his thoughts, his black Friesian stallion snorted a hot, steamy disapproval for the long wait and shook his handsome head. The long hair that surrounded the hooves defined the distinctive breed.

"Soon, Yorath," Alex quietly comforted his horse with a calming hand. The name meant *Handsome Lord* and was appropriate for the magnificent warhorse. Emily, one of his many lady friends, had named the horse when he was still a young colt. The horse was formidable in battle, and just his presence would make the warriors shudder in fear.

Well over a hundred heavily armed warriors waited for the command to attack. It was an adventure of a lifetime. Gideon, Alex's younger brother and their doctor, had assured him that every warrior was physically fit and ready for battle.

Their instruction included several months of training on horseback under the strict supervision of Rebecca, their Master Horsewoman. The warriors lovingly called her their Rebel. It was a nickname Daniel MacKenna, Alexander's younger brother, had given her when she offered to knock him in the nose for falling off his horse and trying her patience.

Daniel was in love with her. It was a well-kept secret that everyone in the world knew, except Rebecca. They had known her since she was a child, and her father had trained their horses. When he retired, Rebecca continued the family business and trained their warriors. To the MacKenna's she was the sister they never had, and they all loved her.

She had a crush on Alexander since she was fourteen years old; but Alex was well aware of her affection and Daniel's secret obsession for her, so Alex kept his distance. Daniel adored her from afar, hoping some day she might look his way. His younger brothers just snickered and suggested he get her into bed.

The warriors all forgot about her striking, crystal blue eyes as she taught them about English saddles, bits, and bridles. They couldn't remember her perfect alabaster skin as they rode until their backsides ached and their hands were blistered from the reins. They griped about her methods, but when Rebecca was done training them, they could direct the horse with their legs so their hands were free to hold a shield and sword and not fall on their bum.

If the warriors fell from their horse, she worked them harder. If they complained, they got a fifty-mile jaunt on horseback. She had no mercy for whiners, no tolerance for insubordination, and never let Alex down. It was pass-fail, and if Rebel failed a rider, Alex respected her decision and wouldn't allow the warrior into the game.

As one exhausted, bruised, limping warrior put it, "If Rebel wasn't so beautiful, I'd throw her off a cliff."

Of all the riders she had trained, Daniel remained her biggest challenge. He preferred his horse power in the size of automobile engines and even though she tried her best to teach him how to ride, he was obstinate and seemed to forget everything she taught him.

Alex sighed again. Daniel wanted her attention and knew very well how to ride a horse. He was a fool in love, and Alex admired his determination.

Where have all the years gone to? His thoughts drifted in sentimental daydreams.

The first battle of the season was at hand. Over a thousand warriors had applied for the month long reality game but only five hundred could be selected to participate. The Laird and the Prince each had 250 men and a year to plan their battles before they would meet in the Highlands. The warriors were chosen on their physical abilities, loyalty, and dedication.

Alex demanded perfection from the men who were from every walk of life worldwide. They would be rewarded handsomely. The winners would take home £10,000 for the month and the losers would get £1,000. There was a vast fortune at stake – thousands of pounds were bet with the Bookies in London, and Alex was certain this year he would win.

His gaze roamed the horizon, but his mind was filled with the ramifications of his decisions. He knew in his heart if he didn't make the necessary changes now, he'd never get the life he wanted. Part of his soul didn't want anything to change.

Alex longed for a cup of Starbuck's coffee and a copy of the London Times. It was difficult to give up their fast-paced, 21st century lifestyle for a month. Other than an emergency helicopter that would take an injured man to hospital, they rode on horseback and didn't have electricity at the cottage. Most of his warriors slept on the ground covered with a tartan just as their ancestors did centuries ago. He didn't mind not having his comfortable feather bed, but he sorely missed his favorite coffee shop.

The warriors were restless, shifting in their saddles. They had trained hard under the tutelage of a Master Swordswoman, Agotha, for a year to earn the right to sit in a saddle beside their champion, Laird MacKenna. Her world was rigid as steel, and her insults could cut a man down as easily as she could slice off his leg. Lethal, non-lethal, and killing zones were drilled into their heads until they could execute the moves in their sleep. The warriors were given scimitar swords for Florentine style fighting. Since this was a game, serious injury to their opponent meant immediate forfeiture. They fought for points, not a body count. Agotha made certain the warriors knew the limits. Injuries were not uncommon, but it took strong leadership to keep the warriors from skipping over that edge to inflict mortal blows.

She explained the rules while they challenged each other inside the lists. They watched in rapt fascination as she demonstrated how to swing a blade and block an incoming blow. Their swords were deadly and could cut right through the gorget around their throats.

The warriors worshiped the gorgeous brunette and never dared to call her by Agotha, her legal name. She was nicknamed VixenBlade, reincarnation of Scathach, the Warrioress from the *Isle of Skye* who trained the Gods how to fight.

They were half-crazy in love with her but it was Robert, Alex's third brother, who stole her heart. If any warrior extended his admiration past her litany of rules and regulations, they faced an angry Robert MacKenna.

Robert had heard a warrior commenting on her luscious bum, and Robert had sent him flying into a thicket of thorns.

"She's mine, ye ken?"

The warrior had spent the next day in Gideon's hospital tent picking thorns out of his bum.

They all ken'd, quickly.

When Robert entered the lists to fight, he bowed to Alex and then dropped on one knee in front of Agotha, kissed her hand, and asked her permission to strike her in battle.

The warriors were equipped with armor for the game with both knee and elbow cops; however, most of the warriors chose not to wear the bulky gear to enable maneuverability while on horseback. Their Laird and Prince George both carried ancient Claymores, which were swords carried by their ancestors and much heavier. The curved design of the scimitars was reminiscent of the days when Attila the Hun ruled over a vast region of the known world.

The Prince had arrived that morning and formally issued the challenge that was accepted by Alexander. The warriors stepped back into a time gone by and became legends from the past. They were expected to speak Gaelic and live as warriors lived.

There were no modern conveniences during the game, and they were not allowed to leave once the challenge had been accepted, unless it was a dire medical or a personal emergency. Contact with their modern day world was strictly forbidden. Breaking the rules meant forfeiture to the Prince. Once the game began, they were honor bound to remain inside the perimeter during the entire month of July. Any man absent from the game for more than a day had to be disqualified. Only one man was allowed to bring the points to be tallied.

Alex discouraged the warriors from speaking to the curious tourists who lined the roads surrounding the *Balquhidder*. The press hounded them for quotes, and Alex remained silent during the game. He warned his men to keep their opinions about the outcome to themselves. To disobey meant possible humiliation for the entire Clan if they were misquoted.

Send me an Angel, Alex silently pleaded with the Celtic Gods, and then frowned, unnerved that his most secret desire had suddenly surfaced in his daydreams.

The wind suddenly changed direction again and brought a mist from the shore. Thunder growled a warning in the distance.

The memory of his father haunted him. He was a mighty warrior and descendent of a French Baron that had escaped the revolution. Alex's father had played the bagpipes to announce their victory, and the memory filled Alex with sentimental foolishness.

It was good to be in Scotland again. The scent of the Highland heather that permeated the air around him always made Alex feel lonely. *Aye*, he thought sadly. The years were melting away. He had sacrificed so much to his duty and his position that he no longer felt anything. He had raised his brothers and built a fortune so they would never need to go hungry.

His father had died that summer eighteen years ago after a lethal heart attack on the battlefield. Alex let out a long sigh. His mother had delivered William, their seventh child, that day when she heard the news. The doctors had awakened Alexander that night and told him she had passed away. The grief of losing her husband had been too much for their beautiful mother. He looked into her eyes when he looked into the mirror.

Alex had dropped out of his first term at University and assumed responsibility for his brothers. He had become a Champion in the Celtic Warrior Game and a father figure to his six younger brothers all in one day. He revisited his grief at the beginning of the game every year and brought flowers to the ancestors' graves at the Kirk. The inscription on the stone crypt read: *Tugaim mo chroi dult go deo, I give my heart to you forever.* He wanted the kind of love they had shared and had found only heartbreak and disappointment.

For eighteen years Alex had devoted himself to raising his brothers and managing their business interests. He was finally ready to settle down and start a family of his own. It was time he took care of the demons that haunted his past. It seemed like an eternity had passed since he had time to consider his personal life.

Work filled the days, but he longed for the scent of a loving woman to fill his nights. His frown deepened when he realized he would need a miracle to find love in the arms of an Angel. He had more money than he could spend in a lifetime, more power than one man should hold, and no one to come home to at the end of the day.

Only one, he asked silently and raised his eyes heavenward. *You can spare one little Angel.*

The time had finally come when he would pass the honor of Laird of the Celtic Warrior Game on to one of his six brothers. He reviewed the mental checklist once again to assure the choice wouldn't be changed. Next in line was Gideon, but he had one year of his internship left to complete before he could open his medical practice. His next hope was Daniel, but he was their Barrister and already too busy to accept any additional duties. Robert handled all their building and demolition. The twins, Iain and Evan, were in law school and wouldn't be finished for another year. That left William who had just turned eighteen. William was reckless, but he wouldn't be alone. William was the best choice.

The direction his life would now take was still a mystery to him. Alex never had time to explore other options. The Celtic Warrior Game had been played every year since his birth and Alex had made a fortune on his personal business interests as well as for his brothers.

The press hounded their every move and had called them wealthy international playboys with a lusty desire for lovely ladies. Discretion for the MacKenna boys was learned from being implicated in numerous, scandalous liaisons. For Alex, it meant he protected his younger brothers from the world that would prey upon them. The thoughts reminded him that his brother, Iain, had another paternity suit pending; it was a good thing Daniel was a fine Barrister. William still had to be protected from the paparazzi and educated at University in Glasgow. Alex wanted time to search his soul for what he would do with his life. The game had consumed him, and he wanted something more.

Alex wanted to love and to be loved.

A shadow crossing the meadow flickered in the corner of his eyes, and Laird Alexander G. MacKenna's attention was pulled back to the matter at hand. He had a sixth sense when it came to routing out their enemy.

He mounted the fearsome black, Friesian stallion and whispered the command. "Prepare for battle." Silent hand signals directed the warriors mounted on horseback to their positions. The surprise attack would catch the Prince and his army off-guard, set them on the defense — and on the run!

They moved silently to the ridge, tensed as the enemy came into view, and quietly drew their swords in bloodthirsty anticipation.

***

Melissa had wandered away from the tour group and explored for over an hour along the craggy shoreline, glens, and hills of Scotland.

She was enchanted with the ancient castles, but loved the people who were the heart of this lovely country, and thought maybe the legendary Rob Roy may have walked this way three hundred years ago.

It wasn't the first time she had wandered off and failed to return. The guide had already scolded her once when she got lost in search of the Loch Ness monster.

The gentle afternoon breeze picked up long strands of her hair and tickled her nose. "This is so beautiful."

A wave caught the hemline of her blue and white dress but she didn't mind. A warm afternoon sun would dry out her new dress in no time, she thought, happy with the purchase from a lovely shop in Glasgow. It fit her like it was hand-made for her petite form.

Melissa still had time to get back to the group. She had planned to spend some time painting, and this was a lovely location. Her bare feet left wet tracks along the rocky shoreline.

A roll of thunder followed a brilliant streak of lightening. The hair on her arms prickled with the intensity, and mist from the shore engulfed her and then quickly evaporated.

The sounds of sea gulls calling in the distance and the ageless motion of the sea turned her thoughts to her most important issue. The wonderful man she dreamed about just didn't exist and she had to accept the inevitable; she was lonely with a seagull for company.

Mist rolled in from the ocean, swirled around her, and then cleared. She felt dizzy, but it passed quickly, and her feet were solidly under her again.

Thunder rolled in the distance and pulled her attention to the horizon. Ferocious looking men on horseback galloped down the shoreline toward her. She stood motionless and her throat tightened in a strangled scream. The trilled battle cry of another clan echoed down the shoreline as what instantly appeared the meanest, most fearsome warriors that ever walked the earth, descended on Melissa.

She clamped her hands over her ears to dull the deafening roar of shouted commands. The warriors rode toward them shrieking and screaming. Somehow, she had stumbled into a clan war and they would surely kill her for trespassing.

It was as if she had stepped back in time. Without a sword she couldn't fight them, and surrender seemed a frightening option to men who bared their teeth and screamed as if the *Banshee* was on their heels. Melissa didn't think they'd quiet down to hear her politely ask if anyone had a cell phone hidden under their kilt, or a VISA card to order lunch while they negotiated terms of torture and incarceration. Perhaps she didn't have enough caffeine this morning, and this was all an illusion of withdrawal from her coffee crazed mind?

Ancient Celtic, sword-wielding, warriors with their faces painted in vivid blue and red streaks surrounded her. She heard tales about the legendary Fae that wandered the hills, but these men were far from a fairytale. They were very real and terrifying.

Chapter Two

Melissa was at their mercy.

But this was modern day Scotland, not 1745! Tourists were encouraged to visit the local establishments but also warned not to wander off or they would encounter the Highlanders. The tour guide had warned Melissa several times; the consequences were dire for being caught on private property. The bus had disappeared from view, and she was alone.

Their leader had to be a Celtic God. He looked magical, as if he had stepped out of the pages of Celtic lore as he held his sword aloft in a challenge.

Melissa was certain she *had* stepped back in time as hundreds of ancient warriors surrounded her. The legends were just stories told beside their campfires that you could take a step the wrong way and get captured by the Fae or ancient Fenian warriors. *It's just a myth*, she silently prayed.

The clang of swords echoed around her. A man's body dropped unconscious at her feet. Mythological or not, the blood coming from his mouth was crimson red and very real. She let loose a high-pitched, ear-splitting scream that would have awakened the ancient Gods.

Yorath reared at the high-pitched scream.

"Bloody hell," Alexander took a second look at the lovely lady stranded in the midst of the battle. His Angel had been delivered — but to the wrong army!

The Prince fought his way toward her, certain he would claim her.

Alex would get to her first. He directed his warriors to break the circle and send her toward him. He had every intention of claiming this pretty token of war for his own.

Melissa bumped into one of the warriors and turned. The opening was only for a moment, but she took that opportunity to jump over a fallen man and run toward the ridge. Her bare feet were bleeding within seconds, cut on sharp rocks as she made her way up the slope. Her foot slammed into a branch of thorns and she screamed again.

Moments later she was airborne, lifted by a strong arm that caught her around her waist, and she landed in front of a powerful warrior. His steed hadn't slowed down as she was plucked off the ground.

Alex felt the tiny lass shiver and fought the fury to beat the Prince senseless just for scaring her. He would find his answers after he had her under his protection.

"You are mine!" He yelled in Gaelic over the sound of battle in her ear. He quickly draped his red and blue tartan plaid over her shoulder. The black horse thundered up to the ridge. Melissa was dropped to the ground. She moved out of the way as the battle continued right in front of her. Her head spun, and she was close to collapsing from sheer terror as the two warriors met in combat. Even their horses battled, biting and rearing. She was mesmerized by the magnificent black stallion. The warrior who had picked her up— protected her, the thought that he had saved her— mingled with fear. Her hero was agile with a strong arm to wield the heavy Claymore sword.

The wind changed direction and blew dust into her eyes. Alex yelled at his brother, Evan, to protect his prize during the battle. Evan rode to her side and held his sword up ready to fight anyone who would challenge the Laird's claim to the woman.

Time and again their powerful Claymore swords clashed. Everywhere she looked there were warriors in the midst of battle. There were clouds of dust from a hundred horses galloping past that blurred her vision. Ferocious warriors blocked any hope of escape.

If she weren't looking directly at an ancient warrior, she would never have believed that she had stepped back in time. "This isn't happening— it's not possible."

Alex decided to end the battle quickly and brought his sword down heavily one last time against the Price. He saw her pale, and the look of shock that made his heart race.

"Evan! See tae the lady," Alex yelled. He saw her reach out to steady her world.

The warriors moved in slow motion. Pins and needles prickled against her skin as Melissa reached out, grasping at anything to support herself and then gracefully fainted.

Evan caught her before she hit the rocks. He gently laid her down and guarded her.

"I found her first," the Prince challenged.

"She has already been claimed," Alex roared with fury and landed a mighty blow. "The victory and the points are mine!"

The Prince conceded with an ominous growl of "revenge!" The Prince's men were pressed back to the shore. He rode off to regroup his warriors.

Alex commanded his warriors to follow the Prince.

Evan followed his Laird's orders and remained at her side. "I think she's coming around."

Alex dismounted and tossed his helmet and gloves onto the saddle.

Melissa groaned, dazed and confused. There were men shouting in the distance and horses thundering past her. She remembered she was in the middle of a war, had dropped to the cold hard ground, and wondered if she had been mortally wounded. She opened her eyes and forgot about being half-dead in a war with ancient savage warriors wielding swords. A rider dismounted and sheathed his sword.

He stood there sweaty and dusty, and she thought him to be the most handsome male specimen she had ever seen. Even from a distance, his striking gaze made her breath catch from a flash of tenderness veiled under long dark lashes.

Did she actually see him wink at her or was it a trick of sunlight? The straight line of his nose was reminiscent of the aristocracy and, oh that sensuous mouth! He had to be sprinkled with fairy dust and stars glittered in the heavens to herald the moment he graced the earth. He had to be descended from the ancients and graceful as a willow branch, yet broad shouldered, tall, lean, and stunningly elegant.

He moved his head and thick wavy hair cascaded down his powerful neck and graced his shoulders. She wanted to run her fingers through his long, dark-as-midnight hair and then continue to slide her fingers over that broad, muscled chest. Dangerous, wild, and exciting all at the same time, he defined desire when he moved, muscled thighs in ripcords of strength.

Yet, he had total control of his masculine, smooth body and walked with an arrogant swagger that exuded confidence and announced to the world that he was master of his domain and defeat was crushed into oblivion.

"My God, what a beautiful horse," Melissa said breathlessly. Her soft moan had nothing to do with an injury.

Alex looked over his shoulder at Yorath and frowned. The horse had followed him and appeared to be peeking over his shoulder at her as she lay on the ground. It was humiliating to see the powerful stallion act like a lovesick puppy, and he hoped the warriors didn't notice, or he'd never hear the end of it.

Too stunned to move, she sighed dreamily when he bent his magnificent head down and nuzzled her hand. Instinctively, she reached out to touch him. The dark as-a-raven's-wing horse touched her hand with his soft-as-velvet mouth. She was certain he was a Prince who wanted to kiss her hand in greeting.

Alex crouched down next to the lady to check for injuries and touched her cheek to confirm that she was alive and breathing. Sunlight cast a halo on golden blonde curls. Mesmerized, he sifted the silky strands through his fingers. He touched her bottom lip with his thumb and noticed a slight cut. There were thorns embedded in her foot that would need medical attention, and several buttons of her dress had come undone to reveal rounded breasts under a lacy slip.

Alex had to push Yorath aside to continue his examination of the lady. The stallion stood guard over her as if he had to protect her and snorted warnings at anyone who approached. Alex yelled instructions to the stallion that sulkily moved away from the woman.

Melissa finally noticed the shouting warrior in front of her. He wore a kilt and a white saffron shirt. And then she noticed the most penetrating, piercing jade eyes imaginable. To her horror, he was staring right at her.

Alex lifted her head and gently held the back of her neck in the palm of his hand. Her astonishingly beautiful blue eyes made time and space cease to exist. His mind drifted in that sea of blue and violet that rose and fell in endless motion. It brought images to his mind of their island in the Caribbean, *the Isle of Mor. A man could get lost in her magic,* he thought.

"Are ye my Angel?" He asked in Gaelic.

Melissa shook her head. "I don't understand what you said." She hoped he understood her. "I've never seen a horse like that. He's beautiful."

Alex frowned. Well, at least she liked his horse.

Her mind couldn't accept the possibility that she had stepped back in time. Yet, an ancient warrior was right in front of her. Melissa carefully asked her next question.

"Are you one of the legendary Fenian warriors?"

Alex had to bite his lip or he'd laugh. Her American accent had taken him completely by surprise. "Why certainly, I am. And are ye one of the mystical Merpeople?" he teased in reply.

He seemed very interested in the delicate buttons on her dress that had wrapped up around her thighs and exposed the length of her bare legs.

"Who were those barbarians? I had no idea the clans in Scotland were still at war."

She had to be joking. It was the twenty-first century not medieval times, and the clans had not made war on each other for over a hundred years.

"Who are you?" she softly whispered.

"Alexander." The stern edge of his voice hid his mirth. "Wha' are ye doing in the middle of a battle? I just stole ye from the Prince, and he's goin' tae ha'e tae steal ye back. Dinna fash yourself. He willna find ye."

Melissa shook her head. "I don't understand you. Are you the Prince of the Fenian?" she asked again enunciating slowly and hoped he understood her.

He looked at her carefully. "Are ye daft?" Perhaps she was wounded worse than he thought.

Melissa groaned. Prince and Alexander were the only two words she could make out of the Highland burr in his voice. She wasn't certain, but she also thought he was looking for a raft to find the Merpeople.

"I'm lost."

This woman looked dazed and confused, not at all like a sultry spy for the Prince.

"Wha' is yer name, lass?"

His Scottish accent fell over her senses and wrapped her in ancient fairy magic.

"What is my name?" It had to be true what they said about meeting one of the Fae. The man crouched down next to her was ruggedly handsome and beautiful.

"Do ye ha'e a name?" he teased, and his lips curled in a soft grin. "Or should I just call ye my Angel?"

Shouting warriors surrounded them, and yet she saw nothing but the light in his eyes. She suddenly felt embarrassed at her reaction to him. He took her arm and helped her stand. Melissa discovered how badly her feet hurt when she stood on the embedded thorns.

Alex noticed that she was still very shaky and quickly lifted her into his arms. He stood still, awed at the gentle beauty in his arms. Her hair fell away from her face, and he noticed long silken lashes that framed her sensual blue eyes. She had to feel the strange sensation, too, because he was certain that a lightening bolt had just struck him.

The warriors who rode with their Laird were witness to his claim. But what Alex would do with his prize still mystified him. He couldn't seem to look away or put her down. At the moment, all he could think about was the enticing curve of her mouth. Alex bent down until their lips were a heartbeat apart. She gasped as his intention became apparent. Perhaps she really was an Angel or just adorably daft.

The quirky, charming smile of his dimpled his left cheek. Perhaps he was the Prince of the Fenian warriors or just the sexiest man she had ever met.

"Prince Alexander, it's lovely to meet you."

So she felt the magic between them, too, he knew when he bent his head to kiss her. Their lips met, and she wrapped him in her enchantment. He caressed and claimed her hot, sweet lips.

Alex advanced to taste and explored this exciting new world. His tongue pressed deeper into that warm luscious sanctuary and his hold on her instinctively tightened. His eyes closed, the sensations racing through his body ignited a smoldering passion.

Her arm around his back pulled him closer. His lips tormented hers, and he bit her tenderly, causing a moan in the back of her throat. He lifted his head, to let her catch her breath.

Her hand wound around his neck. The velvet soft caress of his kiss awakened something deep inside her that delighted and intrigued her senses until it became a tantalizing ache deep inside her belly that curled her toes. She teased his lips with feather-light kisses and then discovered a blazing passion when she delved into his warm mouth and caressed him with the tip of her tongue. His ragged, heated breath against her cheek verified the affect on him.

She took his breath away. Alex knew one kiss would never be enough. He wanted everything she had to give and would give her anything she asked. He surveyed the response. Her lips were moist, flushed crimson, and slightly swollen. Passion simmered in her wide, misty gaze. At the moment, he wanted to devour her.

He was an amazing man that showed only a hint of emotion if she looked deep enough into the soft shimmer of his jade colored eyes as his gaze held hers for what seemed like an eternity in an endless storm that sparkled and raged, whispered and caressed. She felt warm all over when he kissed her. But when he looked at her, forever and always twinkled in his eyes and wrapped her in his magic.

She hadn't believed in love at first sight until now.

"I'm Melissa Johnson."

Alex felt like a blithering idiot. He defined the irritating new emotion that turned his loins to lust and his insides to jelly — it was joy!

At the moment, Alex was mesmerized. He watched the unleashed emotions flicker across her features in absolute awe.

Evan waited beside Alex. He scribbled notes in his journal about the battle, and the points to be claimed. "Dinna fash yourself abou' all of us waiting for ye tae kiss the lass."

"I've never seen a man so smitten," one warrior noted and shook his head.

"*Aye*," Evan agreed. "He looks as if he's go' moonbeams shoved up his arse."

Alex heard every word, but chose to ignore them. A thought crossed his mind and Alex had to stop himself from laughing out loud; 285 points and one heart won during the morning battle. It was a glorious day. Her capture earned them fifty extra points.

But Alex refused to believe victory was assured. An Angel kiss had just claimed one of their mightiest warriors.

Yorath would never be the same.

Chapter Three

Alex lifted her onto his saddle. He mounted behind her and pulled her close, circling her waist with his arms to hold her in place. The exotic scent of Iris and Patchouli wafted from her hair and filled his head with her luxurious scent. She rested her pale cheek against the warmth of his chest. The light touch of her small hand that slid around his waist caused a slow burn of desire to spread like wildfire through his body.

He yelled out commands in Gaelic and the warriors quickly responded and circled their Laird to protect him and the lady in his arms. Evan signaled and they moved into two columns on either side of Alex. Not a trace of the battle remained behind on the shoreline. Twelve warriors would ride with their Laird while the others were sent out on patrol.

One blazing look from Alex and the warriors ceased their stares at the beautiful woman in his arms. The warmth from her full breasts against his arm became a torture that thrilled him. His arms held her tightly to his chest in an act of protection and possession that stunned him. Alex felt amazingly alive for the first time in a very long while.

The strange new feelings and emotions annoyed the hell out of Alex. His pulse had gone completely haywire;

and his stomach felt suspended in mid air as if he had just skied off the edge of a cliff and was airborne upside down and about to drop into an endless abyss.

No one spoke the commands and yet the warriors changed direction at the same time and kept pace in perfect formation. She tipped her head to get another look at the man holding her tightly against his chest. His jade green eyes were fringed in dark lashes that made them appear even more striking. *He is magnificent beyond belief,* she thought, looking at the curve of his lower lip. The feel of his warm skin drew her closer to him. Taunt, rippled muscles under his shirt invited her touch and she realized she had been caressing his back while they rode.

"Where are you taking me?" she asked above the thunder of horses moving fast over rocky terrain. "Am I your prisoner? Are you going to turn me in to the authorities for trespassing?"

"You're not my prisoner," he answered, amused.

His English was broken and spoken slowly, as if he struggled with the pronunciation. She shivered from the cold rain and he wrapped his tartan blanket from his saddlebag around her.

Alex needed to get her to out of the battle quickly. If the Prince decided to counter-attack and try to reclaim her, she wouldn't last through a second battle. He guided the powerful war-horse with his thighs and a flick of his wrist. Yorath responded as if he didn't need to be told and tossed an indignant snort in the morning mist.

Butterflies danced in her stomach as if they were performing some ancient rite of passage that left her feeling like she was floating on air. The next thought took shape. Melissa was lost in the mountains of Scotland. Her shoes and bag had been left behind on the shore along with her passport and identification. She had no way of knowing if she could contact her sisters. Her vacation had turned into an unexpected adventure in a very remote setting.

It was unnerving to be held by a man who looked better in a skirt than she did. His muscled legs were warm against her backside. No matter how hard she tried to blot the thoughts from her mind, Melissa wondered what he wore under his Kilt.

The horse was amazingly smooth for riding at a full gallop and had the beauty and power of a Jaguar. She reached down to pat his powerful neck.

Yorath responded immediately, he snorted and tossed his head triumphantly.

Alex groaned.

She heard him groan and tried not to think about his affections or the kisses that could drive all thoughts from her mind. She was completely lost, and couldn't figure out the directions their route was taking. They rode up and down hills until she was sure they must be in England by now. They rode past a church and Melissa felt drawn to the lovely Kirk.

Thunder growled an ominous warning off in the distance. A light misty rain and intermittent sunshine turned the sky into a field of rainbows. The lush, emerald world around her held an ancient magnificence. They crossed an arched stone bridge. Melissa couldn't help but notice the beautiful river scene and made a mental note to return there to capture the bridge in a painting.

The view of the Manor house was spectacular from the hill. Built in a meadow, tall peaks graced all sides of the massive structure. It appeared both magical and formidable at the same time. Clearly Victorian in design, it held grandeur from the past and no doubt was as lovely on the inside, as it was impressive from the lawn. She gasped at the enormity of the building. There were over a hundred more warriors camped beside the house.

Alex finally stopped in front of the house, jumped down and reached up, took her into his arms again. She opened her mouth to say she could walk but he quickly silenced her.

"Shhh," he instructed. He didn't want to talk at all. His mind raged with emotions all warring at once to be heard. He struggled to control his passion for the wee lass. If he had his way, he'd have her in his bed in five minutes, and then realized he really had gone daft because he didn't think he could wait that long.

He hadn't asked, just commanded her silence. Her mouth closed, the anxious retort she had thought about giving him was forgotten as he walked up the stairs with her cradled in his strong arms. They passed two men and Alex gave orders for medicine and hot water.

He put her down on the edge of the dining room table and ran his hands down her arms to steady her. She was thoroughly inspected from head to toe.

Melissa blushed profusely when he noticed two buttons on the front of her dress had come undone and the gaping fabric revealed a lacy white slip and an intense amount of cleavage. Melissa tugged the dress back in place. He moved his hands down her legs and she winced when he touched her feet. His warm hands were strong, and yet very gentle.

"I'm all right." She argued.

"Ye're injured."

The two men who stood on the steps when they arrived entered the room and brought the requested hot water and medicine. Alexander began his careful ministrations on her foot.

They look so much alike and yet very different, she thought as they stood behind Alex. Dressed in saffron shirts, blue and red Kilts, and black riding boots they looked every bit the Highland warriors she had read about in books. Their hands were clasped behind their back and their feet were spread apart in an arrogant stance. It was their height, she noticed, that made them resemble monoliths. They were all over six feet tall and the term lean and mean came to mind. They exuded power with their honed physique and devastating good looks. They watched every move she made and Melissa soon found their scrutiny unnerving.

"Who are they?" She whispered, watching Alex intently. He had her bare foot in the palm of his hand.

"My brothers." he answered her question without looking up at her. Both men continued to stare. Alex pulled thorns from her foot and rubbed out the sting.

"Do ye want my help, I am a doctor." Gideon asked in Gaelic. He grinned, amused at the personal attention the lady received.

"No." The tone of Alex's voice was loud and direct. He knelt on one knee in front of her and resisted the urge to slide his hands up her legs to explore the hidden treasures that lay within he folds of her dress.

Melissa pulled away when he yelled and Alex smiled to reassure her. "It's all right," he said gently. "I willna' hurt ye lass." Alex turned his head to glare at his brothers and said in Gaelic. "But I may beat ye all senseless if ye don' find something else tae do."

Daniel and Gideon exchanged a smirk and ignored the threat. "Ye don' ha'e tae grope the lass, Alex." Gideon snickered. "Jus' ask her where it hurts."

"I'd be happy tae take care of this situation for ye," Daniel offered, speaking in Gaelic.

"No thank ye," Alex said softly, trying not to frighten her again.

Evan brought in her shoes and bag that were found by their patrol. He joined his brothers. Iain also strolled in to see for himself what they had found, as did Robert. They all had the same reaction and stared as if she were the last, living female on the earth.

William sauntered into the room. "I jus' beat the hell out of a *mon* who told me Alex found an Angel. I set him straight, that if there's a lass with Alex, she's no Angel!" Seconds later his mouth dropped open and he couldn't speak at all.

Alex spoke in Gaelic. "I hope she doesn't understand what ye said, William, because if ye say one mean thing tae her…."

Melissa was becoming unnerved. "Are those men also your brothers?"

"*Aye*. There are six of them tae pester me."

"My word," she said, looking them over as they crowded in to see her.

"She's American," Daniel said quietly to Gideon.

"Damn." Gideon passed an ancient Roman gold coin to Daniel. He lost the bet with a good nature. "My guess was Swedish from the pale blonde hair and blue eyes." The doctor's reply was also coached in their language, as was necessary during the game.

Alex hoped they would get the hint and leave. "Don't ye all have something else tae do?"

"No." They answered in unison extremely curious about the woman Alex pawed.

Melissa could hear the warning in Alexander's voice, even if she couldn't understand the language. Their undivided attention intimidated her, and yet she was instantly curious about all of them. They wouldn't stop staring at her no matter how fiercely he growled at them.

He knew what claimed their attention, as afternoon sunlight streamed through two large floor-to-ceiling windows and cast an ethereal glow around the blonde woman. The impact of her blue and violet gaze amazed him. Her face reflected her innocence. There was no come-hither look in her eyes when she looked at them, just an honest curiosity. He could tell they frightened her, just a little.

Mesmerized by the lovely lady, Alex could hardly breathe, let alone think. When she looked at him, she could see into the depth of his soul. He thought her smile could warm the coldest feet in Scotland. She was lovely, and he held on to her foot to still his shaking hand.

His brothers were acting like idiots. "She's mine, ye ken?"

Iain was completely enchanted with a stupid grin on his face. "Where did ye find her?" Iain asked in Gaelic. His twin brother, Evan, exchanged a look with him that was incredulous.

William could finally speak again and asked. "Are there any more?"

Melissa laughed softly. "Let me guess. I hit my head when I fainted and I've just stepped into the ancient past with seven Celtic Gods."

They laughed in a deep, rich sound that brought the house to life. It had an amazing affect on her and she couldn't help laughing too. "Can you understand me? You all know English?"

They shook their heads, and didn't want to correct her that English and American were the same language.

Melissa was certain they didn't have a clue about what she had just said. They were the most interesting group of men she had ever seen.

Alex noticed that when she looked at him, it wasn't the same look she gave his brothers. Perhaps it was just a trick of light, but her eyes sparkled when she looked down at him, he was certain.

"Her name is Melissa, and she's in shock," Alex said softly in Gaelic. He knelt to complete the task, certain his brothers would behave, and pulled a thorn from her foot. She flinched and he gently rubbed the pain away.

The tender touch of his hand on her foot was driving her to madness. She could feel the tremble in his hands and wished he would hurry.

"Hell," Evan groaned and spoke in Gaelic. "I'd be in shock if ye kissed me like that Alex. Let go of the poor wee lass." Evan's tone indicated he was genuinely concerned for the beautiful lady. "Alex hasn't let go of her from the moment he first laid eyes on her."

"Alex kissed her too?" Robert asked innocently. "I heard that Yorath go' the first kiss."

They had to turn aside to hide the smirks.

Alex growled out a warning. "We have a lady in the house. Try tae act like gentleman."

Daniel couldn't wait to hear how the lady entered the battle from Evan.

Evan sighed, exasperated. The warriors were already making crude jokes about the little lass that captured the passion of their Laird.

"Interesting," Daniel said softly to Gideon in Gaelic, knowing Alex could hear him. "Alex and his horse are both very protective of the wee lass."

They couldn't hide the chuckles this time and Alex was certain he would have to beat them all senseless to shut them up. She looked down at her hands folded in her lap. He could tell their comments were making her uncomfortable. Even if she couldn't understand the language, their intent was obvious.

Melissa could hear them speaking softly in what she presumed was Gaelic. Alexander had removed all of the thorns from her foot and dabbed on a medicine that stung. She flinched but then relaxed as he caressed her foot in the palm of his hand. Her cold, wet dress caused another shiver and the misty rain had her hair curling into a thousand ringlets.

"Ye'll be fine now," Alex assured her in English.

He looked up when he spoke to her and that quirky smile of his nearly had her sliding off the table. His eyes lit up like a hunter's moon in the dead of night.

Alex stood and decided to redirect his brother's interest in other ways. He spoke in Gaelic, "William, our cousins have arrived."

"Aren't they the U.S. Marines, James and Jonathan?" Daniel asked in Gaelic.

"Back for more and ready for a fight," Robert announced, taking the hint that Alex wanted to be alone with the lady.

"*Och*," William bristled and turned on his heel.

"It will be a good fight," Iain said and followed.

"He'll probably try tae take them both at once." Evan walked out behind William.

"Are ye sure ye don't need any assistance with the lovely lass?" Daniel offered.

"Be off with ye!" Alex yelled.

Gideon went to get his medical bag certain someone would need stitches within the hour.

Robert followed Gideon. "No need tae throw me ou'. I had plans tae meet with the carpenters this afternoon."

Daniel walked back into the Drawing Room. Evan had given him the lady's passport when they brought in her bag. Her sensual beauty lingered in his mind as he shut the door and walked over to his desk. The laptop screen saver disappeared when he entered his password and a satellite link brought him back to the 21st century. He emailed Delores, his Assistant, with the basic information and started his search with her name.

Chapter Four

The Game of Love Starts with a Kiss! It looks like Laird MacKenna brought along some summer entertainment this year. What a lucky lady, and oh – what a kiss! Such scandalous behavior from the Laird himself! Unbelievable! The Bookies are going into overtime to keep up with the bouncing odds that now heavily favor the Prince to win.

On the Streets, with Rosabel

"Can you tell me what year it is?" Melissa was confused as she looked around the room. There were rushes on the floor and clean trenchers on the table.

"*Aye*, tis 1745," he noticed she paled considerably.

She had recently dedicated and afternoon to a museum in Glasgow and spent several hours in the section that depicted the Witch Hunts of Scotland. How could she explain where she was from, when she didn't believe time travel was possible? She didn't dare tell him she was from the future or they would burn her at the stake. There was no one she could contact to help her, or any way she could reach her sisters. Her stomach suddenly felt like she had swallowed a live eel. She had to find the mist that brought her to 1745 and return to the future before they found out she was just a tourist who wandered away from her group and got lost.

Melissa took her shoes from Alexander and placed them on her feet. There was no pain when she stood and only then realized how short she was when she stood next to him. He had to be six feet two or three inches tall. The top of her head was level to his shoulder.

"Thank you for rescuing me." She picked up her bag and blindly stumbled toward the door.

Alex stood with his feet braced apart, his arms akimbo, and looked at her curiously. "Where do ye think ye're going?"

Melissa didn't have a clue. She turned around and shrugged. "I guess I don't know where I am let alone how to get back to my hotel."

"Ho-tel?" he asked, playing along with the charade. "Are ye staying at the Inn?"

"I don't know?"

Alex caught her by her elbow and eased the bag from her shoulder. "Then perhaps ye should stay right where ye're at until ye figure it ou'. Ye go' a wee bit of a shock this morning. Ye canna leave me now. Why don' ye stay and rest awhile? Ye can ha'e supper with us."

His hand went to the small of her back and pushed her up a magnificent wide staircase and took a right turn. "Ye should rest awhile," he said again charmingly.

"I'm not tired!" Melissa was instantly aware of the direction he was taking her and was also relieved he wasn't putting her in a dungeon. The windows in the roof filtered light to the Italian alabaster sculptures, and she couldn't help but notice the antique curios that lined the hallway. Everywhere she looked the beauty of gleaming oak and deep red carpets brought out a feeling of opulence and history.

"Aye, lass, ye need some time tae rest. No one will harm ye. But if ye try tae leave the house without my protection it could be certain death. There are two hundred warriors camped outside," the sexy growl in his voice made clear the implication.

"Where exactly am I?"

He was enchanted by her naivety, to be certain. Alex decided to play along with her question. "Ye're safe for the moment. But the war has already begun. Doona' try tae leave withou' me as your escort."

Melissa wondered who would save her from her own raging passions. She had no idea where she was in Scotland, or how she had stepped back in time.

Alex distracted her gently massaging the small of her back. "Ye should get out of that wet dress and lie down for awhile. Ye can lock the door." He opened the door to his chamber and nearly had to shove her inside.

The four-poster double bed had a red and blue tartan quilt that also had a crest stitched in gold thread in the center. Outside the second story windows there was a spectacular view of the mountains to the north, the glen to the east, and a beautiful dark blue loch.

He stepped in behind her but left the door open.

Alex reached out and took hold of her waist. He roughly pulled her up against his warm hard body. Her head tipped up and his mouth lightly touched hers just for a brief moment. The look of surprise on her face was worth a thousand words. Her unmet expectations were evident in the disappointed frown on her face when he pulled back. Alex was well aware of where he was at the moment and that his last shred of control could snap at any moment.

But don't ye want tae kiss your Angel?

The thoughts tormented him with the memory of her soft lips that he tasted so lusciously before. He touched her lips again with his and began a full-scale assault on her resistance. She held on to his shirt as he plundered and tasted, advanced and retreated. His hand reached up to stroke her neck and gently applied pressure until her mouth opened. He moaned from the intense desire racing through his body. He needed her now. His heart thundered against his chest as she yielded to the kiss and wound her hands around his neck. He felt her press against his thighs and thought he would lose his mind. She felt so good in his arms. His tongue swept into her mouth testing and exploring until she trembled.

Melissa was drawn to the heat that radiated from under his shirt. He made her ache for more and she kissed him back until he groaned.

It took all his inner strength to pull away from her soft lips. He gently kissed the side of her neck and stepped back a pace.

He took her hands in his and kissed her fingertips. "Do you want tae bed me now, and later?"

She finally got past the romantic burr in his velvet voice to hear the shameless meaning of his words. Her mouth dropped open in shock.

"We'll save the bedding for later then."

Alex walked to the door and knew that if she didn't throw him out of the room, he wasn't going to volunteer to leave. "Rest now and I'll call ye in time for supper."

He had been toying with her affections and her fists clenched. Melissa was livid. "I've changed my mind. This isn't the House of Wonders. It's the House of Horrors and you're clearly out of your mind. Get out!" The burr in his voice was like a velvet caress that lingered and caressed every secret part of her, and made the ache of wanting him unbearable.

"*Aye*, I've been called a monster before, but that's usually after the bedding."

He shut the door and strolled down the stairs. The door was locked with a click.

Daniel stood at the bottom of the stairs and shook his head. "...certain death, Alex? Wish I had thought of that when I had Heather here." There was a wicked gleam in his eyes.

Gideon and Robert walked into the house and followed them into the Drawing Room.

"What the hell did ye do tae her this time?" Robert asked. "Yorath tried tae break free from his stall when he heard her yelling."

Alex raised one eyebrow in response.

"The men are hoping to catch her eye now that she finds you so disagreeable," Gideon stated calmly. He picked up the fax and let out a low whistle.

"I don't think she knows about the game, or what's at stake," Daniel said plainly.

Daniel closed the doors to the Drawing Room for privacy. "We have a problem." He handed the fax over to Alex and leaned on the edge of his desk while Alex reviewed the headline from the tabloid '*On the Streets*' that read, '*The Game of Love Starts with a Kiss!*' that included a picture of Alex holding Melissa in his arms and their first kiss. It had been taken that morning and was already on the front page of the tabloid.

"The Bookies in London give your latest *Affaire du Jour* a month and you'll send her back tae the States. There are reporters already crawling all over her hotel waiting for her tae return. I sent someone over tae pick up her things before she finds out."

Alex was furious. "Damn it! Why won't Rosabel leave me alone?"

"Unfortunately, your affair is hot news in London and the odds of winning the game have taken a turn for the worse."

Daniel, Gideon, and Robert knew all too well the reason. Everywhere they went there were photographers waiting to catch a glimpse of their latest girlfriends and then the newspapers would torment the lady. Rosabel was the voice of the Ton, and had followed the MacKenna brothers relentlessly for several years.

"I also checked out Melissa, just tae be certain she wasn't a spy for George. She's an American tourist."

"*Aye*, she said she was lost." He remembered every word she said fondly. "The press will crucify her because of me if she leaves now. I canna let her face that humiliation all alone."

Gideon asked the most obvious question. "What do ye want tae do with her Alex? We could take her back tae Glasgow and check her into a different hotel. Or, perhaps send her tae Paris for the rest of her holiday?"

Alex considered the question. "What would ye do if Heaven put an Angel in your arms?"

"Hold on," Daniel answered. "With everything I have."

Evan was outraged. "No, ye canna bring her into the game. Alex, wha' ye'r doin' tae her is'na' right, ye ken?"

"She seems tae like me."

"She definitely likes your horse," Robert snickered. "I canna wait till Rebecca hears abou' Yorath. She's no' goin' tae be a happy wumman."

The MacKenna's all shook their heads at Yorath who made a complete fool of himself and would never be a terrifying warhorse again.

"I need time," Alex sighed, "and your help tae keep her at the cottage."

"Alex, are ye out of your mind?" Robert asked. "Ye canna go on making her believe she has stepped back in time. If she wanders too far from the cottage, she'll know we lied tae her. Ye canna put one little wumman in the middle of this warrior game. She's too beautiful! We'll be scraping the men off her every day."

"Starting with us," Iain stated.

"She was caught in the middle of a battle this morning and fainted she was so terrified." Evan's concern was founded in facts. "*Och*, let her go before ye break her heart."

"We're no' going tae tell her this is all a game," Alex instructed. "I won't allow any warrior or battle tae frighten her again. Let's give her a holiday she will never forget." Alexander's bravado was all show. He stared out of the window for a few moments to collect his thoughts. The wave of guilt knotted his stomach into a painful reminder of the heartache a deception could cause, but he didn't want to lose her.

"She will ask questions." Evan brought up a tactical problem. "What do we say tae her if she asks why we don't have guns in our battles with the Prince?"

"Highlanders were disarmed after the Rising of 1715. Ye can direct all her questions tae me. Tae Melissa, it is 1745, and at tha' time there were very few weapons in Scotland. The English had confiscated most of their black powder pistols. One of our men had to go home for an emergency, so we do have an opening to add her name to the list. We are abou' tae become the warriors of legend no' just play the game. What say ye?"

"We'd better remember all our history lessons." Gideon exchanged a frown with Robert.

Daniel proceeded cautiously. "Alex, it will be very hurtful when she finds ou' ye have deceived her."

"I accept the responsibility for my deception."

"There could also be other complications," Gideon warned, fully aware of the tension between them.

Alex clearly understood the implication and the corners of his mouth raised in a wicked smile.

They all looked at a smiling Alex in wide-eyed disbelief and finally understood that regardless of his circumstances, he was a man in love.

Alex walked to the door. "The alternative is tha' I leave the game with her because I willna let her walk away from me." He saw the look of horror on their faces. "Ye can forfeit the game or join us for supper."

"Weel then, supper sounds lovely," Daniel said.

His shocked brothers nodded in agreement.

Chapter Five

Melissa walked into the bathroom and found that it was nothing more than an old-fashioned water closet complete with a wooden-handled, handcrafted chain to run water through the system. How could they survive without a proper bath and a candle for light? The modern day facilities she had come to depend on didn't exist yet, and she suddenly felt overwhelmed.

She wandered around the room, unsure what to do next. Her sisters would help her if she could contact them, but how? There were no telephones or a radio in the house. At the moment, she missed her family and the comfort of her own apartment.

She fought back a tear when she thought about her sisters. Amber and Sarah would be frantic when she turned up missing and Melissa could just imagine the anguish they would go through while searching for her. They would not give up, no matter how many mountains they had to search. And yet, Melissa also felt drawn to this warrior in ways she had never experienced before now. Did she have to make a choice in either living in the future without him or hurting her sisters to stay in the past? Could she stay in the past even if she wanted to?

She considered Alexander's actions and then had to admit that what annoyed her most was that he was accurate. He had unleashed her passions and then laughed at her innocence. With so much to think about, she was getting a headache and decided it wasn't an answer she could find without a witch doctor or a magician. Perhaps it was all a dream and she would wake up and find that she had never left her hotel room?

She was fatigued and happy to have a little time to herself to regain control of her turbulent emotions. It was his room. She could tell by the scent. It filled her head and started an ache deep inside her belly. It wasn't possible to desire him so completely, her mind reasoned.

She took off the wet dress and hung it over the back of a chair to dry. Her shoes were dropped in the middle of the floor. She crawled in under the covers, moved into the center of his bed, put her head down on the pillow, and fell asleep instantly.

**

He stood there, watching her sleep for a few moments before he had to wake her for supper. Alex had bathed and changed and then realized she could sleep through an entire army battling inside that room, she slept so soundly. She looked feminine in his warrior world and luscious beyond belief.

The house staff brought in an antique copper tub and filled it with steaming water. The home made soap was scented with rose petals and a bath sheet was laid out for her use, and then the staff left with instructions to prepare the cottage for their arrival later that day.

He took a deep breath. "Trust me, darling," he said softly. Alex sat down on the edge of the bed and gently nudged her arm. "Wake up, Sweetheart."

Her eyes bounced open, and she rolled out of bed, stood, and stretched.

The sight of her standing there in a very short, clinging slip was a distraction that made him swallow hard and force his line of sight to her face. He wanted all of her, not just her body, but at the moment, his body was already fervently responding to hers. For the first time in his life, Alex wanted to matter beyond immediate physical pleasure to someone.

"Alexander!" Melissa had heard him call her sweetheart, and it shocked her right out of bed. "That door was locked."

He held up a key. "It's my room."

"I knew it was your room. You said…"

"How did ye know it was my room?" He was intensely curious. Their casual conversation would probably have gone on for hours while he admired the sight of her curvaceous body in an opaque slip. She was confused and adorable with a hurricane of curls falling soft on her bare shoulders. It was a delight to watch her struggle with consciousness.

She waved her hand in front of her. "The entire room has your scent. You are avoiding the question."

"What was the question?" He enjoyed the feminine sound of her voice. Her slip was skintight, and he got the most perfect view of her body when she stepped over by the window and sunlight highlighted her curves.

She ran a hand over the rage of curls that fell over her face. "I can't remember. I'm a little groggy, and it must have been a question in my dream."

"Ye have an hour tae wake and get ready for supper. I will be back tae take ye downstairs."

Alex walked out of the room and shut the door. He stood there for a few moments and then heard the scream. He was certain she had just figured out that he wasn't a nightmare.

He strolled down the stairs. Iain ran toward him.

"What the hell was that?" Iain stopped next to Alex.

Alex casually kept on walking.

Iain let out a long breath. "*Och*, with a scream like that, she can scare the hell ou' of the Prince. It's a good thing she's on our side."

Melissa spent the hour bathing, and cursing without a blow-dryer for her hair or a mirror larger than her compact to put on makeup. She waited for Alexander to return, but it was his younger brother who knocked on the door.

"My brother asked me tae bring ye downstairs." He looked instantly flustered at finding the English words.

Alex looked relaxed leaning up against the white marble fireplace. She walked over to stand next to him and waited for him to finish his discussion.

The room was elegant, and she couldn't help but notice the painted tiles of sailing ships. There were several comfortable sofas and chairs, and large bay windows let in plenty of light. The oak floors gleamed next to oriental rugs of deep blues and greens.

Melissa wanted him to kiss her again and had come to that realization an hour ago. Until she figured out how to go home, she'd better start acting like an Angel, even if it killed her.

What's wrong with me?

She felt terrible for yelling at him the way she did and very embarrassed at her behavior. How often do you get a chance to meet a beautiful Celtic God who could kiss like a dream?

Melissa had only one choice for her wardrobe for the evening and wore the outfit she had packed in her bag for the supper she was going to attend with the tour.

"The warriors have already been told you are a jealous maniac who won't allow anyone to talk to her." Daniel shrugged off Alexander's glare. It was the best scenario they could find to keep the lads from approaching her. "She's going to need time period, appropriate clothing, he commented in Gaelic.

Alexander nodded. "See that it's done quickly." His brothers had already noticed her attire was a short black mini-skirt that draped low on her hips and pleated to sway provocatively when she walked. The swell inside the black lace top was the object of all of their attention.

Evan walked into the room and his gaze focused on her. "Wha' do ye think ye're doin', lass?" Evan spoke in Gaelic. "If ye're going tae romp aroun' in those under things, we'll have a fight tae the death if the warriors lay eyes on ye!"

Alex yelled at his brother and then continued talking as if nothing had happened.

Evan swallowed an entire mug of ale without taking a breath and belched.

Out of the corner of his eye, Alex saw Gideon flip Evan over the back of a chair for his poor manners while they had a guest in the house.

Melissa held on to Alex with a steel grip on his arm. One of his brothers looked very upset, and she wanted to run and hide. The man was obviously distraught.

When she arrived, Alex could barely breathe, let alone think about what Daniel was telling him. He possessively draped his arm around her slim waist, pulling her up close to him.

With every breath he took, he was reminded of white flowers. He inhaled several slow, deep breaths to regain control of his desire for the lovely lass, and the provocative scent of her was imprinted on his memory.

Alex was delighted to touch her again. She was so soft against his calloused hand. "You were saying," he repeated for Daniel and couldn't help but overhear the "bloody hell!" that came out of William's mouth when he walked into the room.

Melissa peeked out from behind Alexander's back to see another brother sailing over the back of the couch. She tugged on his shirtsleeve, anxious about the number of bodies being tossed about, but he just patted her hand, as if this type of event happened every day in their lives.

Two younger brothers rushed the older one and tried to take him down but were tossed off like flies. Melissa gaped, wide-eyed as they tried to regroup and take him down by the knees, but the older brother sent them tumbling across the floor.

Alex sighed and frowned at Gideon, who was having a little fun with the boys.

He gave up any pretense of being able to hold an intelligent conversation. The warm blush on Melissa's lovely bare belly was a severe distraction. The lace top was skin-tight, and there was absolutely nothing left to doubt, she had a beautiful body.

Melissa clasped her hands lightly together in front of her. They all looked at her legs, as if she had a blazing neon sign on her knees that said 'take me' on one, and 'please' on the other. She was suddenly very aware they were all staring at her and inched closer to Alexander.

He finally acknowledged her presence. "Good evening, Melissa."

"Good evening, Alexander. You didn't mention if supper was black tie or white slip."

"Do we get tae choose?" Iain asked anxiously.

Gideon gave him a hard shove with a warning to watch his manners.

The room had become amazingly warm, Melissa thought. Alex had placed his hand on her hip. She couldn't think the caress was so intimate, and yet so casual everyone else in the room wouldn't notice. The affect it was having on her was enough to make her knees buckle. She thought she must have hit her head this morning when she fainted. It was the only logical explanation to her bizarre reaction to him.

Daniel excused himself and had to walk away before he broke out laughing. The tension between Alex and Melissa could crackle glass. Alex appeared to touch her with a casual indifference, and yet, was seducing her right in front of all of them.

She felt the impact of his touch, he knew by the pink flush on her cheeks.

William had walked into the room and stood as if he were made of stone, glaring at Alex.

Alex pulled her closer. "You look beautiful," he whispered against her ear and applied pressure to her hip. "And verra sexy," he added with a low, soft growl.

She was delighted he thought so. She fluttered her eyelashes at him and asked. "What does one wear while dining with Celtic Gods?"

"Hopefully, nothing," Iain suggested.

'I think she just abou' managed tha'," Evan said. Gideon knocked him off the back of the couch with a flick of his muscular arm.

Melissa cleared her throat and tried a different approach. "How about giving me an introduction to these fine gentlemen?"

Alex slipped his arm around her waist so her back was to him. She was firmly anchored against him. The heat of his body made her tremble slightly. He bent down and spoke softly in her ear. "Don't say I didn't warn ye, lass. They can be a wee bit forward at times, especially when they meet a beautiful wumman."

His compliment, spoken softly against her ear brought out a hot flush of excitement on her cheeks.

"Daniel," Alex called, and his brother returned. "They do know some English," he said and shrugged. "Ye can help us learn a lot more since ye speak with such a funny English accent."

Melissa was about to tell him her accent was from America when a handsome young man stood in front of her, picked up her hand, and kissed her fingertips.

His dark wavy hair gave him a very sophisticated appearance. Daniel was elegant, she thought to herself. His emotions were held tightly in check, and the outward smile was practiced and meant to deceive. The depth of this charming man captivated her.

His smile slowly changed, and she got a glimpse of the excruciatingly, gorgeous man beneath the facade. His devastating green eyes reflected a smoldering sensuality that was just barely held in place. His physique was made for a sculptor, with fine lines in his face, lean waist, and broad shoulders. He could be her David and pose for her any time.

"Beautiful lady," Daniel said gently.

His scrutiny was as intense as hers and had similar results, she guessed. "You see way beyond the sight of most men, Daniel," she said with a voice that was suddenly wispy.

Her gaze held his for a moment and Daniel felt wonderful from her attention. They were well aware of their charisma when it came to the ladies. The four older brothers were well acquainted with the boudoirs and social functions in London.

"Gideon," Alex growled in her ear.

Gideon bent and kissed her lips. "Cherished one," he said gallantly. Melissa gazed up at him and smiled. His resistance perished instantly.

"You have a special gift, and I am honored to meet you, Gideon." He was also tall and lean like his brothers but also had strength in his spirit. His presence had a calming affect on her, and she felt like she could sit down and tell him anything and he would listen and care. He, too, hadn't shaved in awhile and had the beginnings of a dark beard and mustache and much longer hair that was tied with a leather thong at the base of his neck. He was ruggedly handsome and very sensual.

"Robert." Alex watched her carefully as Robert stepped forward. He was a special favorite with the ladies in London. Tall, lean, and muscular, his reputation for pleasing women was well earned.

He had long straight hair that was loose around his shoulders and gave him a look of untamed sultry sexuality, just waiting to be caressed. His eyes, she noticed, were a green and gray fringed in dark lashes. He bowed and then kissed her lightly on the lips.

"You are a maker of worlds, Robert."

Alex tightened his hold on her waist. "Are ye all right, lass? Do ye need a glass of water? Take a few deep breaths. That will help."

Melissa thought a fire hose would be appropriate to cool her down. She nodded and let out a long, slow sigh.

Alex noted his brothers were pleased with her reaction. They weren't called playboys because they were monks. He looked at his brothers with his mouth set in a grim line and his eyes narrowed. It was a, *don't you even think about it* kind of look that made them back down.

They were testing her and his patience. He was proud of her. So far they hadn't managed to persuade her to leave his side. Of course, he did have an iron grip on her. The reaction was expected. It was their best effort, and she seemed only mildly affected, compared to the reaction she had when Alex had kissed her.

"Iain is one of the twins."

"My escort," she mentioned. It was Iain who had come to bring her downstairs. His dark hair was also curly and down to his shirt collar. His eyes were almost blue-green and long dark lashes that gave him a look that said: *I am in that secret garden waiting for you and will make love to you beyond your wildest dreams.*

Iain dropped on one knee in front of her and kissed her hand. "I am yours for eternity."

Alex knew he was just looking at her bare belly and growled a warning in Gaelic.

"Evan is the other twin," Alex said.

Melissa's smile was radiant. "I remember you. You are intuitive, Evan."

Evan smiled in that devil-may-care way that Alex used on her. Their charisma was genuine, she surmised, and Evan bent down, gently lifted her chin with the tip of his finger, and planted a kiss on her lips. He then withdrew slightly, groaned, and was about to take her into his arms when Alex shoved him aside.

"And at last our William." Annoyed, Alex tightened his grip. His brothers wouldn't get another chance to slobber on his beautiful Angel.

William stepped forward with his hands clasped behind his back, with a swagger that was almost identical to Alex's, she noticed.

William leaned down and rested his forehead against hers so their eyes were level. "I'd be happy tae show ye what's under my Kilt."

He quickly stepped back to get out of Alex's reach.

Alex turned her around to face him again. "Are we finished with the introductions?"

"Not yet," she corrected. "Who are you?"

Chapter Six

"Laird Alexander G. MacKenna," he said with authority. "My brothers call me Alex."

"How very nice to meet you all," she said cordially. "Now, how do I find my way back to the shore?"

"We thought ye might stay here for awhile. We noticed ye brought painting supplies."

Melissa was tempted. "I must get back."

Alex shook his head. "The only way tae get here is on horseback, and it's getting too late tae take ye back now. It would crush Iain. He made a special supper tonight for our guest. If ye left, he might be insulted and start a fight. Then I would have tae beat him senseless."

She wasn't thinking clearly. She had no idea what the local customs were and certainly didn't want to start a brawl or insult any of them.

"I wouldn't want that," she said softly.

Alex decided to let her relax. She was waffling between flight, fight, and surrender, and he had made a mental note of what had set her off each time. When he kissed her that action had sparked surrender. She couldn't deny what they could be together. When he taunted her, she fought, and it was a good fight, he thought, happily remembering their battle earlier in his chamber. When he had her trapped by her own desires, she took flight. He couldn't bear the thought of her leaving him and so soon.

Gideon brought her a glass of white wine. "We don't often get a chance tae ha'e a visitor." He gave the silent hand signal for 'slow down' to Alex, and his brother gave him a nod. "Where are ye from lass?"

Melissa gulped the wine and avoided answering the question. She had a feeling if she said she was from about 250 years in the future, they'd burn her at the stake and roast a Yak on the bonfire. "Is this house your home?"

"Playground is more like it," Evan stated. Daniel handed him a glass of ale and strongly suggested he drown himself or choose his words more carefully.

Alex felt her tense. "Wha' has upset ye, lass?"

Melissa chewed on her bottom lip. How did she broach the subject of time travel without coming off as a lunatic? They waited for her response, and she was certain they didn't have any idea her torment. "It's a little overwhelming to meet seven Celtic Gods all at once."

They all had a good laugh, but Alex could tell she meant what she said. "It's time for supper." He changed the subject to ease the tension.

William shoved Iain toward the dining room. "When she said we were handsome, she wasn't talking about you, ye ugly bastard!" He spoke in Gaelic, as was required.

Alex thought again about beating some manners into his younger brothers. He hugged her close for a moment. "You feel verra good."

He leaned over and kissed the left side of her neck and radiated heat that spread over her like a protective blanket. The effect he had on her pulse was amazing. One look at the man, and she could barely catch her breath. It was his mouth that caught her attention, and she couldn't help but look, knowing the magic he could create with a single kiss. The room began to grow warm, and she could feel the flush turn her cheeks hot.

"Are they upset about what I'm wearing?"

Alex smiled at the concerned look on her face and raised one eyebrow. "We may ha'e tae get ye a new dress or put ye in a convent tae keep ye safe."

Don't you dare smile at me again, Melissa thought to herself. He had to be the most handsome man in the world! And right smack dab in front of her waiting for another kiss. Her lack of experience in enticing men became a moment of concern. What do you say to a Celtic God who can mesmerize you with his gaze, set your body on fire with one kiss, and make you feel like you were walking on air? 'Please' came to mind, and she had to laugh out loud.

He watched her face with rapt fascination. Her eyes sparkled with mischief, and her luscious mouth curled in a smile. "I'd give just about anything tae know what ye are thinking right now." He gently squeezed her hip, and she turned a new shade of pink.

"No, you don't want to know what I'm thinking," Melissa said honestly.

"Oh, yes, I do," he said with a wicked glint in his eye. His hand slid to her backside. "I'm just checking for hidden weapons."

One silken eyelash dipped in a provocative wink. "My garters are upstairs." Melissa felt he could read her mind. "I've never had a man buy me a dress before."

"I was right," he quickly changed the subject. He could taste her she was so close to him, and that wink had just about crumbled his last bit of resistance.

His hand was at the small of her back as they walked into the dining room.

Iain served supper, and they spent the next hour discussing the fights that broke out during the day. Melissa strained to keep up to the conversation and Alex translated for her benefit. It seemed as if the three younger men were trying to outdo each other with the number of fistfights they had during the day.

Alex sat back in his chair as they told their stories. He listened, but his full attention was on her hand that he held in his. She stroked his fingers with her thumb, and he found the innocent touch charming. It was as if she didn't think about the contact and it came naturally. He felt needed and wanted for the first time in his life.

She had his brothers completely under her spell by the end of supper. Once she had relaxed, they found she had a sense of humor and could parry verbally with them as easily as they could with each other. More than once the younger lads had let loose with a few curse words that emphasized their battle that day. She didn't bat an eyelash at the profanity and listened intently. Every once in a while they spoke English, but for the most part, their language was foreign to her.

The wine slowly disappeared from her glass. Her small hand wrapped around the crystal. Alex wasn't about to let her get drunk. He wanted her in control of her senses later that evening when he took her upstairs.

Her feminine scent drifted over him. He would have her, of that fact, he was certain. But he also wanted something more from her. He held her passions in the palm of his hand, and now, he wanted her heart.

Melissa felt at ease. The conversation was spirited and light-hearted. She expressed her gratitude to the cook. "Supper was delicious, Iain. Thank you."

He blustered with pride. "Wait until ye taste my honey cakes."

They all laughed again, and Alex explained the humor. "It took him a few tries tae make thin cakes. We recommended he follow the instructions again verra carefully."

"We could ha'e shoed the horses with them." Evan laughed and held up his fingers to indicate they were at least two inches thick.

"We used them for target practice," Alex explained.

"I appreciate a good cook, believe me. I've never had the time to learn." Melissa was amazed at their shared camaraderie. There was a lot of shoving, swearing, and name-calling, but they always seemed to blow it off and came back for more.

Alex sat at the head of the table and kept everyone involved in the conversation. Robert had been quiet throughout supper, and Alex asked him how the renovation on the cottage was progressing.

"I'm about finished," Robert assured him. "The outside walls are fortified and we now have the steam engine tae heat water for the roman bath at the cottage."

He was proud of the work he accomplished. "Some of the floorboards are rotted out, and we need tae replace them with oak planks."

Melissa was intrigued. "Are you a builder, Robert?"

"Aye." He beamed, happy to be noticed, and then it dawned on him what he had said, and he looked around the room in horror.

Evan, Iain, and William all looked aghast at the horrendous slip. Gideon coughed, and spoke in Gaelic. "Perhaps she doesn't know steam engines weren't used until 1807."

Robert finally let out a long, slow breath, and Alex distracted her with a wink while his brothers stopped visibly shaking.

She couldn't help but notice the look of contentment on Alex's face. There was tenderness in his eyes when he looked at his family. The smile was a window to his heart, and the view dazzled and took her breath away. It sparked something deep inside her. Crazy as it seemed, she fell deeply in love with him at that moment.

But what did she really know about Alex? He could kiss like a champion and stunning jade green eyes that could turn a hue of blue when he was riled. His dark, wavy hair gave him a rugged, sensual look that made her want to run her fingers through it. He hadn't shaved in awhile, she surmised from the beginning of a beard and mustache that made him look wickedly handsome.

She had witnessed his strength in the battle that morning. Alex had total control of his powerful body and she fought the desire to run her hands over his broad, muscled chest. Just looking at him took her breath away.

Her sisters would probably be in shock if they knew Melissa was crazy about a man she barely knew. Normally, she was far too cautious when it came to relationships to even consider something so spontaneous, but she was hardly in a normal circumstance.

Alex watched the emotions war on her face, her expressions betraying her every thought. He held his breath waiting for the outcome of her internal battle, noticing a flash of fear as she looked around the room at his brothers. She was at their mercy. Confusion etched a frown on her forehead and then she seemed to come to a conclusion of her inner battle and a warm glow reflected in her eyes. He thought she couldn't look more beautiful.

The evening ended, and the boys joined the *ceilidhs* at the encampment. Daniel and Gideon had reports to write, and Robert was reminded that he too had things to get done that day. Alex and Melissa were finally alone.

Alex stood and pulled Melissa gently to her feet. He hugged her close and pulled her up several inches off the floor to savor the touch and taste of her lips.

Her heartbeat hammered wildly in her chest. She was consumed with the heat of his body.

He groaned against her lips. "I've wanted tae do this for hours." He brushed his lips over hers and tasted her sweet mouth before she could think. His hand slowly slid up her silky thigh, and the skirt inched its way up.

She took hold of his hand to stay his advance. "Not here." Melissa had to choose between fleeing and passion, and she didn't want to leave. She had already lost her heart to the tall handsome warrior and now wanted all of him.

The advice her sister had given her came to mind. Melissa was always very predictable, and Amber had told her to follow her heart. This was a once in a lifetime chance meeting, and she knew either way there was a price to be paid. What choice would bring her happiness or a lifetime of regret? She suddenly decided to trust her instincts and wrapped her arms around his neck to pull his head down for a kiss filled with reckless abandon.

Alex lifted her in his arms and took her up the stairs to his chamber. He put her down in the room and locked the door. His shirt was torn from his muscular shoulders and quickly thrown aside.

The touch of his bare skin was her undoing. His lips tormented and tantalized hers. His hands moved up her back, and he had her skirt dropped to the floor before she knew it was gone. She moaned as he tugged her lace top over her head and then gently kissed the base of her throat, touching his lips against her full, hot breast.

Her back arched, and her breathing became ragged. He tormented her body, touching her everywhere. He tossed his belt and Kilt aside, and the full heat of his naked body flamed hot against her skin.

They were on the bed, and Melissa couldn't remember crossing the room or how she had lost her slip that now lay in a pool on the floor. His hand slid down her flat belly and into her velvet heat. She called out to him, quivering with desire.

Alex had almost completely lost control. When he touched her, she responded with such fire. He leaned down and continued to caress and conquer her lips until she moaned softly against his mouth. His fingers slid into the slick heat of her, and her back arched when he slid his thumb over the tiny nub.

She was so hot and sweet. He wanted her more than anything else in his entire world. Alex couldn't wait any longer. He parted her thighs, and his arousal slid deep into her tight velvet heat. The momentary resistance stunned his desire-crazed mind.

Melissa tensed and held perfectly still. The shock hit Alex like a thunderbolt from hell. My God, she was a virgin. She sure didn't kiss like a virgin, he thought, and then realized he hadn't been able to have a coherent thought since her arrival.

He braced his weight with his arms and looked down at her beautiful face. He wooed her with soft words whispered against her lips. He paused and stroked her face and hair. Alex talked softly in her ear. "*A Grá*, shhh. It won't last long, I promise. Ye're so beautiful." His voice was choked with emotion.

Melissa's hands unclenched as she began to relax. "Alex," she spoke softly.

"*Aye*, my darling." He kissed the tip of her nose.

Melissa was overwhelmed by own raging emotions. Tears streamed down her cheeks, and she didn't have a clue why she was crying. "I've never done anything like this before now."

He kissed her chin. "Now ye tell me." He continued to stroke her hair. "I didn't know, sweetheart, or I might have slowed down—just a little. My Angel, ye take my breath away." He kissed the base of her throat and then steeled himself to say, "Do ye want tae stop now?"

He touched her lips gently with his, and she forgot about everything but the aching intensity within her. "No," she raggedly whispered against his mouth and moved her hips against him.

He crushed her lips with his and was beyond thinking or reason. He withdrew a little and then returned to the tight heat within her. A tidal wave of emotions flooded Alex's heart. He didn't know if there could be a more perfect moment in life and wanted this to last forever. They looked deep into each other's eyes, and he watched the pupils in her eyes grow big in absolute wonder.

He searched his heart for the right words to soothe her fears. He realized just how bleak his world had been. Somehow, he sensed she loved him from the first moment they looked at each other, and he wasn't about to lose that gift.

Alex had spent too many years of his life without the perfection he now held in his arms. She held him tightly, and he knew in his heart that he loved her. He leaned down and gently kissed her lips. While in this intimate embrace, he knew he would do whatever it took to keep her beside him forever. If she left him, he would shatter into ash and drift away with the wind.

He smiled against her lips and moved forward again. She gasped in a delighted surprise. He had waited until the shock had passed. His forehead had broken out in a sweat. His body could no longer be denied. The ecstasy was an agony of control. He slowly took her down that path of fulfillment until he felt her shiver deep inside and her muscles tightened against him. She called out to him, and he released his seed deep inside her.

Heavenly bliss descended upon him He kissed her fingertips and held her small hand against his. As the passion ebbed and he could think again he became very serious for a moment. "Did I hurt ye, sweetheart?" His grip tightened on her hand.

Melissa's cheeks flamed with embarrassment. "It was a surprise more than anything else."

He understood why she looked so fragile. "My sweet lady," he soothed. "I'm never going tae let ye go." His mind wandered for a while consumed with guilt at what they had just done. He experienced another emotion that was foreign to him. He was content with the feel of her body next to him.

"Melissa," he said softly. "Ye're not lost any more."

Chapter Seven

Melissa gently touched her hand to his cheek. "I'm so happy it was you who found me."

He gently kissed her shoulder.

"Aye, lass, I am happy it was me who found ye." His hands lazily stroked her hair, not wanting to break the enchantment that had surrounded them.

"What happens now?" She was truly mystified by his gentle voice. Her hands slid down his back and felt smooth and warm to the touch.

"Beautiful, wonderful things happen now."

"You are amazing. Is it this exciting every time?"

"It gets better," he assured her. "The next time we make love there won't be any painful surprises for you." He kissed her face again. "Ye're not going tae leave me, ever." He made the statement with absolute fact.

She was bewildered by his strong words at such a tender moment. "I had to make the choice to surrender to this passion or regret it forever. Alex, no matter what happens next, we have this moment together." *And if I can stay beside you, I will love you all the days of my life*, whispered in her mind.

Alex kissed her temple and thought silently, *you'd rip my heart out if you left me now.* He rolled to his side and took her with him. Perhaps if they hadn't made love he could have watched her walk away, but he too would have regretted it forever. They had both made a choice, and he could not bear to go through the pain of her departure when he had just come back to life again.

"I'm afraid once you get to know me, you'll hand me over to the Prince." In one short day her world had turned upside down. Melissa didn't want to leave him, ever! She could barely remember her name, let alone where she lived and any other pertinent details of her life. It all seemed so inconsequential compared to the way that she felt when she looked into his eyes. The world fell away, and it was the two of them alone.

"I can be very stubborn," she warned.

He was certain he had proved she was most amiable. "I don't have any intention of handing ye over tae anyone. Ye are mine, and I am yours." He reached over the side of the bed, pulled out a strip of tartan, and wrapped it around her hand that held on to his. "There ye go, lass. We belong tae each other."

"That's all it takes to be officially yours?"

"*Aye*. I know I want ye, and ye want me, too. I'm no' the sharing type of mon." Alex was already deep in thought about the future and what he would have to accomplish to keep her beside him.

"What is this called?"

"Handfasting," he said between kisses. "Ye are mine now, forever."

"That makes me very happy." Melissa was getting sleepy. He was so warm and his hand gently caressing her back had her dozing off in minutes.

75

Alex walked across the room to pick is plaid off the floor where he had dropped it. Their clothing was strewn around the room. He had only minutes to come up with a plan of action before he faced his brothers. He knew he would never give her up. He would have walked through the fires of hell for her, and that fact rattled him more that facing a hundred warriors in battle.

"Rest now, my Angel," he murmured and pressed his lips against her forehead.

Most of the men were on duty or sleeping outside. His brothers were all present in the dining room.

"Good evening, gentlemen," Alex stated in a matter of fact tone as he entered the room.

Daniel and Gideon had their hands clasped in a death grip arm wrestling, and neither one moved an inch in either direction. They already knew, from all the years of watching each other's backs, what had transpired in his chamber.

William stood by the fire and glared at Alex. "She'll probably throw herself off the cliffs tomorrow once she finds out what a bastard ye are. The rules in the Highlands are absolute and binding, even on you, Alex."

"Hell," Evan growled. "What were ye thinking, *mon*? She was under all of our protection."

"We didn't know ye would take it all this far, or we would have stayed here and protected the wee lass," Robert said in a gruff tone of voice.

Alex stood by the hearth and listened to his brother's comments. He accepted their fierce threats were all bluster and any one of them would have been happy to bed her. "If any one of you touches her, I swear by the

Celtic Gods you will live to regret it. I accept full responsibility for my actions," he stated for the record. "She's not leaving. Not tomorrow. Not ever. I have found my *Anam Cara*."

"What makes you think she will want to keep ye?" William scoffed.

Alex took a swing at him. William was younger and faster and hit Alex hard in the mid section, taking him down to the floor.

He was quite serious, and outlined his plan when they lay in a heap, gasping and sweating from the struggle of a wrestling match. When Alex could catch his breath, he said, "She is coming with us."

Melissa woke with a jolt to the sound of shouting voices. The room was dark, and her clothing neatly folded on the chair. A search of his wardrobe produced a shirt to wear and she instinctively followed the noise and the light. "Excuse me." Melissa stated from the doorway. She was amazed at the tangle of men on the floor.

They all stood up and looked at her with wide-eyed stares, thinking she had heard every word. Alex released his stranglehold and Evan crumbled to the floor. Melissa stood still, as mesmerized by them as they were with her.

Alex was certain they were just checking to make certain he hadn't permanently damaged her in some way. She had one of his shirts on and noted the bare feet as well. She had a beautiful, serene smile on her face, and he was instantly thinking about stripping her naked.

"I heard a fight break out," Melissa said. "Is there going to be another battle?"

She stood on one straight leg with the other bent slightly, and Alex forgot to breathe again. She looked verra good in his shirt, he thought.

One of the younger lads stood up and ripped the sleeve off his shirt. "It's only fair tae warn ye lass—"

Melissa felt her heart sink to her toes.

Alexander found his voice again. "The lads think ye should know we are at war with Prince George. The battles *could* go on for several weeks." Alex made the implication clear, that it could also be ended this evening.

"Ye have nothing tae fear, sweet lass," Gideon assured her. "We will protect ye!" He put Evan in a headlock so his brother wouldn't say anything else to upset her.

"You would do that for me?" She was overcome by their generous offer.

Alex exhaled slowly. "I think my brothers adore ye, almost as much as I do," he said charmingly, and let William fall to the floor with a thud. Iain squirmed under his boot, and Alex finally lifted his foot.

"It's no' a secret any more," Iain said, and Evan agreed. They commented on the pink panties held by a tiny slip of satin and lace around her lovely backside. From where they were crushed on the floor, they couldn't help but notice.

Robert fell backward on the couch, unable to speak at all. Four weeks with a beautiful, nearly naked woman in the camp would be a test of their stamina. The remaining brothers exchanged a knowing glance.

They all fascinated Melissa. She had found seven of the most perfect men that had ever graced the earth. It was a little unnerving to be in their midst, and she worried they thought she was too forward. Perhaps she had just broken every social rule in their book, to say nothing of the thousand or so she had just broken in her own time.

William glanced out the window and noticed their camp had company. "We need tae go now!" He nodded toward the front doors and muttered, "Rosabel!"

Alex grabbed her hand and dragged her up the stairs. "Get your things. We are leaving right now."

"I'll get the horses," William announced.

Her dress was stuffed into her bag of painting supplies. "Where are we going?" She was suddenly terrified. "Are we under attack?"

"We're moving our camp tae the cottages in the mountains where the Prince won't be able tae find us." It was a tactical move, to give them as much distance from the local cities as possible.

He took her quickly down the back staircase and out into the courtyard. William had the horses saddled and waiting for them. Alex mounted his horse, and Daniel put his hands on her waist to lift her up before she could protest. She landed on Alexander's lap.

The Laird growled out commands to his warriors in Gaelic. The camp bustled as they moved quickly to break camp. The warriors would cause a diversion and then catch up with their Laird at the cottage.

Gideon stayed behind to command their army. Luckily, one of the warriors had been called home for an emergency and they didn't have to ask for a volunteer to leave. Melissa wouldn't fight, but they could have no more than two hundred and fifty warriors each, or they would have been disqualified. Melissa's name was included on the roster as a warrior, and Rosabel – no doubt – wanted to question the addition in the game.

They set out at a furious pace. Melissa noticed that once they cleared the grounds surrounding the house the terrain got steep. The horses slowed to a walk, and they moved in single file up and down hillsides.

The shimmer of moonlight cast a magical appearance on the hills around them. There were millions of stars overhead on a clear night. The heat of the summer had quickly faded, and a cool evening chilled her bare legs. She leaned back against Alex's chest and took a deep breath, feeling very safe in his arms. His hands were in front of her, holding the reins, and she held on with an arm around his waist.

Alex reached back into his saddlebags and took out a plaid blanket to warm her. If she didn't stop squirming they were going to have to stop for—fifty or sixty years before he could say he had enough of her.

He leaned down and kissed her neck. She was a luscious temptation that filled his head with her scent. He thought back to his comments earlier that day and had to say a silent prayer of thanks for his Angel.

Melissa leaned back against his arm so she could look up in his face. She didn't dare close her eyes, afraid her Celtic warrior would disappear.

Melissa heard William humming softly behind them, and looked back over Alex's arm. "I think I know that song." She just couldn't place it at the moment but recognized the melody from somewhere.

"*Aye*," William agreed. "The lady has excellent taste. I still can't figure out why she'd want tae take up with such an ugly bastard like Alex."

"They're drunk," Daniel explained.

Adding credence to Daniel's words, Iain bobbed, almost falling off his horse.

Melissa looked back at William. "I'm amazed how much you look like Alex."

"*Och*!" The resounding chuckle from the brothers indicated she had hit her mark. But then he began to hum again in a happy drunken state before starting to sing.

"Her beauty in the moonlight overthrew you."

Alex bent his head to kiss her again. The warmth of her lips was gentle and searching. It was as if she too needed the reassurance that what they shared was real.

She put her arms around him and he pulled back to survey the sweet innocent in his arms. For the first time in his life, Alex was truly terrified. It was a void in his life to have not known love, but to have found it and then lose it, would crush his spirit into a numb oblivion. He wouldn't allow that to happen and would risk anything to keep her there with him. The fear that clenched his mind caused him to tighten his grip on her and bury his face in her hair. The night hid the torment on his face, and the anxious moments passed.

She instinctively snuggled up against Alex, allowing his warmth to lull her to sleep.

The last thing she remembered was Alex whispering *hallelujah* in her ear.

Chapter Eight

Laird MacKenna has managed to elude reporters and refused to comment on the lady or the progress of the game. MacKenna is still in the lead, but it's early in the game and perhaps the Laird is a little distracted. Prince George has plenty of time for a few surprises.

On the Streets, with Rosabel

Melissa heard male voices from across the room, turned over, and stood up with a jolt. Her warm feet were on a cold wood floor. She was in a tiny cottage, and five men were standing around a table staring at her. The mist cleared slowly, and she remembered their late night arrival, and being tucked into bed. The dream was real. She sighed.

"Sweetheart, um, ah," Alex stammered.

"Good morning," Melissa said sleepily and stretched.

They all pointed toward the water closet. She stumbled in and shut the door.

"Ten seconds," was the bet between Iain and Evan. She screamed in four seconds, and Evan won. She had just figured out she had nothing on but a blush.

"Alex!" Melissa yelled. The door opened a few inches, and he handed her a wrapper.

Gideon appeared unaffected and shrugged. "I went tae medical school. That's nothing I haven't seen before."

His hands were slightly shaking. "I've just never seen it look that good before now. Wow!"

"Its not too late tae change my major. " Iain stated in a harsh groan and stumbled blindly out of the cottage.

"Did I miss anything?" William sauntered into the cottage, his head pounding from a hangover. Evan walked blindly into him and mumbled an explanation.

Robert's eyes were glazed over. "The sight of that wumman naked takes your breath away."

Melissa was mortified. She vowed to live the rest of her life inside that tiny room, too embarrassed to ever face his brothers again. Alexander coaxed her out of the water closet with an assurance they hardly noticed.

Attendance at their morning battle meetings improved drastically during the next week. Every one of the ten commanders insisted on being included in the meeting. By Friday there wasn't room inside the cottage to turn around, and Alex had to move the meetings outdoors.

Melissa, they all noted, slept right through all the meetings, and didn't have the decency to stand up and stretch even once. The anticipation had nearly driven them all to madness.

Her clothing was packed away in her bag and a full-length dress was found on the table with a note from Daniel that the soft wool would keep her warm. His thoughtful gift brought a tear to her eyes, and she didn't want to think of what he had to sacrifice to purchase the fine fabric. She put on the dress, and then hugged Daniel when she saw him by the lists, even though he told her the dress was actually from Alex.

They were always so affectionate with her. It seemed as if he never wanted to let go of her. Alex had to yell at him several times to get Daniel's arm pried from her waist. She had heard the camp gossip from Iain that the Laird was a raving, jealous maniac. She tried in vain to tell him that Daniel was a gentleman.

"Let go of my wummun!" Alexander challenged, and Daniel finally released her.

He was about to beat Daniel senseless when she distracted him with a soft, warm kiss on his lips, and he forgot about murder and mayhem for a few moments.

During the week at the camp, she was escorted to several "scenic" areas to find a location for her next painting, but she had something special in mind and asked Evan to take her to the lovely stone arched bridge.

Evan was impatient, she noticed, and walked with her everywhere they went at a brisk pace instead of taking a horse from the stables. He told stories of ancient battles, valiant warriors, and heartbroken wenches while she painted. He was known as the camp Bard and entertained them beside the evening campfires.

Melissa loved sitting beside Alex and listening to the burr in their voices as the brothers exchanged tales. They sounded ancient next to her American accent. Melissa was also beginning to feel a sense of possessiveness toward the family as her Celtic Gods commanded the army that surrounded them. They taught her Gaelic while she taught them English. They learned their lessons quickly and be the end of the week they could communicate without Alexander there to act as an interpreter for her.

She was always under one of their protection, as they called it, and she knew it was because she couldn't find a sense of direction. One way seemed as good as another to her. More than once she was told she was on her way to England and to turn around. To her, one ridge looked just as beautiful as the other.

To the MacKenna's, she had frayed every last nerve they possessed. She had nearly discovered their helicopter, parked on the launching pad on the ridge and nestled into a secluded glen, and Gideon's medical instruments were lying out on a table when she entered his tent to speak to him. They had managed to keep her from inspecting the livery while she visited Yorath, and concealed the stamped leather saddles from view.

The warriors were instructed not to talk to her, or Alex would go into a jealous fits and beat them all senseless. They feared Alexander's wrath and avoided her religiously.

Iain cooked their breakfast every morning over a wood-burning stove. The entire clan was so poor they had to steal their food from the Prince.

Melissa worried she would be an added burden to them and couldn't bear to tell him she hated mutton. It was their mainstay, and she nearly choked it down for supper every evening. She would give just about anything for a burger at the Lion's Tap and a frosty mug of root beer instead of the tea they drank. Her diet had drastically changed, her clothing was lost in the future, and hair was giving her fits with the lack of products to tame the frizzy ends during a humid July afternoon. Gideon made her a leather thong to tie her hair into a pony tail, but it was Robert's gift of hand-made hair pins that let her put her hair into a coil, that she finally had it under control.

Wearing the same dress every day was also getting on her nerves and laundry facilities consisted of dipping a garment into a tub, beating it with a rock, and tossing it over a tree branch. They all wore shirts and Kilts, so she found Robert to discuss a proper place to do laundry.

He suggested it was women's work, and the way women had always managed.

"Chauvinist!" She ran after him to beat him senseless. Alex caught her and tossed her over his shoulder to hold her back from wrapping her hands around Robert's throat to strangle him.

It was a week she would never forget. No wonder the women didn't live very long, she thought as she hauled water for the roman bath at the cottage from the Loch. The women didn't paint their nails, because their hands were raw from chopping wood, she reasoned and gave up any pretense of managing the sharp axe. She had to learn how to do the simplest tasks all over again, like washing dishes, without the turbo jet propulsion of her Kenmore dishwasher. With no electricity, they made love by candlelight every night, and didn't stay awake past sunset – too exhausted to see the moon rise.

If she ever made it back to the future, Melissa vowed to check herself into the Sanctuary Spa for a month to undo the damage to her manicure.

How did these people survive? The warriors would return from battle fatigued and exhausted. They dropped on the rocky, hard ground and slept where they fell. It seemed as if everyone had a cut or a bruise, and the hospital tent was always full of bleeding men. Melissa was excused from bandage wrapping duty and encouraged to paint.

Alex sent out patrols twenty-four hours a day. They had four major battles and one minor skirmish. Their points totaled 600 for the week, which gave them a 250-point lead over the Prince. They trained in hand-to-hand combat every day and spent many more hours in a saddle. Alex was relentless. He didn't back down after a victory, and challenged the Prince in every way possible on foot, horseback – during daylight and the night. The warriors answered to their commanders who reported to the Laird. It was an army in motion at all times, and throughout all of the bustle and activity, he never lost sight of his lady. He knew where she was and who she was talking to at every moment. By the end of the first week, the strain had taken a toll on him, as well as his brothers.

He found her sitting beside the Lock with her head down, crying. When he asked what was wrong she mumbled she was homesick for her family but still wouldn't tell him where she had come from or why she couldn't send a letter to tell them she was all right.

"I'm beginning to look like I was dropped from a cliff and rolled in mud," she sobbed against his shirt. Her dress was mud splattered and her hair made Godzilla look like a pretty boy. "I look like a gerbil. Gideon won't give me a razor to shave my legs – he cringed when I told him what it was for and refused to give it to me."

Thank God, Alex silently prayed!

He picked her up and held her in his lap to comfort her. It was late in the day and they were both tired. He dried her tears with his shirt-tails and kissed her swollen, hot lips. The wave of guilt that tore through his heart made his throat tighten. He wanted to tell her everything, and just couldn't watch her so upset without feeling like a monster.

"Melissa," Alex asked while he stroked her back to calm her. "What's a gerbil?"

It broke the tension and she chuckled. "It's a hairy little rodent."

"I like your legs just the way they are," he cooed in her ear, and also cringed at the thought of her using Gideon's razor on her lovely skin. "We will have the Prince routed out of the mountains soon enough. In a few weeks we can go looking for your mysterious family?"

"You'd come with me?" Melissa was shocked, and her head popped up to see his face.

"I will follow ye where ever ye go lass." He tugged on the piece of tartan that he had given her that first night together. "We belong together, and if ye want tae see your family then we will go verra soon."

She felt a tingle run up her spine as she contemplated taking him back to her home in the future. But, could she find the magical door that had brought her here? Could they both pass through that door to return to her life? Her arms tightened around him, and she forgot the misery of missing her sisters.

"Were they so horrible tae ye, tha' ye still canna talk about them lass?"

"No," Melissa said quickly. "They are so far away it will take a miracle to reach them."

"I believe in miracles," he said wistfully.

**

William was ordered to lead an overnight raid. Alex paced the camp at dawn, anxiously waiting for him to return and report on his progress.

Melissa could tell Alex was annoyed by the harsh commands and gruff tone in his voice.

She sipped her coffee, grateful that Iain had found some in a raid. It was unnerving to see them so poor. They stole nearly everything they ate, except mutton, and rarely replaced anything unless it was on the verge of falling off their body, or about to crumble into dust. The coffee was a luxury to them, and she would never look upon her opulent world in the same way again. Sugar was nearly impossible to find, but Gideon traded fresh goat milk at a local village for the treasure. He was grinning like a bobcat when he presented her with the small leather pouch filled with raw brown sugar. She nearly cried it was such a lavish gift and a tender moment with Gideon when he hugged her and said she was sweet as honey.

The first sign of William's return was yelled through the camp. Alex stood like a statue. He could tell there was something wrong. The warriors that rode up to the cottage were deathly silent. William was last to enter the camp and explained the battle didn't go as they hoped.

"The Prince almost caught the pup," a warrior said in Gaelic. "William was so drunk he fell off his horse."

Melissa couldn't understand the words in their heated discussion. Because he was so much younger than most of the warriors, William tried harder than the other ten warriors who had ascended to the rank of Commander. He trained relentlessly and worked long into the night on his sword skills. He had to be exhausted, she reasoned.

Alex was livid!

"It was an ambush," another warrior stated. "The Prince trapped William. We lost one hundred points to keep him from getting captured."

"William! What where ye thinking? Ye know better than tae let the Prince put ye at a disadvantage." Alex had William backed up against a tree. "That could have been a penalty for your capture," Alex shouted in Gaelic.

William shouted just as fiercely. "We executed this plan exactly as commanded."

The warriors scoffed. "We executed the plan all right, right up tae the point where ye fell on your arse."

Alex grabbed William by the shirt and tossed him back at the tree. "You're going tae have tae sober up if ye want tae stay a warrior in my camp. I won't tolerate your drunken mistakes again!"

Melissa was terrified Alex would actually hit him. She ran forward and threw her arms around him. "Please don't hit William!"

Alex looked down. His frown should have warned her she was treading on dangerous ground, but her earnest plea got through the anger, calming him.

"I have no intention of hitting him at the moment, Melissa." Later, he would beat some sense into his brother. The thought made him feel better.

William looked at her in shock and at Alex in anger. "I almost go' trapped by the Prince because ye wouldn't listen tae me, Alex. I warned ye!"

"Ye almost got caught because ye were drunk, and drunks make stupid mistakes."

Melissa could feel his muscles tighten. She tightened her hold on him, and he looked down again. "Please don't kill him," she implored Alex.

He felt a tinge of jealousy. It was a damned difficult transition in his life to allow anyone else to interfere with his family.

The warriors noted his reaction and disappeared into the morning fog before the Laird turned on them. Gideon had warned them the Laird was insanely jealous.

William turned and walked away. The defeat had cost them dearly. The warriors wouldn't let him forget it as they worked even harder to make up the points.

Melissa wasn't about to let go of Alex. She held on tightly until she knew he had calmed.

Alex put his arm around her, deciding to take her to the Loch where they could speak privately. The camp was bustling with warriors.

"Ye can let go of me now, sweetheart." He looked down. Melissa released her hold on him, and her smile warmed his heart. They set off for the loch, his hand firmly holding hers as he dragged her down the path.

Melissa was afraid of what he would say to her. He appeared to be upset at the moment, and she wasn't about to ask if they still flogged women in this time period. He was so tender and loving to her; she couldn't imagine him beating William senseless but had seen enough of their playful shoving to know it wasn't too far from what they were already doing to each other.

She didn't want to think about the upcoming battle. Alex could frighten most men into defeat, but the Prince wasn't about to back down. No matter how many times Alex bested the Prince, he came back for more. The battles were getting increasingly dangerous. Injured warriors were taken directly to Gideon's tent.

"Would it be possible for me to come along with you?" Melissa asked while they walked.

"If we brought ye along, I wouldn't think about the battle, lass." He had thought about that possibility a hundred times. Alex didn't like leaving her at the camp. He worried about her when he was gone and couldn't stay away from her when he returned. The warriors were trained, but it wouldn't take much of a distraction to throw a battle.

Alex explained his reasons why he couldn't take her with him. "The warriors often drop their kilts tae the ground and go into battle half-naked, with only their shirts tae cover their 'parts' during the battle. It might be rather shocking for a lady." While this was historically accurate, Alexander had not personally witnessed such a display. In fact, he didn't want her to see all the tourists who line up to watch the battles.

"I hadn't thought of that's." She hadn't considered what it would be like to watch a battle with hundreds of half-naked men.

"Are you angry with me?" She didn't like to think about the long hours he was gone.

"No. I'm no' angry, *A Grá*. My brothers and I fight all the time, so we forget what it must look like for someone new tae our way of doin' things."

"William tries so hard to please you, Alex. You push him harder than anyone else."

"I know I do and for good reasons. William has more training than most of our warriors. He needs tae learn how tae take command and earn the respect of the men who will fight hard for him."

"How could anyone measure up to you? Alex, you worked hard for a long time to become the mighty warrior you are now, but William is still very young. I'm sure you made a few mistakes when you were younger."

"No. I didn't," Alex said, and his voice raised a notch. "William has got tae stop thinking he is alone and learn how tae draw from the power of all his warriors. If he takes on this war by himself, he will be defeated."

"Then teach him how to do that," Melissa insisted.

"What do ye think we're trying tae do with him? He has tae know there are consequences if he fails. I'm his Laird, and he answers tae me. The men who trusted him tae lead them into that battle won't let him forget his disgrace. They will be ten times harder on him than I was. I canna protect him every day of his life. He must become a man, ye ken?"

She looked at him in wonder and heavily sighed.

They had only a few moments left before he had to depart and Alex didn't want to spend those precious moments arguing. He backed her up to a tree for a kiss.

The warmth of her tender lips caused a jerk in his stomach. How could he think about anything else but her warm and wonderful body under him in bed?

Melissa wound her arms around his neck and leaned into his warmth. He could make her forget just about anything, except that he was about to leave her again. She wanted to beg him to stay with her to keep him safe. She couldn't think about losing him in battle.

The anxiety caused her stomach to drop to her toes. It felt horrible to have to let go of him, even for a few hours, knowing he was going into a dangerous battle.

The touch of his lips was bittersweet. Every goodbye could be their last words spoken to each other, and every hello was as joyous as their first. She loved him in those few moments with her heart and soul. There were tears glistening in her eyes when he pulled back, but she forced a smile.

The warriors led his stallion up to the Loch and waited for Alex. It wasn't easy to concentrate when an army watched your every move. Alex kissed her quick and walked away. It unnerved him to see her upset.

The army rode slowly past her. Her hands were in her pockets. She wanted to go with them, just for the sake of knowing Alex was all right.

She climbed to the top of the nearest ridge to watch them ride away and waved them all on to victory. Melissa yelled as loud as she could "Alex!"

He stopped and turned back toward her. He was at the front of the army, and they halted.

Melissa blew him a kiss.

Iain and Robert were riding behind Alex and noticed the kiss she threw. "That kiss was meant for me," Iain said fondly, smacking his lips, and leaning back in his saddle. "She adores me."

Robert scoffed. "Why would a beautiful wumman throw a kiss tae a toad? No, little brother, that kiss was meant for me." He grinned. "She likes me more than ye."

Daniel knew better. "Sorry, lads, that kiss was meant for me. She likes me better than both ye ugly bastards. She told me yesterday that she thinks I am charming."

"Charming?" Iain teased. "*Aye*, and aren't we the lucky lads that get tae fight next tae his Highness today," the warriors agreed with howls of laughter.

"Ye can kiss my royal arse," Daniel growled.

It started again down the line of warriors. Every warrior claimed that kiss was just for him, and occasionally, a fight would break out in the ranks when one warrior was absolutely certain she was looking directly at him when she sent the kiss.

Alex just shook his head and pressed onward. It was a daily ritual with his warriors that he had come to accept. Alex knew she liked him best of all, and that was enough, he thought with a smug smile.

It was a good fight that day. The warriors had plenty of energy to wear off on the battlefield. By the end of the day, they had made up the points lost earlier that day and had an easy 200 point lead over the Prince.

Alex didn't lift his sword once and sent William in to meet Prince George. It caused quite the upset on the battlefield as the Prince faced William MacKenna. Alex was testing them both. William was brilliant, fast, and strong and took the opportunity to trounce the Prince. Alex beamed with pride.

Later, Alex and Daniel discussed the battle from the edge of the glen. "What do ye think George has planned?"

"George isn't the type of *mon* who makes a boast of that magnitude without a plan in mind. Perhaps it was a psychological threat and no' one that he intended tae carry ou' with action."

"Double the patrols and put the question again tae the Commanders who are baffled at what the Prince has in mind. I suggest we contact Rosabel tae find ou' if she knows the answer."

"We should send Gideon...."

Knowing Gideon, he would have her in bed within the hour, and she would tell him anything he wanted to know. Rosabel had an ardent interest in Gideon, if what he heard about their meeting on the steps of the Manor House was true.

"Have Robert take Gideon tae London for the day tae pick up medical supplies." For the first time in eighteen years, Alex was worried.

Daniel conveyed the instructions to Gideon and Robert. Alex reminded them both they were needed in the game and not to be gone too long.

"And ye will distract Melissa so she doesn't notice a helicopter taking off?"

Alex smiled. "Aye, I'll keep her distracted."

Chapter Nine

Melissa's thoughts wandered. Painting had become her obsession. The inspiration overwhelmed her at times, and she couldn't help thinking that being in love for the first time in her life had brought a light and life in her work that hadn't been there before she left for Scotland. She sketched if she couldn't paint. In her heart, she knew her time in the mountains was limited, and she didn't want to miss anything. There were days she produced only one painting, other days she managed to complete two and had watercolors to fill in when she was waiting for the paint to dry.

It didn't surprise her that for every painting she completed, a new canvas magically appeared. The warriors cherished her paintings and fought about who she was thinking about when she painted the battle. Alex and his brothers all seemed to anticipate her every need, but she finally broke down in tears when Daniel had given her a new canvas.

"Please don't spoil me so." She sobbed against his shirt. "The clan is so poor I just can't accept your expensive gifts when you need the money for food."

Daniel was charmed speechless.

She loved watching Alex command the warriors. He instinctively knew what each person was good at and drew them into the decisions. By night Alex was loving and tender. By day he growled out commands, yelled like a demon, and pushed the men to their limits. He was every bit the powerful Laird and expected his commands would be carried out without complaint.

They were daunting to look at and fearsome when they challenged their enemy. Alex had four eagle feathers in his cap, Daniel had three, and every other warrior was only allowed to have one. It was custom, Alex explained to her one evening when she asked about their garments, belted kilts, and the distinction of the eagle feathers.

Robert reminded her of a fierce Native American warrior with his long black hair and dark eyes. The MacKenna brothers all held a rank of Chief, but they honored Alexander as their Laird. When he went anywhere, he was guarded by warriors, and Daniel said it was called his *tail* so that no man could do harm to their Laird.

Alex had four warriors who flanked him during battles, and those warriors were hand picked as the most daring and able to protect the Laird. They all also wore dirks, which she came to learn were small sharp daggers that were often tucked into their stockings and pulled out in the crush of battle.

Evan was their Bard or *Seanachaidh* as they called him. His duty was to write down and remember the history of the clan, and he often gave oral dissertations that could drive a nun to drink. He was exact, precise, and would brook no deviation from the historical facts.

There were pipers and drummers in the ranks that entertained them in the evenings. Alex was stunning in full regalia with a black velvet doublet with silver dolphins for buttons.

Their dogs were great black hulking beasts that were tended by the warriors and given free reign of the camp. They were larger than any dogs she had ever seen, and they could be as fierce as their masters and as gentle as a kitten when Alex gave a command, and the animals obeyed without a whimper.

Gideon was teasing her on one occasion and said they had left the lions at the castle and didn't bring beasts to the battles any longer.

When she questioned Alex about the lions, he broke into laughter and walked away.

Evan and Iain were tactical geniuses. They planned the battles with Alex looking over their shoulders. He would listen to his Chief's recommendations before making the final command.

The Clan hunted for food but lived primarily on mutton, much to Melissa's distress. She saw a chicken tucked into the belt of a warrior that had returned to the camp but couldn't stomach the thought of preparing the bird for supper.

She wondered if the Olive Garden would consider delivery. She was almost desperate enough to eat tree bark, and fettuccini *alfredo* was constantly on her mind. If only she could phone in an order. Her cell phone battery had gone dead, and she wasn't sure if they could cross the same time barrier but thought she was almost desperate enough to try.

Alex could tenderly hold her at his side and then bellow commands to the warriors at the same time. He was magnificent, strong, and dazzled her every time he looked at her. Melissa loved him more than she ever thought possible, and had to admit she was proud of all of them. They were fierce, strong, tall, and so handsome.

She was having an amazing impact on all of them. By the end of the second week, their English had greatly improved, and she could understand them all, even with the burr in their deep, rich voices.

Evan especially had a knack for picking up languages, she learned, since he could curse louder and longer than all of them, in a variety of languages. He took his position as the Clan *bladaire* very seriously and hailed their victories to the camp.

The camp was very quiet one evening, and Alex told her they had lost an important battle. She nearly broke into tears, hugged all his brothers, and gave them some words of encouragement. They were more than willing to lose a few more battles, just for the attention, and Alex had to remain beside her or he was certain she wouldn't make it back to the cottage.

Alex softened his directions to the warriors because Melissa was present. When they suffered a defeat, he drilled battle tactics into their heads for hours. Their third defeat brought them dangerously close to losing the game. Alex pressed them harder to think faster while they had the opportunity to turn the battle into a victory.

Melissa found it was a good time to visit Yorath rather than worry. She adored the magnificent stallion and always saved him a piece of apple or a carrot for a treat. He followed her everywhere she went.

She didn't see Alex put his head down and cover his face with his hands, "She's ruined my warhorse," he choked, "and I'll have tae put him ou' tae stud."

"Tis sad tae see a stallion act just like his master," Gideon clamped a hand on Alex's shoulder, smirking.

By the end of the week, Melissa had heard every curse word possible, in two or three different languages. She never berated anyone for cursing and asked Alex to translate the list.

He took the list from her and spent nearly a half an hour yelling at his brothers for teaching her how to curse in Gaelic, Chinese, and Russian.

Melissa worried about them all when they went into battle. When Alex walked into the cottage at night she put her arms around him and nearly broke into tears she was so grateful he was still alive. She was so much in love with the man she couldn't think about anything else. Her previous life and her family were forgotten in the arms of her love. She sensed there was something dreadful that he wasn't telling her, and the apprehension of what that could be was leaving her a nervous wreck.

She had also become terrified of the mist. They walked along the Loch one evening and the mist rolled in to the shore. She was nearly hysterical, and dragged Alex back to the cottage. Melissa was torn between going home to her sisters, and the man who loved her so completely. Either way she would lose some part of her heart. She wasn't ready to return to the future – not yet. The first week had been hell, but she didn't want to leave unless Alex was going with her.

Life in a war camp was far different than anything she could ever expect. There was more than one fistfight Alex had to step in and settle. Almost every one of the fistfights were instigated by William, but they were all certain it was just because he had been sober for at least two days in a row and was a little touchy. The warriors feared and respected Alex and Daniel who were also trained in martial arts and were masters with a sword in their hands. A fight would break out in the camp, Alex would barely flinch, and the warrior would crumble to the ground or land five feet away.

Alex demanded perfection of his warriors. Training in his camp was mandatory, and he personally supervised most of the physical training. The men would train with scimitar swords and then their abilities were tested until they got the moves down where they could do them without thinking. Daniel was also revered and feared in the camp, she found out because no one wanted to fight with him except Alex.

It came as a surprise to find out they were all trained to fight by a woman. They called her VixenBlade and always put a hand over their heart in salute to her many talents when they made the comment. Melissa couldn't wait to meet her.

Alex spoke of her with absolute respect and admiration for her skill with a blade. Robert perked up the moment her name was mentioned. Melissa guessed he was madly in love with her but didn't want his brothers to notice.

There were also craftsmen in the Clan who made and repaired shields and swords. Their shields were not much more than a circle of leather on a wood frame. Some of them had a *targe* in the center, and Melissa was told it was the center spike.

Melissa announced she wanted to do a painting of the church she passed, and it was decided that Iain, who had more to confess than all of them put together, should be the one to take her to the Kirk. Iain was delighted for the opportunity to spend the day with Melissa.

They rode on horseback to the lovely Kirk set on a hillside. Melissa quickly found the perfect point of view for her painting. Iain went inside to see the priest with a long list of his many transgressions.

Melissa chose the side of the Kirk where a tall statue of an Angel was surrounded by flowers. The contrast of stone against brilliantly colored flowers caught her eye, and she quickly sketched the scene on the canvas. The canvas was placed on the easel, and she began in earnest.

She had been painting for over an hour when she heard someone approach. Melissa looked up and smiled as a gentleman walked up to her and stood behind her to look at the painting.

"You're an artist," he said, and she was instantly drawn to the silky sound of his voice.

Melissa noticed a dazzling smile, and the paintbrush lay idle in her hand. "Yes," she said and returned his smile. "Are you a wandering art critic?"

He laughed softly. "No, Sassenach. I'm a man who appreciates true beauty, like you."

She was stunned. "Thank you." Melissa felt a little uncomfortable. She had heard the term before and knew it meant that she was English.

He reached out, gently took her hand in his, and kissed her paint blotched fingers. "I can see why my cousin, Alexander, is enchanted."

Melissa couldn't help but notice the heat from his ardent perusal. She was horribly embarrassed at the paint splats on her hand that he stroked, gently and admiringly in his.

"I'd love to take you dancing in the moonlight," he said smoothly, devastating her defenses with another smile. "I'd give just about anything to see your gorgeous blue eyes twinkle in the starlight. We'd dance until dawn, and then...."

He was standing right next to her, and she had to admit he was one handsome man. He had dark, straight hair with a tinge of silver at his temples and smoldering deep blue eyes.

Tall, dark, and dangerous was her thought as he reached out to brush the backs of his fingers against her cheek. He wanted to take her dancing. The thought whirled her stomach into a knot. Wasn't that what she had asked for—a man who could love with a passion and could dance? If she hadn't met Alex first, she would have agreed to a date with him.

But Melissa wouldn't betray her affection for Alex. "I'm not available."

"I'm truly devastated. Would you please deliver a message to Alex for me?"

"I'd be happy to deliver a message, but you could probably find him later this evening."

"I'm sure he's out riding with his warriors," he said. "Give Alex this message; tell him his cousin says *touché.*

He will understand the meaning." The stranger brushed past her on his way back down the path.

Melissa thought he was a very confusing man. "By the way, what is your name?" she called out after him, but he had disappeared from sight. She returned her attention to her painting, and the hours slipped away. Her thoughts wandered back to the handsome man, and she couldn't help thinking she had met him before now. It was late afternoon when she discovered Iain had fallen asleep in the church and gently shook him awake.

They walked back to the cottage with the horse in tow, and Melissa noticed Alex across the field. She looked at Alex and could feel the heat rising in her body. She waved and walked on to the cottage, certain her face was glowing like a 500-watt light bulb. How could he get her pulse throbbing through her veins with just a look from across a field?

The intimate relationship they shared at night was so vastly different from their lives during the day. It was his ability to reduce her to mental mush every time he kissed her. Damn he was good at kissing, she thought and her body tingled in response.

Evan met them on their way into camp. Iain left her in Evan's care.

Evan chatted about directions, and her eyes glazed over. It was useless to point out the sun rose in one direction or set in the other.

"Ye aren't paying attention," Evan scolded. "We will review my instructions, ye ken?"

Melissa looked at him with a frown. "Instructions?"

Evan was frustrated beyond belief. "*Och!*" he scoffed and threw his hands up in the air. He had to walk away at that point or he was going to do something drastic like strangle her. He left muttering he had witnessed a miracle—she had somehow on this huge planet, managed to find them. It had to be divine intervention because she couldn't find her way to the glen.

She frowned again at his back because she honestly couldn't remember what he was talking about. When Alex looked at her, she couldn't think about anything. Evan was still ranting at her when he reached Alex at the list, and Melissa could see Alex laugh and give Evan a shove toward the training field. Evan shoved Alex back, and the fight began. Moments later Evan was running from the field, as both Alex and Daniel were about to teach him some patience.

At supper that night they recounted their valor and Melissa listened intently. They had lost an important battle. She could tell by their quiet manner.

Alex noticed her painting and looked at her wide-eyed. "Why did ye decide tae paint this?"

She became alarmed at the look on his face. "It seemed the perfect view of the Kirk."

The painting got the same reaction from all of them. They looked at Iain who didn't have an explanation because he had been detained inside the Kirk all day.

"Do ye know what you've painted?" Alex asked.

"The Kirk?" She didn't have a clue what upset them.

"The graves are for our ancestors," Gideon said softly from behind her. "It's where the Baron and Lisette are laid tae rest."

Melissa looked at the painting again. "The language on the markers was Gaelic, and I didn't understand what it said. I just found a beautiful site and was captivated by the stone Angel and lovely garden."

Alex put his arm around her shoulders. "This painting will be treasured by all of us."

She sighed in relief. "Then it is a gift to your family."

Alex looked at it thoughtfully and swallowed past a painful lump in his throat. "Ye ha'e a wonderful talent."

They were called to supper, and Melissa sat down between Alex and Daniel.

"By the way, I met your cousin today." The emotion was thick in the air.

"My cousin?" he said casually, but every muscle in his body tensed, and it was very quiet around her.

"Yes. He stopped to chat while I was painting at the Kirk. He said to give you a message." Melissa didn't like the silence. They all waited to hear the message. "He was very charming and polite," she reassured them.

"Wha' is the message?" Alex asked. His teeth were clenched together, and a muscle rippled along his jaw.

She couldn't help but notice that Iain looked like he was going to faint. "He said to say, *touché* and that you would know what it means."

"Did he touch ye, sweetheart?"

"No—well he did touch my cheek."

They all stood at once.

"That sneaky bastard," Evan growled in Gaelic. "Where were ye, Iain?"

"I was in the church keeping the Priest busy so he wouldn't come out tae ask her any questions—as I was instructed tae do, remember?"

Alex mentally tallied the points and then spoke quietly in Gaelic. "George gets the points even if he didn't kidnap her. That's a loss of 250 points. Prince George has just taken the lead. He expects retaliation tonight. Call a meeting of the Commanders."

"Are you upset with your cousin?" Melissa was confused.

"I've got an idea," William said from the far end of the table.

Alex leaned forward. "Yes, William." He smiled at Melissa and held up a hand to indicate he had heard her and would answer her shortly.

"Send in two or three warriors and steal all of his horses," William suggested. "We can engage a battle while they're roundin' up their beasties."

"That's brilliant," Alex commented. "Take the Marines, James and Jonathan, with ye."

Alex switched to English for her. "We will retaliate because he touched ye," he explained to Melissa. It was only a slight exaggeration of the truth. They had lost points, but it also irked Alex to know that the Prince could have walked away with her today, and Alex would have forfeited the game to get her back. They had come too far to turn back now. His brothers were also thinking about that possibility and gave him a worried frown.

"No one touches ye. With so many men around, it would be dangerous tae start something ye couldn't finish. My cousin will no' get away with that insult."

William stood and followed his orders. He called out to James and Jonathan on his way to the stables. There were two patrols coming in for reports, and William met them to get the latest information about troop location.

Alex kissed her, and she couldn't remember her name when he set her back on her feet. She felt like she was floating on air.

***

At sunset, James and Jonathan were saddled and waiting for William. They rode out and would spend the entire night collecting horses.

They had to sneak directly into their camps and that earned them fifty additional points. William and his cousins corralled the horses in a glen several miles from the Prince's camp. The additional points almost put them back in the lead.

The next morning, Melissa noted that Alex could give praise when a task was completed as planned. William received the recognition he deserved in proclaimed victories from the men.

By mid-morning, the Prince had a chance to collect his horses and Alex rode out to meet him in battle.

Melissa walked into the cottage to collect her paints, and William followed her inside.

"I'll only be a minute," she said quickly and reached for her bag next to the table.

"Melissa, I want tae speak tae you." William's voice was tender.

The cottage grew smaller by the moment, and she bolted out the door. Distance, she thought and nearly ran out of camp toward the hills. Melissa couldn't wait for

Iain. She needed to put some space between her and William immediately. There was no logical explanation for her haste, but Alex was a jealous man and she wasn't about to give the camp more gossip.

Daniel, Gideon, and Robert were all Chiefs and led out three bands of men to harass the Prince, who was just about to find all his horses were missing.

Daniel noticed Melissa running out of camp and then saw William come out of the cottage. They had three important battles to lead, and Daniel caught Evan and sent him in her direction to watch over her.

"You've got tae have a talk with William," Daniel said quietly to Gideon. His warriors waited for his command. "He listens tae ye, and he's abou' tae make a terrible mistake if he tries tae bed Melissa. She doesn't seem tae reciprocate his adoration."

Gideon had noticed as had the warriors. He mounted and let out a long sigh. "I'll have tae talk tae him some time soon abou' him following her around. Alex is bound tae notice even if she doesn't."

"Do it soon, Gideon, before Alex finds out she just bolted out of the cottage."

"*Och*," Gideon became alarmed. "That boy is goin' tae get his arse kicked."

"Aye and he'd deserve it to." Daniel confirmed. "Evan will keep her safe today."

Chapter Ten

Laird MacKenna's ladies have loudly voiced their disapproval that a woman was allowed in the game. His Personal Assistant, Bridget, set fire to his office when she heard the latest gossip. I'm thinking, she didn't take the news that he had found a new love, verra well.

On the Streets, with Rosabel

Evan knew every blade of grass in the surrounding area. He caught up to her just in time to turn her away from walking into a nearby village.

That evening, Melissa waited for Alex at the stables. She found out from Evan that Alex wouldn't allow any other women in camp and asked him to explain.

"We'd all quit fighting," he said and took the saddle off his stallion. "If ye give a Scot a choice between a good fight and his lady, you might no' get a fight out of him."

"I didn't know Scotland was such a passionate country. The warriors are known to be fierce in battle but I had no idea they were also devoted lovers." She lovingly stroked Yorath's neck.

"I'm a very devoted lover," Alex agreed with a glint in his eye. They walked back from the stables, and she put her hand in his. She brushed the dust off his shirt, and he playfully reached down to bite her neck.

They could hear Daniel yelling from across the field. "Iain, I'm goin' tae have ye gelded! What were ye thinking? Are ye trying tae break all family records for the highest number of paternity suits?" Daniel yelled.

He met Alex and Melissa on the path. I hae' tae leave and meet with the parents of yet another young lady. Keep Iain in the camp."

Melissa asked, "How many paternity suits can one family have?"

Alex realized the horrible blunder as Daniel rode away. His mind went blank. He just couldn't think of anything to say to cover up the fact that they didn't have paternity suits in the year 1745.

She wasn't sure if they didn't have an accurate count or didn't want to discuss such a delicate subject in front of the warriors.

Alex had just enough time to eat, and he was out with the warriors again. This time, he wouldn't be back until very late at night since it was already supper bells in the camp.

Melissa was asleep when he dropped into bed next to her. Alex was asleep before she could even say goodnight. By morning's light, he was gone from camp and leading another battle.

Gideon's gentle manner always soothed her loneliness. She didn't visit his hospital tent too often because she couldn't stand the sight of blood. By Thursday, the hospital tent was full of warriors, and they needed the cottage table to sew up a cut on his leg.

She had just walked back from the loch and found the cottage filled with warriors. The small table was turned into an operating room, and Gideon brought in several candles for light.

Melissa noticed the open wound and gagged. She could see the muscle protruding from the man's leg and blood gushing everywhere.

It suddenly got very warm inside the cottage and, she couldn't seem to breathe at all. Her vision got fuzzy, and the room started to spin.

"Melissa, good we need another pair of hands," Gideon said. "Here, hold down his leg, while I — "

Evan caught her before she hit the floor in a faint. He put her down on the bed tucked into the corner of the room.

"There are smelling salts in my medical bag, but perhaps we should wait until I'm finished tae wake her."

***

Alex returned to the camp that evening to discover Melissa in an unconscious state. His anger was curtailed when he found out the reason and instructed them to set up an auxiliary hospital so Gideon had some extra room.

Alex closed the door to the cottage and went over to the bed. Melissa's complexion was still pale, and he gently lifted her head with a hand on the back of her neck. Her eyes fluttered open, and she looked up at him.

"Alex," she spoke in a broken whisper. "That man on the table nearly had his leg cut off."

Alex tried hard not to distress her by laughing. "He go' four stitches and they let him keep his leg."

"The wound looked far more serious than a few stitches," she said frostily.

"Are you feeling up tae supper now, or would you like tae wait until later?"

"I can think of other things I would like to do later," she said with a silky voice. "So you better eat now to build up your strength."

He liked the sound of that challenge. Their supper was out in the camp that evening, and Melissa got a chance to meet several of the warriors, including their cousins, James and Jonathan. Alex didn't allow too much conversation with the warriors, she noticed beyond a casual greeting. He explained that if she were to favor one over the other, fights would break out and then he would have chaos on his hands.

Alex also noticed she wasn't eating very much, if anything at all. She nibbled on a slice of rye bread, and he realized it had never dawned on him to ask her if she was a vegetarian.

Their supper was always boisterous with warriors walking around and shouting across the camp. His brothers ate with the group they commanded that day or sat with them.

Alex usually didn't eat with the warriors. During the previous eighteen years, it was his few moments of solitude. Since Melissa had joined them, she preferred sitting outside. The men appreciated her encouragement and enthusiasm, and it gave Alex a chance to see the warriors in a much different way. They were fun, friendly, and helpful to each other. Also, rude, crude, and ready to beat the hell out of each other if pushed.

Evan was called upon again for a tale, and he stood in the clearing, looking thoughtful for a moment.

"I think I have the perfect tale for this evening," he started, and the warriors settled down to hear it. Evan spoke to Daniel for a moment and then nodded.

Alex sat on the edge of the table and held Melissa close to his side. She never went very far away from him, enjoying their moments together beside the campfire.

"My tale this evening will be in English for the lovely lady." Evan bowed to Melissa. "The Guardian at the Well," he began. "Or, Tae kiss a Hag."

Melissa groaned loudly. "Hag?"

"'Tis a good story." Alex smiled at her response. Melissa got worried where this story was going, but Alex only laughed and nudged her closer to his side.

"Niall of the Nine Hostages," Evan began his story.

Evan's voice was smooth as silk when he was telling a tale and there was a light in his eyes that Melissa loved to watch. He was their Bard; there was no mistaking his love of a fine tale.

Evan waited until the crowd had settled down. He loved the drama and winked at Melissa. He cleared his throat and began in earnest.

"Niall and his brothers were lost in the forest and they needed water tae cook the game they had killed. The oldest was the first brother who went in search of water. He found a Hag guarding a well who told him that he could have his water, but for one kiss." Evan held up his pointer finger for emphasis and the warriors groaned in response.

"Just one kiss," Evan continued now that he had their attention. "The oldest brother took one look and couldn't bear the sight of the old hag and returned tae his thirsty family empty handed." Evan was looking directly at Alex, who only smiled.

They all groaned. Evan strutted in that MacKenna swagger with his hands clasped behind his back around the circle of warriors.

"The second brother went tae the well for water and the Hag again said yes, ye can have the water but for one kiss. The second brother looks at the hag and cringes. He canna bear the sight of her." Evan held up his arm, shielding himself, but with a smile.

There were more cheers. Melissa groaned.

"Ye can imagine what that poor bastard was thinking," Evan interjected his own thoughts into the story and there was a resounding agreement from the warriors. "If I can just close my eyes and kiss the hag I get the water. But no, he couldnae do it tae save his family. The coward walked away, and the old Hag still hadn't been kissed."

Melissa choked. "Old Hag?"

Evan enjoyed her discomfort immensely. He continued with his tale. "The youngest lad, Niall, journeys tae the well and finds the hag who tells the lad he can have the water, but for one kiss."

"Niall thinks about the offer for a moment and asks the hag, I get only one kiss? Now," Evan interjected again. "He looks at the same task and instead of saying I canna' kiss her even once, he wants tae kiss her," Evan looked fondly at Melissa, "over and over again. Niall looks at the old hag and asks her again for the water."

"Aye!" Evan loudly proclaims and the warriors joined in with a resounding "Aye!"

Evan paused in front of Melissa for affect. "The lad kisses the hag."

There was a lot of cheering and whistling as Evan leaned down and kissed Melissa for effect. The kiss was more than an innocent peck on the lips. Alex noticed Melissa also accommodated Evan's creative license. He scowled a warning at Evan.

Evan straightened and let out a long, shaky breath. "Whew!" Evan smiled and continued. "And the old Hag turned into a young, beautiful, enchanted woman whose name is Sovereignty! The lad was given the water that saved his family. She told him that some day he would become King of Tara. The moral of this tale is tae look beyond what we see on the surface." Evan bowed.

"Ye stole a kiss," the warriors yelled.

Evan beamed. "Aye, I did! And I'm still alive!"

"Smart lad," was heard across the camp.

Evan still had their attention. "Now, for my *encore*."

"Ye better think twice abou' any more kisses from my beautiful wumman, ye ken?" Alex warned.

Evan kept his distance and beamed. Daniel passed the gold coin to Evan. Evan had bet him that he could kiss Melissa right in front of Alex and he wouldn't get killed. Daniel thought this was a fool's bet because Alex wouldn't allow anyone to kiss Melissa, especially in front of all the warriors.

Melissa wound her arm around Alex's waist. "That was a good story Evan. Thank you."

Alex stood and took her with him back to the cottage. He didn't want anyone else getting ideas about stealing a kiss from Melissa. The camp was winding down for the night, and the evening patrols were checking in for reports and instructions.

Robert took the reports and issued the instructions. It amazed Melissa to see them all work together. They shared the burdens and responsibilities of the camp as well as the ongoing battles.

"Alex," she took his hand and led him away from the cottage. "Let's take a walk in the moonlight."

He walked beside her, thoughtful for a few minutes while they exited the camp. They would be watched by one of their patrols, he knew, because no one got near that cottage when they went to bed at night. The guards that surrounded them were very discreet. She didn't notice the men stationed around the edge of the forest or along the rocky ridge to their South.

Melissa got to the top of the ridge. "This is so beautiful, Alex. Why couldn't we just stay here for the rest of our lives?"

Loch Voile was calm and reflected a half-moon and stars like a mirror. "Aye darling, it's beautiful and peaceful. But cold in the winter in the cottage."

"You'd keep me warm." She snuggled into his embrace and tipped her chin so he could see her smile. "Wouldn't you?"

"I'd never let ye get ou' of bed. Don' ye think you'd get lonely ou' here?" She snuggled up to him, and he kissed the top of her head.

"I love it here. It feels magical and ancient." Her hands caressed his back. The warmth of his skin under his shirt drew her like a magnet.

"Aye, darlin', tis beautiful, but ye'd better watch out for the fairies coming out tae steal a beautiful wumman. They'd take ye into their magical castles, and we'd never see ye again."

"Well then I have nothing to worry about! I'm just an old Hag."

His body shook from laughter.

"Would you, my handsome darling, kiss a Hag?"

The simmer in his jade eyes sparkled in the moonlight. He bent down and brushed his warm lips across hers, and it was all the invitation she needed. Melissa wound her arms around his neck and held on as his tongue touched and caressed hers. The sensation was warm and had a dizzying affect on her.

His arms held her tight and lifted her off the ground while he tasted and tempted her. The ache deep within her was already at a fever pitch, and yet, he could make her burn with desire. He released her slowly, and she slid down the length of his warm body. Melissa took several deep breaths to calm the rage of passion. Her cheek rested against his chest while his arms held her tight.

"Ye sure don't kiss like a hag," he teased.

Melissa bit him lightly on the chest.

"Och! Ye're in a playful mood. Now I am going tae get ye into bed fast!"

Alex took her hand in his. They walked back to the cottage and it was their nightly routine to take a hot bath before bed. The bath was a marvel of ancient Roman design, Robert had explained, and heated by stones in the sunlight during the day.

Alex was already in the bath. He could strip off his clothing faster than anyone she had ever met. She hung up her dress, and she stepped in behind him. Melissa put her hair up with a comb so she didn't have to try and dry it before she went to bed. Alex reached for the bar of soap that he used on his hair, and she took it from his fingers, and reached up to wash his hair.

That left Alex with two free hands to apply soap to her body. He had her right where he wanted her, settled on his lap. His lips caressed hers while she massaged the soap in his hair. It was a delightful sensation, he thought and continued to plunder and taste her soft lips until the soap started to run down his face. Alex dunked his head under the water and rinsed off.

He shook his head and water splashed in her face. She sat on a ledge and involuntarily gasped as his hands slid up her thighs. The water wasn't very deep and he was on his knees in front of her.

"I canna remember a time in my life when I've been so happy," he murmured, and his body responded, hungry and demanding as his fingers found the heat of her.

"I love tae watch ye sleep," his voice was pitched deep and low. He knew where to touch her to bring her comfort, and so much pleasure she purred and her head fell back. Her legs wrapped around his hips, but he would not cease the rhythm, or let her pull away from him. He slid deeper and he could feel her muscles spasm against his hand.

"No, no' yet," he stepped out of the bath and stood her before him to dry her with his kilt. Her knees buckled from the heady pleasure of his tongue against her hardened nipples.

The heat of his body excited her. He took her hand in his and kissed her fingertips. Alex lit a candle and put it on the table.

Alex didn't seem to mind the cool room and waited for her to crawl into bed. She was settled in the small bed, and he crawled in next to her, rolled over and had her pinned under him.

"Just where I want ye," he said softly and brushed the hair from her face. His weight was braced with his elbows as he studied her face in the candlelight. The shimmer of love in her blue and violet eyes always brought a wild joy to his heart. Her skin was softer than the finest silk, and she responded so intensely to his touch that it delighted him to know she desired him.

Melissa didn't give a little of her heart; she poured it all into their world. He savored that moment of ecstasy as the wet heat of her enveloped him. He tried to remember every detail, every feeling, all the turbulent emotion he felt when they became one, and yet found every night he had forgotten her beauty and the raw passion that engulfed him. In this physical embrace, he was beyond thinking while her small hands roamed his body to caress and explore.

He claimed her lips and wound his fingers through her soft hair. The glimmer in her eyes mesmerized and tormented him. Where had she been for all those lonely years? The timeless rhythm of their bodies brought out a glow in her gaze that was just for him. It was a carnal act of possession to drive his throbbing shaft into her again and again.

Her mouth opened to his, and he tasted and caressed her lips with the tip of his tongue. Melissa moaned softly, and he could feel her body trembling from passion held at bay to prolong the moment. Her back arched and he thrust into her hard. He met her soft moans with a hand at the small of her back to bring her closer.

"No, not yet," he said again, and turned her over onto her stomach. The damp sheen of perspiration glistened in the soft glow of candle light. He was going to explode from wanting her so much and slid into the depth of her womb while he caressed her, filled her, and brought her to spasms of ecstasy. His hands slid over her hips and the mind-shattering release left him gasping and crushing her soft body beneath him.

He sagged onto the bed next to her, spent. Slowly they could both breathe again.

She turned on her side to put her head on his chest. "Now?" she teased and it made him chuckle.

In truth, he realized, he was awed at her gentle beauty. He had intimately known beautiful women in his life, but never one who could speak to his heart and soul with nothing more than a smile on her sweet lips and a sparkle in her eyes.

The candlelight sputtered, and the room went dark. They were wrapped in each other's arms when they drifted off to sleep. Alex was certain he heard a bagpipe playing softly somewhere in the hills out beyond the mist and the fairy mounds.

Chapter Eleven

Prince George jumps into the lead! Laird MacKenna was caught off guard and lost a two hundred-and-fifty point lead. It was reported by the Prince's men that William, the youngest MacKenna, fell off his horse during a battle. The Bookies in London are dropping from exhaustion.

On the Streets, with Rosabel

Amber was in the checkout lane at the Safeway Grocery Store in Boulder, Colorado. Her mind was on summer school and the upcoming exam. The last thing in the world she expected was to look over the magazine and tabloid display and see a picture of her sister kissing a man who looked like he had walked out of ancient Scotland. She reached out and took the tabloid in one hand, and the other hand speed dialed her sister in Minneapolis on her cell phone.

"Oh my God, Sarah, you have to get a copy of this tabloid. "It's Melissa! There's some wild barbarian who's got her cradled in his arms and he's kissing her. This guy is wearing a skirt in public. There is some serious gropeage going down on my sister."

"I've been trying to reach you. The hotel called this morning and said there have been reporters looking for her. Isn't she with her tour group? She said she wasn't going to call home during her vacation, but I really want to hear from her to know she is all right."

Amber loaded her groceries in her car and got behind the wheel. "I'm going to call the Embassy right now. See if you can find out something online about this guy and where he might have taken her."

Amber finally made it through to the Embassy office. They explained that Highlanders don't have a permanent address and were difficult to locate. The local Constable would have to be sent out on horseback to find them.

"If a tabloid can find her, so can the Constable!" Amber raved, exasperated. "Find my sister!"

***

It was Evan's turn to command the camp on Tuesday, and she hadn't checked in with him before she left for the loch. He found her, and she quickly discovered Evan had a temper. He backed her up all the way to the cottage by yelling, non-stop in Gaelic.

The burr in his voice was hard to understand, but somewhere in his ranting she guessed he thought she had gotten lost.

Wednesday, Gideon's easy-going nature got riled when the warriors offered to pose for one of her paintings. He slung her over his shoulder like she was a bag of wheat and dropped her on the cottage doorstep with a warning to stay put until Alex returned to camp.

Gideon swore his hair was going to turn white. She didn't understand the language well enough to know the warriors were offering to pose nude for her.

It was Robert's turn to command the camp on Thursday, and he nearly had a nervous breakdown. Melissa walked down the path to the loch and was intercepted by warriors several times before she had made it out of camp.

The warriors were always gracious, she noticed. Most of the men were out with Alex in battle and it was a hot, lazy afternoon.

Robert yelled at her from across the camp. He was furious, she noticed when he approached and glared at the warriors who had come out to greet her.

"Melissa! Where are ye goin', lass?" Robert fumed. "And have ye though' about putting on your proper dress instead of romping around in your under things?"

She was wearing the only other clothing she had, her skirt and lace top that she wore to supper with his family when she arrived. "My dress was washed this morning and it's drying on a tree branch."

"It's a ten point penalty to be caught out of uniform," a warrior commented and Robert blanched. He barked out orders for the warriors to get on with their duties, aghast at the slip.

His long, straight hair was unbound and gave him a fierce, untamed look. "You will not wear that skirt outside without Alex here, ye ken?" Robert was not going to argue.

She didn't think he was being fair. "I don't have a uniform like all of you do." She wanted to cry. "I don't have a tartan!" He pointed back to the cottage, and she returned — fuming.

Robert was so badly frazzled he had to blow up a bridge before he could calm down.

Her short skirt was mentioned in several prayers that evening.

Iain came in to prepare her breakfast, but Melissa assured him she wasn't hungry. He left the cottage to take care of his duties, and Melissa sat with her legs tucked under the warm wrapper. She sipped her coffee and thought about her day. Alex was often gone at first light, and she spent her days painting or tidying up the little cottage.

It didn't take long to straighten up the room, and in fact, most of the clutter was hers. Alex never made a mess, and she found that fact disturbing. She swept the floor with a hand-made broom and sat staring out of a small, four-pane window while she was lost in daydreams.

There were shutters on the small window, and she couldn't imagine a storm so fierce that it would tear them off and send them into the field outside the cottage. The black house was thatched with bracken and was so sturdy it could withstand just about any fierce storm. A small fireplace heated the room quickly and took the chill out of the air. It was a beautiful life, she thought—simple, serene, and lonely without Alex beside her.

It was funny how something so simple as sweeping the floor could make her burst into tears. She desperately missed her sisters, and had been yelled at for most of the week by Alex's brothers for every minor infraction possible. She put the broom aside and sagged onto the bed, sobbing with her face covered by her hands. When Alex returned to camp and found out she had been outside in her short skirt, he was furious with her and told her stay inside where she was safe. They had their first fight, because Melissa refused to be held hostage. He also found out she wouldn't back down from his steaming-hot temper, and had yelled right back in his face. She refused to join them for supper, and by sunset, there was a small bouquet of wild flowers on the doorstep with a note that he loved her. He didn't come back to the cottage that night and she spent the long hours in tears of frustration. She wanted to go home, and yet didn't want to leave without him. She had almost talked herself into going to the shore to find the mist again, when she fell asleep.

Melissa decided on sketching to quell the loneliness while he was gone. She took out her charcoals and watercolor pencils. She had to light a candle and put it on the table beside her paper. It was dismal and rainy today, and the weather matched her melancholy mood.

She didn't think about what she was sketching, the subject matter chose itself. Her drawing was a nude of Alex sleeping on his stomach on top of the covers. He looked so beautiful, she remembered, and ran her fingers lightly over the curve of his body as if she could touch him wherever he was now.

The quilt over the bed was his tartan colors of blue and red with gold threads, and it added a little color to the drawing to put in small pieces of the world around them.

An old stone Irish whiskey bottle sat on the window ledge that she used for wildflowers, and the floorboards were worn smooth and gray. The cottage was sound and had only three rooms to clean. The kitchen fire was in the middle of the main room, and their bed was tucked against the wall.

There was a pantry against one wall that held some items in an icebox that had a hand-made handle, and ice was brought down from the mountains, Alex had told her. The ceiling was made of beams of cleft oak placed close together and then covered with sod to keep them warm and dry. The cottage roof was thatch, overlaid with fishing-nets weighted with stones to keep them in place.

This was her home with Alexander. Melissa didn't want to think about her world in the future. Hot tears dropped on her cheeks. She didn't want to leave him, but didn't think she could survive living in the past. He had promised to go with her when the Prince was sent back to England, but that was a week ago already and it didn't seem as if the fighting was ever going to end.

It frightened her to think the mist could find her and whisk her back to the future. The anxiety was taking its toll on her. If she left without Alex, her heart would shatter and break.

She ran her fingers over the sketch. Was it possible to love him any more than she did at this moment? Every day they found out something new about each other and, their nights were intimate and searching.

Would the day come when they had discovered all there was to know about each other and look elsewhere for the intense pleasure they found in each other's arms?

There had never been the kind of intimacy that she had with Alex. He only had to look at her with that wicked smile of his, and she would lose her mind. But would he ever want another woman?

Melissa broke the charcoal in half just thinking about Alex in bed with another woman. The thought rattled her terribly. She had never been possessive about anything or anyone else before now.

The rain had let up, and she decided to go down by the loch to paint. Gideon wouldn't allow her out of the cottage without an armed escort. The camp was nearly deserted, and she walked down the path and set up her easel. She had been working on a painting of Alex and had the sketch on the canvas and was ready to go to work. It was still the morning hours, and he wouldn't be back until supper.

The paint eased on the canvas, and she worked frantically to get the light right before it faded. She painted until the image that was inside her mind was on the canvas.

Alex was unusually late getting back to the camp, and Melissa was getting worried. She cleaned out her paintbrushes and stood back to admire the painting of Alex standing on the top of a hill looking out at the ocean. He looked magnificent with his dark wavy hair just below his shirt collar, tartan kilt, and sword belted to his side. He looked every bit the handsome ancient warrior. He had that far away look in his soft jade eyes. The tormented emotion she had seen in his gaze was now captured on canvas.

William sauntered up the hill where she was painting. She hadn't seen him in days and guessed he desperately needed some rest. She continued cleaning up her painting supplies.

William took a long look at the painting. "Ye're in love with him."

The deep, melody of William's voice always unnerved her. If she closed her eyes she could hear William's voice from almost anywhere in the camp.

"Was that a question?" Melissa became uneasy. "Are you afraid that I would hurt your brother in some way, William?" She reached out and touched his arm.

His hand covered hers possessively. "I canna stand tae see ye so upset."

She didn't want to lie to him. "Don't worry. Alex and I will work this out. I took one look into his eyes, and I knew that I loved him."

William looked back over her shoulder and his gaze hardened. He withdrew his hand. "Good evening, Alex." he greeted his brother.

Her heart started hammering in her chest. She knew Alex was standing directly behind her and had heard what she said. His arms circled her waist.

"I've left ye alone too much this week," Alex whispered against her ear. "Forgive me, my Angel."

She didn't see the blazing look between two brothers as William departed.

Alex had victory in the palm of his hand. He had won her heart. The intense fear that had clenched his stomach into a knot for the past few weeks slowly eased.

It was an awkward moment, and she wasn't sure if she should bring up their argument.

"Alex, what is the statue on the hill for?" She had been curious about some of the local history and wanted to break the tension between them.

"That's a *sheila-na-gig*, a fertility symbol. Late at night the warriors strip down and dance naked in the moonlight so they can father many bairns and please their women."

"Did you dance, Alex?"

He growled seductively in her ear. "Till my wee feet were sore and I dropped tae my knees and begged for a beautiful lass with golden hair and blue eyes tae keep me warm at night."

"It seems you got your wish," she tugged him down for a kiss. "You please me very well."

"Ah, lass, ye do keep my feet warm at night. Let's go for a swim in the Loch. I go' a Nessie for ye tae find."

He could be so damned charming and it made her laugh.

He looked at the painting then and let out a low whistle. "I don' look tha' good."

She was pleased he liked the painting. He hadn't said a word about their argument, and she was grateful.

"I don't think it's possible to capture you on canvas."

He ran his hands down the length of her arms and hugged her close to his heart.

Alex was suddenly terrified of losing her, especially once she learned the truth about him.

Chapter Twelve

Alex knew. The knowledge knocked the breath out of him, and his hands trembled a little. William was in love with her. That look in his brother's eyes could not be denied. The lad had fallen deeply in love with Alex's Angel. The flood of jealousy that hit him clenched his fists. It took all of his control not to explode in fury. Melissa belonged to Alex. He had made that clear from the beginning, and he would not tolerate any challenge for her. His mind raged against the thought of her with another man.

Alex was in a touchy mood and his forehead was wrinkled in a frown, she noticed. He dove in and surfaced next to her. The water was refreshing after a hot summer afternoon. The worries of the day washed away. Her arms were around his neck and her breasts pressed against the warmth of his chest. The sensation woke every nerve in her body.

"You have absolutely ruined me." She laughed. He stiffened for a moment and then smiled as her intent became clear. Her legs wound around his waist. "You are tense tonight." She taunted him with a tug on his ear lobe between her teeth.

He growled against her ear.

"So I finally have your attention? You're very distracted, Alex."

"I've ruined ye?" He was afraid to hear the answer.

Melissa touched his cheek and held his gaze with hers. "Yes, my darling. I wouldn't want another man to touch me the way you do."

His lips sought the safe haven of her mouth. She always tasted so sweet, and he found himself always wanting more of her. Tonight, he ravaged her tender lips, claiming them undeniably as his territory. He held her close, and the tension strained the muscles in his shoulders into rippled cords.

"Excuse me," Daniel interrupted them from the shore. "I hate tae interrupt your swim."

Melissa inched lower in the water. Alex held her firmly in place against him. The water was up to their waist, and she had no doubt that Daniel was getting quite the view from the beach. She noticed he was wearing his dress kilt. "You look very handsome, Daniel. Are you leaving again so soon?"

Daniel flushed at the compliment.

Alex groaned. It wouldn't be long before all of his brothers were in love with her.

"Oh, I'll be back again soon. I wouldn't want tae miss a thing." His laughter echoed across the lake. "We were about tae get some company, and I didn't want tae upset the lady."

She looked puzzled.

"The warriors are coming in from patrol." Alex explained. "Make haste, little brother." He called out in Gaelic and continued to nibble her neck.

At the top of the ridge, dust began to spiral into the air and Alex saw the helicopter take off. He didn't think a kiss would cover the whir of the blades so he dunked Melissa under water.

"You beast!" Their laughter echoed across the valley. He slid under the water before she could get the hair out of her face. "Come back here." When he surfaced next to her, she dunked him under. She had the feeling he wasn't fighting too hard because he had more than enough strength to throw her over his head. The oversized shirt he gave her to swim in came off under water, and when she surfaced, she clung to him. Alex laughed and wrapped his arms around her for modesty's sake.

"Now I've got ye where I want ye." He bent down, and her lips were warm and inviting against his. Her smile for him was radiant and loving.

"And I have you right where I want you. You can't possibly let go of me."

"Oh, can't I?" He released her just a little. Melissa screamed and hung on tightly to him laughing. The shirt floated up to the surface and he draped it over her head.

He carried her out of the water and wrapped her in the extra plaid he brought along. The water was cold, and he rubbed her down vigorously to warm her. They walked back to the cottage and locked the door.

Melissa slipped the shirt off and hung it over the back of a chair.

Alex leaned down and kissed her, tenderly at first and then the heat of her breasts against his chest flamed his desire, and he groaned.

His tongue slipped into her soft mouth, teasing and tormenting with a lazy caress against her tongue. He felt her tremble and heard her whimper in the back of her throat. The nipples against his chest had become hard.

She gasped against his lips when he reached up to gently caress the side of her breast. He pulled back to kiss the base of her throat, and she moaned in reply. Her eyes sparkled, and her lips were slightly parted, her breath coming in short gasps.

Alex was beyond thinking. His mouth ravaged against hers with his tongue sliding in, retreating, and driving into that sweet mouth again until she groaned. His teeth nipped at her bottom lip. His lips tormented her until she writhed against him.

"Alex, please."

"Please what my lovely Angel?" He smiled in that devil-may-care way that drove her crazy. She would do anything he asked. He knew the affect it had on her and used it when he wanted to torment her.

"Please don't ever stop," Melissa whispered.

He brushed his lips across her hardened nipples, and sighed. His mouth closed over her pink breast, and her hands clung to his shoulders.

He kissed her flat stomach, hooked a finger into the fabric of her pink panties, and slid the wet fabric to the floor and tossed them over the shirt. He laid her back on the bed, already aroused at the beauty before him. His hands were warm on her cool skin while he kissed the inside of her thigh before kissing the heat of her.

Her hands tore at the blanket for something to hang on to. He took her higher and higher, building an ache that demanded an answer. "Alex, please," she begged again.

He could feel the spasms of ecstasy that wracked her body before she knew what was happening. She called out to him again and then sank back on the bed, gasping with pleasure.

"You enjoy doing that to me, don't you?" She was amazed at his prowess. Her laughter filled the room with a joyous sound.

He hovered over her and smiled. "Aye, I do."

Melissa pushed him over on his back. "You torment me until I beg you to make it stop." She straddled his hips, and his eyes grew big in wonder. "It's your turn to squirm and beg for mercy, sweetheart."

He reached up to stroke her breast. She bit his finger.

Her hair fell across his chest, and the silky tickle across his skin felt very good. She kissed his neck before licking and suckling his nipple.

"Oh, lass, you have my full attention." Alex groaned when her head moved down to his lap. His hands wound into her hair, and he thought he had died of pleasure from her silky tongue moving over him.

He groaned again when she took him in her mouth and stroked the inside of his thigh. "Melissa, my darling, please..." He could hardly breathe the pleasure was so intense.

"Please what?" Even her voice sweetly tormented him. Don't stop!" Alex begged. Her feather light touch moved over his body and sent shivers up his spine. She demanded more of him and took what she wanted with a reckless abandon. She thought of nothing else but his pleasure, and she pleased him beyond his wildest dreams.

She had his full attention and straddled his hips, easing down on him. The heat of her body wrapped tightly around him.

Alex leaned forward and put a pillow behind his head. He didn't want to miss a moment of her passion. His hands slid up her thighs. He loved to watch her face while they made love.

Her eyes would get big and half close when she was close to the edge, and then he would give her that touch which made her fall off the world into ecstasy with him. Every thrust of her hips brought them to the edge, but he held her back to enjoy the battle. She moved against him and whimpered. He put his hands on her hips and lifted her a little, and she found a whole new delight while he moved below her.

Alex couldn't get the thought of her with any other man out of his head. It tormented him. She belonged to Alex, body and soul. The dark thoughts raged across his soul and he unleashed the jealous anguish that tortured his heart. Once before he had believed in ideals but life had taught him some harsh lessons. He had managed to bury all emotions for years, but with Melissa, his barriers came down. Love mixed with desire, and possession defined love. It was wrong, he knew, but at the moment, was beyond guilt, sanity, or reason.

He sat up still tightly joined to her and tucked his legs under him for leverage. Melissa held on to his shoulders. His strength held her, and he loved her in a wildly wicked way. He drove deep within her heat again and again. His mouth covered hers and crushed her lips against his.

"Alex!" Her voice trembled as she called out to him.

He could hear her calling to him from far away. The rage of jealousy burned deep within him and he became almost savage in his desire to brand her his woman. His arms crushed her against him until she could get no closer. He possessed her lips and sunk his tongue into her mouth to claim all of her at once. His hand wound into her hair and wouldn't let her pull back from him. His breathing was ragged against her cheek.

Melissa wound her arms around his neck. "I love you, Alex." she cried out in complete surrender and held on as ecstasy shivered through her body. Alex groaned against the extreme emotions gripping his heart. She trembled and nearly fainted in his arms.

He called her name and brushed his lips against her cheeks. "My sweet Angel," he soothed and caressed. "Ye are so beautiful, so very beautiful. Melissa, my love, forgive me if I hurt ye."

"Alex," she said his name in a whisper. Her hands caressed his back. She had heard him say he loved her and started sobbing against his chest, completely overwhelmed with his fierce emotion. He held her gently now and rocked her with his body until she calmed.

Alex felt a sting in his eyes. She broke down all the walls he kept around his heart and wrapped his tortured heart in her magic. His Melissa was so delicate, and he felt like he had become a monster.

He moved back against the pillows and took her with him to stretch out on his chest. He couldn't let her go, not now. The emotions that filled his heart were frightening because it had consumed him entirely. If she left him, he wouldn't just go numb; he would cease to exist at all. The enormity of the realization made him tremble. His sanity was vulnerable for the first time in his life, and he couldn't control or predict the outcome. Alex was truly terrified.

Melissa's cheek rested against his heart. The wild heartbeat began to calm, and she wondered what had upset him. That far away look was back in his eyes, and he held her in a crushing hug.

She didn't want anything to ruin their beautiful new love. If she knew the answer to that far away look, she might be hurt or worse, lose the man she loved more than life itself. Her head tipped up and rested on the back of her hand. She ran a finger over his whiskered chin. His beard and mustache were dark, like his hair and gave him a very sexy, distinguished look. Her fingertip traced his bottom lip. "I love you, Alex."

Her eyes were a deep violet this evening, and her gaze fell on him like a blanket of warmth and security. He felt safe with her and let the beast in him be calmed by her love. "Ye truly are a part of my life, and I canna thin' abou' ye ever leavin' me."

"Aye, you are stuck with me now." She laughed lightly, trying hard to bring that lovely burr into her voice. Melissa felt immensely proud of herself. She had pulled him back into the warmth of her love. Her body was tender from his fierce attention.

The pain was still raw to him but Melissa had withstood one of his worst moments in his life when all the barriers came down, and his fears demanded her innocent, tender body. For the first time in years, he faced his demons and realized he had buried his heart with work. It was as if a terrible burden had been lifted from his shoulders. She still loved him, he was certain. He stroked her soft skin, in awe of the gentle beauty in her.

"Why are you so upset today?"

"It's nothing," he quickly changed the subject and talked about the battle that had been won that day. How could he tell her everything and risk losing her?

The details of their battles always made her a little nervous. She suddenly got very quiet.

"Wha' is wrong, Melissa?"

She reached up to touch his check. "I don't know what I'd do if something happened to you. I've seen you in battle, and it scared me. I can't bear to think about it every day." Tears glistened again in her eyes, and she put her head down on his chest.

His arms went around her and held her close. "How did I get so lucky?"

"You wouldn't take me back," she answered for him.

He squeezed her again. "If I told ye not tae worry would ye follow my instructions?"

She shook her head and caressed the strong muscles of his chest and arms. She hadn't wanted to think about the future and tried to push the thoughts aside. How long would the fighting continue? Their moments together were precious.

"We were afraid this harsh lifestyle would be too much for such a delicate lady." Alex yawned and wrapped his arms around her.

Moments later he was snoring in her ear.

"I love you, Alex. So much it frightens me," she whispered softly in the dark.

His arms never left her, and she felt content for the moment. They had this moment together, no matter what happened, and she didn't want to shadow the love she felt for him with fears and regrets. There would be time enough for that in the future.

Melissa had Nieman Marcus tastes and wasn't sure she could make the lifestyle change to homemade clothing and growing her food. The enormity of the difference finally registered in her lovesick mind. She had never considered a life where she had to cook.

The last thought she had before she dozed off was; the man didn't have electricity or a microwave. How the hell was she going to survive?

Chapter Thirteen

The Game of Love Gets Hot! Laird MacKenna was seen swimming at Loch Voil with his lady, and it appears that swimming suits, even in the midst of five hundred warriors, are still optional. What a spectacular view. Personally, I can't wait to ask the lady all about her holiday.

On the Streets, with Rosabel

Melissa got up early the next morning and set off to catch the morning light in her painting.

Alex privately expressed his concern about her pale cheeks and her lack of appetite to Gideon. Daniel brought him the latest tabloids when he returned to the game.

"I don't know who looks more exhausted, you or Melissa," Gideon noted. "She's either pregnant or anemic by now."

"I'd say anemic," Gideon reasoned. "Any other changes – say, to her topside - would have been noted by at least a hundred men outside your cabin. I'll get a blood sample and run some tests to find out what she needs for vitamins. We've got to find something she will eat."

Daniel noticed Melissa was missing from the cottage. "She's probably pretty homesick by now. Her sisters called the Embassy, and they are not willing to wait much longer to talk to her. Where is she? Has our lovely lady taken flight?"

"Robert took her tae the glen tae work on her painting," Alex gruffly said, still too shaken by the information he held in his hand to speak without a roar in his voice.

Gideon looked over his shoulder and saw the latest headline plastered across the tabloid. "The Game of Love Gets Hot!" and there was Alex with a topless Melissa swimming at the lake. Her face was tipped up, and her smile looked radiant.

"The photographer's got tae be one of our warriors," Daniel surmised. "No one else could have taken that picture even with a telephoto lens. There were guards on duty that day and no one could slip through our defenses."

Alex remembered that moment all too well. Her shirt came off when he dunked her, and he had wrapped his arms around her. He touched the photograph of her beautiful face and remembered kissing her and their lovemaking had been a turning point for him.

"You both look verra happy," Gideon said. "Perhaps we have been going about this all wrong. Instead of hiding her away, maybe we should make a formal statement tae the press."

"Not yet," Daniel said.

Gideon gave him an affectionate shove. "Try tae get some sleep, will ye?"

Alex smiled. Who needed to sleep when you had an Angel in your arms? He walked over to the bed and fell down, asleep before he hit the pillow.

Daniel put the tabloid back in his briefcase. Gideon and Daniel found Melissa later that afternoon painting while Robert and his crew repaired a cottage. When she saw the two of them approach, she called out a greeting and went up to put her arm around their waists.

"It's good to see you again, Daniel. I feel very blessed to have such handsome men keeping an eye on me." Daniel gave her an affectionate squeeze.

"I brought our lady a present." Daniel smiled and instantly got her attention.

"You brought me a present?" Melissa was delighted. "It isn't even my birthday. Come and sit down. I was just going to pour some lemonade for Robert and his crew."

Gideon walked over to the painting, and his mouth dropped open. She had captured warmth and camaraderie between Robert and the carpenters as they repaired the old cottage.

Robert had his shirt off and was sawing a log to repair the thatched roof. His long dark straight hair was unbound and gave him a mystical look. There was a carpenter on the top of the wall and another standing on the ground and passed the log up to him. The men wore their kilts and laughed while they worked. Daniel had the same response.

"I took the painting she did of Alex and had it framed." Daniel said quietly beside his brother. "It's already hanging at the Manor House."

"She has a gift," Gideon said. "Now, if we can get a blood sample without her ever seeing the hypodermic needle, then we are magicians!"

Daniel nodded, certain it would take a magic trick to get this feat accomplished.

Melissa walked back and handed them a tin cup of lemonade that was kept cool in a wine skin and lowered into the cold water in the well. It was weak, at best, she noted since lemons were almost impossible to find, and most of the fruit they ate were dried berries that had been picked during the early spring and then dried on large woven frames in the hot sun.

"I thought ye liked tae paint flowers," Gideon said, stunned. "This is verra good."

"Everything about this place inspires me."

Gideon was reminded of his reason for tracking her down. "I'm a little concerned about how pale you look, Melissa. I wouldn't want ye tae get sick."

He held the slim blade in his hand and grinned.

Melissa backed away. "Oh, no. You're not stabbing me with any dirks." She remembered the section in the museum where they used to bleed people who were ill.

Gideon smiled, nodded to Daniel, and they put their cups down. He loved a challenge.

"Oh, yes, I am."

Melissa screamed and turned to run. Daniel signaled to Robert, and he caught her around the waist before she had made it ten feet away. They found out she could scream like a Banshee.

Robert had her over his shoulder but soon found out how hard it is to hold on to a squirming, screaming woman. She got away twice before Robert got her airborne on top of his shoulders. She screamed as they managed to immobilize her, and Daniel held her arm.

Gideon had a sash on her arm while Daniel distracted her. She tried to punch Daniel.

"Aye, ye got it lass. That is a good fist for a fight."

Daniel and Robert worked hard at keeping her still while they laughed. It took the help of the other two carpenters to hold on to her feet.

"I'm going to hit you, Robert." She laughed again and then groaned when she felt the stab of the dirk. "Listen, Dracula." She yelled at Gideon. "If you want some fresh blood hang around William. Men bleed around him all the time."

Gideon leaned down and released the sash with his teeth. "Dracula?" he said garbled in mock outrage. "Ye must be talking about Alex."

"I'm going to get you for this, Daniel," she cried out, laughing hysterically.

"Yeah," Daniel laughed heartily. "What army would challenge me?"

"That one," she pointed over his shoulder and Daniel looked back. William, Evan, and Iain had heard her screams and followed the shouting with fifty warriors ready for battle.

The three brothers, William, Evan, and Iain shook their heads. All that noise for one little cut on her arm? They thought she was being beaten and raped.

"You're going tae need some help, Daniel," Alex stated and joined the melee. He too had heard her screams and nearly lost his mind thinking she was hurt. "You get the twenty on the left; I get the twenty on the right." He grinned at Melissa and pulled on her ponytail.

Gideon got the second vile of blood and removed the needle from her arm. He applied pressure with a cloth bandage and then made a tiny cut with the tip of his dirk

146

just to make it look good, and carefully put the precious samples away in his bag.

"Traitor!" she yelled at Alex. Robert had held her firmly on his shoulder until Daniel finally released her arm. She stood on wobbly legs, and Alex put his arm around her to steady her.

"It won't be a fair fight." Daniel shook his head.

"*Aye*," Alex said with certainty. "When they beg for mercy, we'll let them go, ye *ken*?"

Melissa was told later what a unique opportunity the warriors had in fighting with Alex and Daniel. She witnessed the warrior's enthusiasm and stood back, watching Alex and Daniel best each warrior in turn. She screamed once, and Alex got punched because he looked over at her. Their cousins would later boast of that accomplishment.

Daniel and Alex were matched for skill and cunning when it came to hand-to-hand combat and it wasn't until the warriors tried an all out assault that Alex and Daniel finally went down.

There was a lot of back slapping when they finally got free from the tangle of men, and she learned first hand the actions behind their comments of "It was a good fight." There were a dozen bloody noses and numerous cuts and black eyes.

The men all seemed delighted.

"Now, aren't you all a sight. Alex, you beat up the wrong man!" She pointed at Gideon, and he grinned.

Alex walked over to look at the painting. "Did ye paint this today?" He was clearly impressed and hugged her to his side.

"It looks like my ugly brother." Daniel spit out blood and frowned.

Melissa looked at Daniel, concerned. She thought Robert was rather handsome.

Robert was strutting around now that he was 'immortalized' in a painting. He shook his head and walked away before anyone could notice that he got a little misty eyed at her thoughtful gift.

Alex took her hand in his. "Since you started this fight...."

"What?" Melissa scoffed.

"I will expect you tae be very appreciative of your champion, and you may console me for my injuries."

"What injuries?" Daniel asked while Gideon bandaged his arm. "There isn't a scratch on ye, ye bastard. However, I have a severe cut on my arm."

"It's a scratch," Gideon corrected, laughing.

"You had it coming to you for helping Gideon stick me with a dirk."

Melissa walked over to Daniel and gave him a kiss on the lips. "There, do you feel better?"

Daniel's eyes got very big for a moment, and Gideon broke out laughing.

"Your present is on the table in the cottage." Daniel winked.

Melissa whispered in his ear. Daniel shook his head.

Alex growled. "If you're going tae kiss someone, ye can start with me."

Alex had a cut on his lip that she had to kiss several times before he felt better.

"Perhaps a back rub would help sooth your severe injuries." She teased Alex as they returned to the cottage.

Gideon was curious. "What did she say tae ye?"

Daniel flexed his arm and winced. "She told me it was far too extravagant tae spend money needed for food and medical supplies on presents for her."

Gideon collected his medical bag and supplies. He held up a hypodermic needle filled with a crimson blood sample. "She never saw it coming. Damn, I'm good."

Chapter Fourteen

Prince, darling, London is so lonely without you. Do hurry back! The Laird and the Prince are even for points. It's still anyone's game.

On the Streets, with Rosabel

Amber stopped at the grocery store for supplies for a party she was having that evening. She looked at the tabloid stand and let out a scream that nearly brought the Boulder Police Department out to investigate. Amber held the tabloid in one hand and speed dialed Sarah again.

"Sarah! Go get this paper. You won't believe it. Melissa is topless! That barbarian has her swimming half-naked in public." Amber paid for the paper and walked out into the Colorado sunshine, still talking to Sarah.

She put in a conference call to the Embassy and ranted at the man for nearly an hour, stating it was their duty to rescue their sister from those wild barbarians. Poor, innocent little Melissa was probably being held against her will. Amber demanded an answer from the Constable, who had apparently forgotten to find Melissa and speak to her. They were leaving in a few days, and it was apparent this trip was necessary. It was all Amber could do to hold her temper back and speak nicely to the man who was obviously a blithering idiot!

***

Gideon made Melissa what he called his special tea that was laced with vitamins. He also ordered her to bed for rest. The dark shadows under her eyes were from worry, and Iain was beside himself with anxiety to get her to eat something. After three days of bed rest, Melissa was getting cottage fever and begged Alex to take her out for a ride.

Alex had his horse brought up to the cottage. He left instructions where he would be if he was needed, but otherwise they were gone for the day. He reached down and caught Melissa around the waist, lifting her up into his lap. They walked the horse out of the camp, and then Alex turned Yorath loose in a valley. They ran with the wind.

With Alex behind her, she could lean back and relax. Alex laughed and hugged her tightly to his body. The horse gobbled up the earth as long strides turned into distance.

It was a sight of Scotland she hadn't seen until now. The area around the cottage was very rocky with hills in every direction. The rhythm of the horse was magic as emerald green vales and hills blurred past her fingertips. Melissa forgot she was on a horse and not just floating on air. Her eyes closed for a few moments to mentally earmark this moment in time as one of the most exciting things she had ever done.

Her long golden hair wrapped around his arms, and Alex felt free and alive. He slowed Yorath to a gentle pace. Her face glowed in the late afternoon sun, and her deep blue eyes took on a new sparkle.

"You have such complete power over my body. You only have to look at me in that sexy way, and I want you. When you touch me I go crazy with desire."

"Ye have the same affect on me." He was happy he could bring the smile back to her voice.

"What are you thinking, Alex?" She stroked his muscled chest, curling the wavy dark hair around her finger, and peered up at him.

"I was thinking I should take ye riding every day." He kissed her fingers. "I don't think I ever knew what happiness was until ye dropped into my life." He held her hand up and placed his palm against hers. He noted her delicate fingers and brought them to his lips again.

"But it almost seems unreal, Alex. There is a world out there, and while we are here, it all seems so different, almost as if that world doesn't exist." She sighed and looked up at the blue sky. "I am so happy it almost hurts to think about that world. I don't ever want this magical one to come to an end."

She couldn't tell him she didn't want to return to the future. He would think she was crazy, and her stomach was in knots thinking she would ever leave him. It was as if the past, present, and future all melded into one agonizing thought. Would she be able to stay, or would he ever ask her to leave?

"My sweetheart," he said against her ear. The ride back was much slower so he could kiss her again and they could have some time alone. He lovingly caressed her body, amazed at the perfection at his fingertips. She always responded to his touch and with such abandon it made him smile. When they were together the rest of the world went away. Her gaze was magical and held his heart with wonder. Her touch could make his mind go completely daft, he thought, before bending down to kiss her again. The warmth of her mouth beckoned him, and he explored, ravaged, and claimed her for his own.

Three riders approached, and Alex didn't raise his head from her tender lips until they were beside him.

Melissa was startled to find out they weren't alone. Her cheeks flushed hot, and she nudged Alex's hand from her breast. Her face was buried against his shoulder; she was too embarrassed to look at the riders.

"Nice day for a ride, Alex," The man on horseback said in greeting.

"Aye, John it is." Alex acknowledged with a smile.

The riders moved past them, and Alex hadn't taken his eyes off her beautiful face. They heard the men laugh as they rode away.

"Who was that, Alex?" Melissa asked.

"John Stewart, Laird of the Stewarts."

"Do you think we should stop and talk to him?"

"No." Alex bent his head again, and she forgot the question. He growled in the back of his throat and tormented her lips with hot kisses. She never noticed the Stewart Laird was dressed in modern day clothing.

She groaned defeat and slumped back against him panting. "Alex, I want you again."

He started to laugh, thinking about taking her right there. "We'd probably fall off Yorath. But I'd be happy tae accommodate your insatiable desire," he said softly against her ear.

"I tried to warn you. When you smile at me like that, I go completely crazy." His arms wrapped around her tightly, and he slipped down from the horse.

Melissa finally noticed they were back at the cottage and were surrounded by a hundred warriors. The riders who were guarding the Laird also entered the camp, and discretely disappeared from view. It suddenly dawned on her they had been followed.

They walked back to the cottage and Alex stopped to speak to the warriors with instructions not to be disturbed for the rest of the afternoon unless the camp was on fire.

The cottage was cool and quiet. Alex stripped his clothes off and sat on the edge of the bed. He pulled her toward him and took his time taking her clothes off, kissing her soft body as each piece of clothing fell into a pile on the floor until she stood before him flushed. Her eyes had a glow that he knew very well. Alex reached out and ran the back of his fingers against the swell of her breast, and she gasped but stood still with a glow of love in her eyes.

Her arms wound around his neck, and she pressed up against him. Alex wrapped her in his arms and pressed her down in to the bed. They held each other tightly, afraid to let go even for a moment. Their lips touched, and their gazes warmed, touching each other's soul. She was as lost in him as he was in her.

The impact dazzled Alex, and he was afraid he was crushing her, he held her so close. She was his safe haven, and he wanted everything she had to give. She gave him so much more. His eyes closed in complete surrender. He let her take him to ecstasy. She matched his rhythm and demanded more. His body became hers. Alex had never felt anything so powerful in his life. He had set aside his busy schedule with board rooms, and running the vast business holdings that consumed his time, for a summer of personal enrichment. He had found so much more than he had ever hoped, that his modern day business world seemed as if it were centuries away. If only he could get Starbucks to deliver, his life would be complete, right where he was.

Physical pleasure was very different from where she took him. She opened her heart and wrapped him in love. He had faith in her, and she pleased him in ways he never knew possible. The intense love she gave him soothed him and made him whole again.

He could feel the tremble deep inside the hot center of her and she called out to him. Alex fell endlessly and trembled in his own release, spent and exhausted from the experience. He collapsed, and her arms held him tightly to her. She spoke softly against his ear and caressed his back, telling him over and over again that she loved him and he was safe.

He rolled to his side and took her with him. His lips still touched hers as he whispered her name and then fell sound asleep.

Her eyes closed, and she, too, drifted off to sleep, too exhausted to think or feel anything else. She dreamed about the flower beds that surrounded her small home in Minnesota, and about her position as a graphic artist. It was as if she was looking at someone else's life.

***

Gideon entered the cottage shortly before dawn to wake Alex. He put a hand on Alex's shoulder and said his name. Alex opened his eyes. Melissa was curled into his side sleeping peacefully.

"We need you outside," Gideon said very quietly, trying not to wake Melissa.

Alex moved quietly away from her warm little body and stood up. He tucked the blanket around her to keep her sleeping peacefully. He wrapped his plaid around his hips and found a clean shirt to wear. Splashing cold water on his face, he reveled in the lingering joy he'd found in her arms. He looked different, he knew, because he felt very different.

Alex covered her shoulder before he walked out of the cottage. "What's wrong?"

"Daniel found one of the photographers, and the warrior has been sent home on a personal emergency."

"What was the emergency?"

"Daniel."

Alex nodded in understanding.

"It seems there is a second photographer yet to be found."

"Then let's give him something to photograph to draw him out."

Chapter Fifteen

Iain brought Melissa toast, coffee, and fresh wild strawberries for breakfast. She didn't wake when he entered the cottage. Iain suspected she was exhausted and served her breakfast in bed. He left then and she was alone in the tiny cottage.

Alex was already up and gone. The aroma of the toast and coffee filled the room. Her stomach wrenched, and she ran for the facilities, glad Iain had left and she was alone. She stepped into the bath and hoped Robert had fixed the heating stones, and there would be hot water again. Steam drifted up, she smiled, and silently thanked Robert. A hot bath was exactly what she needed to feel like herself again.

She scrubbed her hair clean, the rose scented soap feeling like velvet against her skin. She noticed her body was a little tender today, no doubt from the wild afternoon they spent together. She wrapped her hair in a towel and put Alex's soft woolen wrapper before she went to eat her breakfast. The wild strawberries were delicious and she finished the coffee and toast. Her stomach settled down and she felt better.

Melissa thought back to the night with Alex and how he hadn't wanted to let go of her. She had guessed correctly. Falling in love was terrifying even for a man.

She drew from his strength and had finally been able to give him back some of her own.

She crawled back into bed and was instantly aware of Alex's scent. It surrounded her, and she closed her eyes, just for a minute and fell deeply asleep. Her dreams were vivid and sensual, of a man who swam naked in a warm turquoise sea. She could feel his power and longed to reach out and touch him. The desire was so strong; it caused a moan from her lips.

Melissa didn't hear Iain walk in and pick up the tray. He noticed she was back in bed, heard her moan, and went to find Gideon.

Gideon and Alex walked into the cottage. Melissa could sleep through a tornado, they were certain when she didn't budge as they spoke to each other. She peacefully slept through Gideon putting a hand to her forehead and taking her pulse.

"She appears tae be fine, Alex. She's just a little feverish, anemic, and exhausted. I'm going tae have some more tests run from the blood sample we took, just tae be certain we didn't miss anything. I'd say the drastic change in her diet might be contributing tae her pale complexion, ye ken?"

Iain stood in the doorway. "She hasn't been eating much lately and was throwing up this morning."

Gideon frowned. He would contact his office right away and get those tests done immediately. "Let her rest for awhile, and see how she feels later."

By mid afternoon, Alex had checked on her seven times, and she hadn't moved. He insisted that Gideon examine her again. The news that she was ill raged through the camp until all the warriors were concerned.

Melissa woke to find five men looking down at her. She smiled at Alex and tried to sit up.

Gideon gently pushed her back down and told her to open her mouth. He stuffed a pill soaked in honey between her teeth and told her chew and swallow it.

"I'm fine." She was wide-awake now and looked up at Alex.

Gideon loosened the wrapper so he could listen to her heartbeat.

"You're not going to stab me with a dirk again?" she asked him.

"Don't talk with your mouth full," he teased.

"Alex," Melissa pleaded.

"I'm no' going tae give in tae your whimper." Alex wouldn't budge until he knew she was going to be all right. Iain had told him she didn't eat her breakfast until after a hot bath.

Gideon put his hand on her forehead and diagnosed a slight fever, but nothing serious.

"I told you I was fine. I slept in today." Melissa smiled up at Alex who looked vastly relieved. "What time is it?" she thought to ask.

"Four o'clock in the afternoon," Gideon said concerned. "You've been asleep all day, and we were getting worried."

"She's very pale," Robert noticed. "I think she needs some ale."

"If I had tae wake up next tae Alex, I'd be pale, too," Iain concluded.

She combed her fingers through her hair and was surprised to find it was dry. "What's for supper? I'm starving." Melissa put her head back on the pillow. Alex looked worried, and she wanted to reassure him she was fine. The warm glow in his gaze lingered.

Alex sat on the edge of the bed and covered her hand with his. "I think ye should stay in bed today."

"Not unless you join me," she countered, delighted when he stretched out along the wall and wrapped his arm around her. Daniel and Robert pulled up chairs next to the bed.

"Don't you have something to do?" she asked, hoping they would get the hint.

"No." Daniel answered and sat back in the chair. They were waiting for a signal, and he was comfortable at the moment. The frown he gave Alex was for keeping her up so much she was totally exhausted.

Iain also took up residence and sat on the foot of the bed, looking at her with concern. "If ye went a little easier on the lass, Alex, she wouldna' get sick."

Alex already felt guilty enough and didn't want to upset her by pounding on his brothers.

Daniel got up and went over to the table. He brought over the package he brought for her. "Consider this a get well present. Ye don't have tae wait."

Melissa sat up and leaned back against Alex. His arms closed around her, and she sighed. He felt so good. She slowly opened the package and noticed they watched her every move.

"You must be a nightmare on the holidays," Robert said, annoyed it was taking her so long to unwrap the package. She was thinking about all the holidays with her sisters and the elaborately decorated gifts. It was such a drastic comparison to the plain brown paper and twine tied in a bow that held the package closed.

"I don't often get presents so I cherish the moment." The package opened to reveal a long sleeve, full-length dress made of soft ivory colored wool and a MacKenna tartan tunic that had ties on the side and was the same length as the dress. She ran her hand over the blue and red tunic with gold threads and looked up at Daniel. "The plaid is your family tartan. Thank you. It's unbelievably beautiful and very thoughtful."

"There's more," Daniel prodded her to look further and she found a lovely heart shaped ruby pin. "That's also from Alex," Daniel assured her.

"It's a Luckenbooth pin," Alex explained. The pin had far more significance than he admitted. Their father had given it to their mother when they were engaged. Later Alex could tell her what it meant to all of them to have her wear it.

"It's beautiful." The pin appeared to be antique and very rare. She was overwhelmed at the gift and lovingly ran her fingers over the ruby stone.

Iain brought coffee, and they sipped while she enjoyed her presents.

"Are you going to let me out of bed to try on my new dress?" She gave Alex a hopeful look.

"No," he stated and pulled her back against him. "It will still be here tomorrow, and Gideon said ye needed a day of rest."

"If Gideon had his way with me I'd never get out of bed." Melissa looked upset. "He thinks just because I look a little pale one day that I will fall over. I'm fine."

Melissa crawled out of bed. "I'm going to the water closet." She tossed the covers aside, grabbed her new dress, and closed the door behind her.

She looked at her face in the mirror and was surprised to see how pale she had become. Melissa did feel a little dizzy but guessed it was because she hadn't eaten much in the past few days. Their diet was primarily roast mutton, boiled mutton, mutton kabobs, braised mutton, and baked mutton with cheese. She decided she hated mutton. She felt a pang of homesickness when she thought about chicken and fresh vegetables at her favorite restaurant.

She dropped the wrapper to the floor and tried on her new dress. It was the right length and touched the top of her feet. She had lost a few pounds during the past few weeks, but the dress snugged up nicely with the tunic. She brushed her teeth and combed her hair. Still pale, she pinched some color into her cheeks and put on a sheer red lip-gloss to bring some color back in her face. Her bare feet were cold, and she stood on the wrapper to keep from getting chilled. The dress was soft as flannel, and she wished she had a long mirror to see how it looked.

Melissa opened the door and walked out. Daniel let out a low whistle. Alex smiled, clearly delighted with the results. She turned around and showed them the 360-degree view before she went over to kiss Alex.

"You look beautiful," Alex said, and that sexy sparkle in his eyes lit up. "And don't think I didn't notice how ye wormed your way out of bed." He pinned the broach on her dress.

"Thank you for the lovely gifts, Alex and Daniel. The dress is very warm. I feel wonderful." She closed her eyes for a moment and then looked directly into Alex's soft jade gaze. "Have I told you today how much I love you, sweetheart?" She asked softly.

"Not before now," Iain said and then shut his mouth when Daniel kicked him.

"Supper." Daniel changed the subject. "I'm hungry."

Evan stuck his head inside the cottage. He looked at Alex and said, "It's a lovely evening for a walk. Why don't ye take Melissa down by the loch?"

Daniel and Iain decided to join them. They walked down the center of the small village that was camped outside the cottage and made their way to the edge of Loch Voil.

"Well, now isn't this a rare treat," Melissa laughed when she had Alex on one side of her and Daniel on the other. She put her hand through the crook of their arms and walked down the path. "Ok, guys. What is going on? You're acting very strange."

"It's his nature," Daniel explained. "We've tried tae get him help."

"Unsuccessfully," Iain commented from behind them.

Alex covered her small hand with his. They were setting up the scene to catch the photographer but didn't want Melissa concerned. "I'm just verra content and happy today," he explained for Melissa. They walked slowly down to the loch.

Alex and Daniel both saw William drop from a tree and sneak up behind a man. Melissa didn't notice, and they exchanged looks over the top of her head.

Daniel brought her hand up to his lips. "I hope ye are feeling better, my sweet. I think I'll go see what William is up tae this evening."

"I'll join ye, Daniel." Iain walked beside his brother.

Alex looked down at Melissa and smiled. "Ye are such a delight." He leaned down to kiss her. Her eyes closed, and her arms wound around his neck. The moan in the back of her throat made his breath catch, and he gently nipped at her bottom lip. Her sigh nearly drove him to madness.

She didn't see the man being dragged away by Daniel and William.

Chapter Sixteen

Laird MacKenna has found and removed two photographers from his camp. It appears Prince George had his spies taking photographs of MacKenna's camp and his hot new sweetie. They do look cozy on his horse, don't they?

On the Streets, with Rosabel

As he spoke, Yorath was brought up to him beside the loch. Alex smiled. "There's a lovely little Inn no' too far away that has wonderful food."

He mounted and Robert lifted her to sit in front of Alex. The warmth of his arms was a sweet temptation. Yorath picked his way up the side of the glen to the ridge. They were guarded by a dozen warriors, who also kept a discrete distance.

Excited, Melissa said. "This is wonderful. I can see everything from up here."

Alex pointed out the cottage. "This is the *Balquhidder*." He told her stories of ancient wars and mighty battles, and the sensuous trill of his accent woke every never in her body.

He spoke softly, with reverence for the battles, and then would laugh and tell her a story about his ancestors that fled a revolution to find freedom amongst the savages. An hour later, in the midst of a glorious sunset, they arrived at an Inn. Alex took her hand and led her inside the deserted Inn to a private room.

"Have I told you today how beautiful you are?" He pushed her inside the lovely private room before the press found out they were there. The management at the Inn was expecting Alex and his guest to arrive and had everything ready.

Alex had used the medical necessity loophole to get Melissa out of the camp and some food that she would eat. He was worried about her pale complexion and knew she was at her physical limits from their harsh lifestyle during the game.

Their dinner was waiting for them. There was also a large four-poster bed in the room. She eyed the bed and then looked back at him.

He tried to look innocent, but his wicked smile gave him away. She nibbled a piece of rye bread while she walked around the lovely room. The heavy blue velvet drapes gave the room a feeling of opulence as if it were meant for royalty. The lavish marble and oak facilities made her eyes go big.

"Alex, there's a bathtub in here."

"For you, love. We'll have to try that out later." His voice didn't sound at all serious. "Let's eat. I'm hungry."

There were lovely buttered vegetables and succulent roast beef. Ten minutes later they both came up for air, and Alex opened a bottle of wine. He poured two glasses and handed one to her before sitting back in his chair and pulling her onto his lap.

"Right where you belong." He stroked her back and sat back to take a deep breath. He was worried about her.

She had slept the day away, and he thought twice about bringing her to the Inn. His fears were set aside when he noticed she did eat dinner and looked like she felt better. There was color back in her cheeks again.

Melissa sipped the wine and leaned back on Alex's warm chest. "Now, this is living."

She wound her arms around his neck, and her lips found his, warm and inviting. His arms held her very close. He explored and teased her sweet tasting mouth. He could excite her with a look, and when he touched her, she melted into sizzling flames. His hand cupped her breast, and she softly moaned against his lips.

Alex quickly lost any sensible thought about taking his time to seduce her. He liked the way she felt in his arms. He untied the tunic, but she didn't notice. He smiled in the kiss, and she pulled back.

"What are you smiling about?" She knew all too well but wanted him to admit he could undress her with not much more than a flick of his wrist.

"Ye make me smile," he teased. "I love tae touch ye." His hands moved over her body, and her breathing became erratic.

"How do you always get my clothes off before I know what you're doing?"

"I distract ye with a kiss." He leaned down and brushed his lips across hers. She gasped and clung to him. The affect made her feel dizzy it was so intense. Her eyes closed as the warmth spread through her.

The tunic was in his hand.

Melissa smiled and held up his belt. That got him to laugh. She slowly unbuttoned his shirt and slid her hand down his muscular stomach. The tub came to mind, and she stood and pulled him with her.

Hot water filled the old-fashioned claw foot tub, and there was a lovely scented milk bath potion in a stone bottle to put in the water. The water turned a milky white, and the aroma was of clean air and flowers on a summer morning. Alex leaned back against the door, watching her. She tested the water and satisfied, turned off the tap.

Alex was grateful she didn't ask him about the modern plumbing at the Inn. He didn't want to lie to her but didn't want to ruin the evening either.

He was getting seduced, and she took her time doing it. She took his shirt off and kissed her way down his stomach to undo the tuck in his plaid. She took him to the tub and made him get in first.

"You're being very agreeable." Her hands moved up to his shoulders and started massaging the strain away. *So he liked the attention.*

She took off the dress and hung it on a hook. He held a glass in one hand, keeping the other was on the rim of the tub, totally relaxed. The warm water was soothing. Melissa went back into the bedroom and lit a candle in the fading light, giving the room a warm inviting glow.

She was humming to herself and couldn't help but dance a little wiggle of her hips while the slip came off.

"Nice touch," he said with a growl in his voice.

She slid into the water with him and leaned back against his chest. His arms closed around her, and he held her. The water relaxed her in minutes, and she reached for the soap and turned around.

His free hand caressed her while she soaped down the rippled muscles of his chest. She leaned up against his soapy chest, and her arms went around his neck.

"Your eyes are beautiful in the candlelight," he said softly. Alex was relaxed and smiling.

"You look different today." She looked into his eyes, seeing something new and exciting there. They always had a sparkle of mischief, but now there was also a light that shimmered in the depths. "You're so handsome. You take my breath away." The astonished look on his face made her smile. "Do you know how beautiful you are?" she asked, and he shook his head slowly.

"No, darling. Ye're the beauty. Those blue and violet eyes can drop a man tae his knees and beg for ye just tae look at him."

"You're changing the subject," she reprimanded. "I get lost in your jade eyes. They take me to eternity. And that smile—" she traced a finger down his cheek. "You smile at me, and I forget to think."

"Is it working?" He smiled ran two hands over her backside. The feel of her soft skin was like velvet to his callused hands.

"Yes." She turned over, leaning back against him again. His fingertips brushed against the side of her breast, and she gasped.

Curious, he thought and tried the action again. He touched the side of her breast with the back of his fingers and noticed the change.

She had lost some weight in the past few weeks. Her clothes didn't fit her as well as they had when she arrived, but this new delight got his attention. He made a mental note, and his hands caressed her arms.

The water had cooled, and he wanted to take her into that wonderful bed. He rinsed off and got out of the tub. His hips were wrapped in a bath sheet of soft wool when he ordered her to stand up.

Melissa stood, and he lifted her out of the tub, carefully drying her off. He liked taking the time to notice every inch of her body. He could tell she was still a little shy around him, but for the life of him, he couldn't figure out why. But he liked the way the blush gave her a rosy glow.

He took his time to reinvestigate the delicate curve of her leg and the sensitive backs of her knees. He kissed her there, and her eyes became round with desire. His hand moved up the inside of her thigh, and she trembled. He knew where to touch her to build the passion and ignite her into flames.

Alex dropped the sheets and picked her up. In his arms, she was such a little lady. He took her to the bedroom and pulled the covers down.

He brought the candle into the bedroom and put it down on the table. The dishes had all been cleared while they were in the bathtub, and a midnight treat of warm blueberry cobbler was waiting for them.

Melissa sat on the edge of the big bed, facing him, and her gazed drifted over his beautiful body. He didn't have a shy bone in his entire body. Alex could walk around naked in front of her as if it was nothing unusual. What an actor, she thought to herself. His men feared him, and only she knew how tender and loving he truly was when they were alone. His lean and muscled body had an elegance that came with total control of his enormous physical power. She had witnessed his strength in battle, and it amazed her. He was graceful, and yet could exude fear in any opponent with a change in his stance or a fierce look in his eye.

Alex reached up and removed the pins holding her hair up off her neck. The golden cloud spilled down over her shoulders. She leaned forward to kiss the ticklish area inside his hip, making his breath catch in his throat.

He brushed her hair back over her shoulder and leaned down to kiss her sun golden skin. A soft moan escaped his lips as she closed her small hand over his arousal.

"Melissa." His voice was already ragged. She kissed him there, taking her time to please him. And she pleased him so very well. Alex wound his hands through her golden hair, and all reason and thought escaped him.

She had discovered on her own where to touch him to please, where to caress to torment him, and where to kiss to take him to ecstasy.

He trembled as she took control of his body, and he fought the intense desire to throw her down on the bed and take her fast and hard. Her hot little body was already aroused, and he wanted her beyond sanity.

Alex pulled back and lifted her in his arms to kiss her. Her lips were even softer and hot against his as he sank his tongue inside her mouth, claiming that territory for his own.

They fell back on the bed, and he covered her body with his. Then he sat up on his knees and turned her over on her stomach so he could kiss and explore every inch of her. She had taken command of his body. Now, it was his turn, and he wasn't going to miss an inch of her luscious feminine form beneath him. He kissed his way up her warm and inviting legs and gently eased her back over.

"Alex…" Her body arched in delight as he kissed her belly, and his hand moved to rest on the soft mound between her thighs.

The anticipation nearly drove her insane. He could torment with his touch and his warm mouth. His head bent down to her soft mound, and she cried out. The pleasure was so intense it racked her body with shivers and left her breathless.

Alex took her all the way to heaven in a heartbeat. His body joined hers, covering her on the soft bed. She held on to his shoulders as the dizzying feeling spread over her body. The rhythm of their mating was demanding and fierce.

He tasted her, licked, and demanded more of her, hungry for all she had to give. She ran her tongue over his, and he moaned deep in his chest. Her gaze never left his until he could feel her tremors begin, and her eyes closed in the rapture. He spilled his seed deep into her velvet heat and trembled in his own ecstasy. They were both panting and gasping as they rolled to their sides to face each other.

"I can't seem to get enough of you. I want you again," he said with a wicked smile.

"Right now?" she asked, still panting.

"Oh, yes, right now." Alex moved his hips against hers, and she gasped.

He sat up, still joined to her, and she clung to him, trembling from the rage of passion he unleashed. He could hold her and love her at the same time, and his body thrilled her again and again until she could bear the sweet agony no more and gave in to the ecstasy.

Alex fell back on the bed and held her close. He couldn't let go of her. Her small hands gently caressed his shoulders, and her breathing slowly calmed. Her eyes were closed and there was a pretty smile on her lips.

"What are ye thinking, Melissa?" Alex propped his back against the pillows so he could hold her against his chest. "I want tae know what that smile is for."

"It's for you, my love." She turned her head so she could peer up at his face. Her fingers traced the line of his chin. "My beautiful love," she sighed. "What am I going to do with you?"

"I can think of several things." He stroked her hair that spilled over his chest and arms.

The serious tone in her voice was an instant warning to him. "You're no' going tae leave."

She looked at him with a sad smile. "I do have to work, Alex."

"Why? I can take care of ye?"

Melissa wanted to cry. He was so wonderful to her. She knew the enormous amount of responsibility he already had on his shoulders, and it made her want to work even harder to help him.

"Alex, I wasn't born in this country. I don't know what work there is available for women here. I will have to apply for permission to stay here."

His heartbeat hammered in his chest. He couldn't ask her to marry him just to keep her there beside him and couldn't bear the thought of her leaving him.

"Daniel is a Barrister. He can take care of that."

"Do you ever let Daniel rest?" She laughed. "He is always going somewhere. Alex, I have to work."

"But why do ye have tae work, my lovely lady?"

"So we can afford to buy our own cottage."

He looked at the warm glow in her eyes and couldn't believe how much he loved her at this moment. "You'd go tae work tae buy me a cottage?"

He stroked the hair from her face and got lost in her gaze. He had never had anyone offer to take care of him before now. The thought rolled around in his mind, and he decided he liked the idea of having Melissa take care of him. She was the first woman he trusted with his heart and his body.

"Yes." She laughed at the serious look in his eyes. "We have to put a roof over our heads. We can't stay at the cottage forever. Winter is coming soon. That is what partners do, don't they?" He was smiling at her and didn't seem to notice she had asked him a question. "Alex. We are partners, aren't we?"

He let out a heavy sigh and had to choke back so much, just for now. He wanted to be honest with her. She didn't hold back with anything. Melissa loved like she painted with a passion. "Forever, *a Grá*."

Melissa noticed that far away look in his eyes. They were content for the moment, and she didn't want to break the enchantment that surrounded them. She wanted him to hold her and chase her fears of returning to the future away. She wanted to think she would be beside him forever.

Whatever it was that caused that look in his eyes, she didn't want to know. She couldn't bear the thought of leaving him, and it wrung her nerves ragged to think the mist that brought her to him could take her back to a time when she couldn't touch him. With his arms around her nothing could hurt them.

"Forever, Alex," she whispered, certain that even if she did get pulled back to her time in the future, she would find a way back to him.

Moments later, Melissa thought about the warm cobbler left for them and got out of bed to redeem her treasure. She crawled back in bed and sat next to Alex. "Want some?"

He softly caressed her back. "Aye, lass, ye know I do but…" He grinned and in one sweep of his arm had her on her back and pinned to the bed. "I want tae lick it off your sweet lips."

"That is not my lips." Melissa laughed as he nuzzled her stomach. The tickle of his whiskers was a delight.

He stuck his finger in the cobbler and brushed a dab on her lips. "Just the way I like it," he teased and proceeded to taste her.

She pulled his finger up to her lips and lazily licked the remaining blueberries off. He was spellbound as he watched her pink tongue curling around his finger. She closed her mouth on his finger, and he could feel her tongue moving against his skin. The sensation was clearly meant to arouse. The look in her eyes took on a soft glow in the candlelight.

"Insatiable wench."

She nodded agreement, and the cobbler was forgotten.

Melissa laughed as he stared at her nose. "What are you doing?"

"Shhh, you're making me lose count." She moved just a little, and he was distracted with her warm body wiggling under him, losing his place.

He started humming a Gaelic love song for her, and she was content for the moment. Alex started the freckle count again, but then she distracted him with a kiss on his chin, pulling him down to nibble his earlobe. He groaned and tried to remember where he left off. He was up to nine freckles, and she moved under him, causing him to lose track again.

"Ye're goin' tae have tae stop squirmin'." Her silken lashes brushed against his cheek, and he forgot all about freckles. The touch of her soft lips against his was a severe distraction. Her blue eyes shimmered violet in the glow from the candle.

He joined with her gently, lovingly. Her gaze held his, and he caressed her golden curls and soft skin. Her smile was radiant, and he felt her quiver deep inside, bringing him with her into ecstasy.

Alex collapsed beside her.

She brushed her lips over his eyelids. "Go to sleep, my love. You look tired." After extinguishing the candle, she curled in to his side. They had already developed sleeping habits, she thought happily. His arms went around her, and she put her head on his chest.

Melissa yawned and closed her eyes. "I love you, Alex." As she tried to drift off to sleep, her stomach grew queasy again. The cobbler had been very rich and was the cause, she was certain. It had been weeks since she had any sugar. Their diet was very different from her salad-a-day nutrition. She had decided she hated the smell of mutton. But lately, her stomach was rebelling over almost everything.

"My love, my Melissa," Alex said quietly and drifted off to sleep. He held her close by his side always certain he was going to wake up in the morning and find out his beautiful Angel had only been a dream. His thoughts drifted back to her earlier comment about going to work to buy him a cottage.

Alex had let go some of his enormous control on life, and the result staggered his imagination. She was taking care of him, and it pleased his soul to know she wanted something more out of life than to be a trinket and adored. She was his partner, lover, and friend.

He hoped she would forgive him for the deception.

Chapter Seventeen

Alex was already awake when Robert arrived with the horses. When he touched Melissa's shoulder, she turned over in the soft bed. "Not yet, darlin'," she protested. "It's too early." Moments later, her eyes opened as the covers were pulled back. She could hear the sound of the Robert's whistle, and the sound made her stand, stretch, and head for the water closet.

Alex loved to watch her wake up. There was a battle raging as she struggled for consciousness. It was pure sin to watch her stretch in the morning. His thoughts always returned to their joining. Reluctantly, they got dressed and met Robert out on the lawn.

The ride back to the cottage was spent snuggled in Alex's arms. He put her back to bed the moment they arrived, with a promise to join her soon.

He then met William at the stables. "Ye are taking command today, William. I am taking the day off tae get some rest."

William looked at him in shock. "You want me tae command the warriors?"

Alex smiled at him. "Yes, little brother. You've earned the right. Make war upon the Prince!"

Alex finally noticed Rebecca, their horse trainer, standing on a bale of straw beside Evan. He walked over to her and smiled.

"Tis good tae see ye, Rebecca." Alex had no idea he was about to get punched, and the blow completely surprised him, knocking him to the ground with a thud. He rubbed his jaw. "Wha' was that for?"

Rebecca glared at him. "Ye ask me? The answer is plastered all over the bloody world!" She threw the copy of the tabloid at him. "Ye sent me off tae find an Andalusian stallion for William's birthday present, and I find ou' while I am in Caracas that ye have a woman in the game with ye. And then, I find out that ye have ruined Yorath!"

"Tis a special circumstance, Rebecca," Alex tried to explain. She was obviously furious with him for excluding her from the game, when he had brought Melissa into the game with them. They had known Rebecca all her life, and he had never seen her so angry.

"I love the present, Alex," William said quietly and led the beautiful white Andalusian stallion over to be saddled. "I'm going to name him Phantom of the Opera."

"Ye're welcome, William." Alex frowned, his jaw still stinging. He had no idea Rebecca would take the news this hard. He stood up and brushed the dirt from his Kilt.

Rebecca shook the sting out of her hand. Hitting him was like striking a brick wall. Livid, she jumped up to ride bareback on the Andalusian mare she'd brought to breed with William's stallion. How could he just break her heart and act so casually about it? Devastated, she wanted to scream.

Moments later, when Daniel walked up, he knew there was something very wrong. Rebecca had tears streaming down her face. Alex had no idea she was in love with him. Daniel knew she loved Alex and had kept his own affections for her to himself. He couldn't stand seeing her so upset. "What's wrong, Rebel?"

Rebecca took one last look at Alex. "Go to hell, you miserable bastard!" She kicked the horse into action and sped off toward the hills.

Daniel shook his head at Alex. "Ye haven't figured it out? She's in love with ye!"

"Yes, I know. But I've never been able to figure out why." For Alex, it would have been like falling in love with his sister and just not possible. He watched Rebecca ride off, mystified.

Daniel walked up to the saddled Andalusian stallion. "William, I am going tae need your horse tae catch up tae her." He ran to the horse and was off in an instant to find her.

"Good. When you find her, tell her thank you for the horse," Alex said softly. Rebecca didn't know how much Daniel cared about her.

Rebecca's mare had reached the cliffs when he caught up to her. She was headed straight for the edge, and his heart jumped into his throat. Daniel envisioned her riding straight off the edge, and her broken body at the bottom of the cliffs.

"Rebecca, no!" he yelled and raced to intercept her before she did something really crazy. He was angry, too, because in all the years they had known her, she had never done anything so wild. The stallion picked up speed, and he managed to head her off just as she came to a screeching halt on the edge of the cliffs.

Her heart broken, Rebecca didn't care if she ran straight off the cliffs.

Daniel turned the horses back to the grassy hillside and dismounted. He held her reins in his hands, unwilling to let her try that foolishness again. He was furious with her and roughly pulled her off the horse in front of him.

"If I wasna a gentleman Rebecca — ye scared me half tae death!"

Her tear streaked face turned up to his. "Alex does no' love me. I've waited all these years for him."

Daniel put his arms around her — to comfort her, he told himself. He had dreamed of this moment when he could finally touch her, a few too many times to trust himself.

"Alex never knew ye were in love with him, Rebecca. Ye are like a little sister tae him. He is verra fond of ye lass, ye know we all are, but he is no' in love with ye."

At that moment, he decided he would kiss her. She needed kissing, and he was going to have that one moment of heaven with her in his arms that he had dreamed about. He bent down and touched his lips against hers. Her warm, soft lips felt swollen.

Rebecca opened her eyes and pushed him back. "No, I canna do this now." She withdrew from his embrace and walked back over to her horse. The intense desire that suddenly raced through her confused her. How could she be in love with Alex and still desire Daniel? The emotions derailed any attempt she could find to talk to Daniel. His kiss still tingled on her lips.

Daniel's eyes narrowed. The sting of her rejection was bittersweet on his lips. He could still taste her, but knew he'd never get another chance to kiss her again. He helped her onto the horse and handed her the reins, avoiding eye contact with her. She had hurt him, and he wasn't about to show her how much.

Rebecca caught his hand when he gave her the reins. "Daniel, thank you."

The wave of relief that hit him almost washed him away. He squeezed her hand and smiled. He had hope again and would give her some time to work through the feelings she had for Alex.

She gave him a sad smile. "I'll race ye back tae the stables, and then I won't see ye again until the party."

"I will look for you there," he said softly, hoping she understood his meaning. He couldn't help but notice the sadness in her blue eyes.

***

Alex rubbed his jaw and glared at William. "Go, make war on the Prince!"

"*Och!*" William bristled. He quickly assembled his team. Evan and Iain gave him strategies for the day, and William took command. The warriors were already saddled and waiting for their commander. William was given a new mount, and they rode off to find the Prince and their battle for the day. Now that he had sobered up, William was excited to be a part of the game again.

Alex returned to the cottage to find Iain checking in on Melissa. He a stack of papers for her to sign—for her identification that she lost, he explained. Melissa signed where he pointed. He looked very pleased with his meddling and tucked the papers back into a satchel.

She didn't read all the paperwork, and Alex realized just how much she trusted them not to take advantage of her. He had to hide the grin as he closed the door behind Iain. "Robert said the heating stones are working again." He followed her into the bath.

**

A rider approached, and Gideon immediately recognized him as the local Constable. "Oh hell, now what's wrong?"

The Constable approached and asked for a word with the MacKenna brothers.

Gideon introduced himself and Robert.

The Highland Warriors looked ferocious. Gideon's hair was shirt collar length, dark and curly and his beard had grown out during the past weeks. His gray-green eyes were narrowed, giving him a dangerous appearance.

Robert's long straight dark hair made him look wild and wicked. They were all lean and powerfully built, and the Constable had dreaded this visit. But he had a duty to perform, and his superiors expected a report.

"I'd like tae speak tae Alexander MacKenna," he said with authority. "The United States Embassy is looking for Melissa Johnson. Her hotel said you picked up her things, and no one has heard from her since."

Robert knocked on the door to the cottage. The brothers heard Melissa scream and giggle amidst the sound of splashing water. Robert knocked again, much louder. Alex answered the door with a yellow bath sheet wrapped around his hips.

"This better be damned important," he growled, his hair dripping.

The Constable pushed him inside. "I am here on behalf of the United States Embassy. We are searching for Melissa Johnson."

Alex could feel his heart lurch inside his chest. In that split second of time, he watched his world fall apart. The Constable was not something they had considered. "Aye, she's here."

Melissa called out from the bath. "Get back in here, Alex. The water is getting cold."

He smiled innocently and shrugged.

The Constable wouldn't be deterred. "I need tae know the lady is no' bein' held against her will."

Alex walked over to the open door that led to the roman bath. "Melissa, sweetheart. There's a *mon* out here who wants tae know if ye are all right?"

"Tell him to get lost. I plan on getting you in bed for the afternoon," was her reply, certain it was Gideon, and he would order her back to bed for the day.

Robert choked. Gideon had to leave the doorway before he burst out laughing. *Leave it to Melissa to always say the right thing.*

"Excuse us, gentlemen." Alex firmly pushed them out of the cottage and locked the door. He braced himself against the door and had to catch his breath. His heart was beating like a jackhammer on a New York City street. "That was close," he said softly and went back to the bath. His knees were still trembling.

The Constable was clearly disconcerted. "I would say that it seems she is a willing partner."

"She certainly has been an enchanting guest," Gideon said, now that he had regained his ability to speak. "As ye have witnessed, she's a little demanding of our Laird."

"I'd say your Laird is being very accommodating, considering." The Constable snorted, satisfied he had a reasonable answer for the Embassy.

The United States Embassy reported that Melissa Johnson had been found, and it was ascertained that she was not being held captive. The report did go on to tell them the Constable had spoken with Ms. Johnson and was told to "get lost". The local authorities are certain Laird MacKenna has been very accommodating to the young lady and suggested this was a private matter.

Chapter Eighteen

Ye can run, but ye canna' hide Laird MacKenna. The Prince has ye on the run.

On the Streets, with Rosabel

Daniel laughed for hours when Gideon and Robert relayed the events of the afternoon to him. He received a copy of the report from the Constable and was going to have it framed for his office.

He walked out to the stables toward his brothers. "I have tae see the Stewart Laird. It seems our Iain has another paternity suit pending."

"Not again," Robert groaned. "Isn't that the third or fourth one for this year?"

"Aye." Daniel found a sturdy horse to take him to their neighbors. "It's always the quiet ones who get into trouble. Keep him out of sight until I get things calmed down with the Stewarts."

He rode off at a gallop, eager to get out for some exercise. He needed some time alone to think about Rebecca. She hadn't said a word when he brought her back to the stables and had taken her own Friesian mare to return to the city. She needed time, he thought again.

Gideon and Robert exchanged a frown. "We need tae teach Iain how tae play and not get caught," Robert said. "Or rent him out for stud."

Gideon agreed. "Tis a good thing one of the previous blood tests came back negative, or he'd be in trouble."

"Alex will be furious anyway. He told me he saw John Stewart riding back from the cottage and wanted tae know what he was doing here."

"Aye," Gideon agreed. "Alex will kill Iain this time. Daniel is already working on the other law suits and has promised tae have Iain castrated if he isn't more careful."

"From the look on Daniel's face, he didn't tell Rebecca he was in love with her." Robert changed the subject.

Gideon raised an eyebrow. Daniel's secret love affair with the red-haired horse trainer was obvious to everyone, except Rebecca. She didn't notice the longing in Daniel's eyes or the tenderness in his voice when he spoke to her.

The brothers knew she was in love with Alex, but Alex had enough on his mind during the past few years not to notice her love for him.

***

Alex knew his time was running short. The game was about to come to an end, and with it, his lovely lady would find out the truth and leave him. He couldn't bear the thought of the days in his life without her. She had such a sweet innocence about her that filled his heart with hope. He loved her and hoped he could get through the next few days without losing her precious love.

While the warriors were all out fighting battles, Alex was raging a battle of his own with his soul. He couldn't give her up, not now that he held her trusting heart in his hands. He hoped she would understand and forgive him. Her scent wafted lazily over him, reminding him she was still with him, loving him tenderly.

Melissa saw the sadness in his eyes and fear clenched her stomach. Something haunted him, and she feared losing his love. Her hand caressed his powerful chest. They had bathed and made love, but she could tell there was something distracting him. He seemed so far away.

The ache in her heart nearly choked her. What could she say to him to get him past that pain? She had shown him in every way she knew that she loved him, but her own fear of losing him kept her thoughts and fears secret. His eyes closed, and he wrapped his arms tightly around her. Her cheek rested against his warm chest, and she fell asleep in his arms.

It was much later that afternoon when Alex and Melissa walked out of the cottage and made their way through the army so Alex could check on how the battle went that day with William in command.

Melissa noticed that Alex's brothers were all in a very good mood this evening and kept breaking out in laughter. It was good to see them happy. Daniel had private news to tell Alex that also had him laughing. She guessed the news had to be about the battle and that Alex was pleased with the results.

She wore her tartan tunic over the wool dress and had brushed her hair until it shimmered in the setting sun. They had supper under the stars that night next to a campfire with an army beside them. Since she had been so ill, they treated her gently. Curse words were muffled, and more than one warrior got reminded to mind their manners.

William made a rare appearance at dinner and was called up to honor them with a song for their entertainment that evening.

Melissa was delighted. She leaned into Alex's possessive arms. The warmth he radiated every night was enough to keep her cozy in the embrace. She smiled at him for reassurance and noticed he didn't tense up and look threateningly at William. They had passed that jealousy, she reasoned.

"What song would ye like to hear?" William asked of the army that surrounded them.

Several titles were yelled out, but William had something different in mind. He selected one of his favorites and brought out a stringed instrument.

Melissa was content yet, she felt the sadness in the hauntingly soft tune. Her mind wandered with the image of misty mountains in the distance. The music reminded her of an ancient Gaelic song of lost battles and fallen warriors.

She thought about Scotland while he played and the weeks she had spent with Alex. She looked up at the stars and couldn't believe they were the same stars from her sky on the other side of the planet and from a different time.

Her world had changed drastically during the past several weeks, and she was deeply in love with a magnificent warrior.

Robert and Iain were noticeably missing from the evening festivities. Daniel mentioned that Robert had to pick up supplies, and Iain had agreed to help. He didn't mention that picking up the supplies would only take about an hour. Both Robert and Iain had other plans for the evening and would be delayed, depending on how drunk they got.

She leaned her cheek against Alex's warm chest. Tomorrow, she would do a painting of William and his fellow warriors. The bonfire cast a warm glow on his profile. There were other instruments brought out to the clearing, and they soon had three guitars, a violin, and a keg of ale to limber up their voices.

Their festive mood was contagious, and they soon had the camp up and dancing to a wild Highland jig. Alex pulled her into the dance with him and showed her the steps. They laughed and danced to a spirited song before applauding the musicians and catching their breaths.

William was in a good mood, smiling as he played. He had won several important battles that week, and the warriors all made comments about their pup that had grown up right before their eyes—now had the roar and teeth of a lion. When he finished his song, he bowed to Alex and took a seat with the warriors.

Suddenly, the patrols came back into camp and brought news the Prince was secretly planning to raid their camp in the morning. Their cousins had overheard the plan while they lifted some supplies from the Prince's camp.

Alex held Melissa firmly at his side. "Call the commanders for an emergency war council," he said to William. His orders were carried out quickly.

"Melissa, I don't want tae keep ye up all night. Why don't ye go tae bed and wait for me?" He added the last part softly in her ear.

She shivered against him. "No Alex, I want to stay with you."

He looked down at her blue eyes and couldn't think about anything else. She looked so innocent and trusting. Alex didn't want to leave her alone again, but he knew he must. "If ye get some rest now love, I'll wake ye up when I get tae bed."

"Tease," she answered softly. "I'm taking my responsibilities seriously, Alex. I will waive them on to victory." She collected her coffee cup and sat down at the table so Alex could concentrate on his upcoming battle.

She didn't want him to see the tears that glistened in her eyes. She couldn't bear the thought of any of them going into battle again. Lately, everything seemed to upset her, and she longed for the day when the war with the Prince was over.

Alex and his brothers had come to mean more to her than life itself, and she just couldn't think about any one of them going into battle nor the possibility that one of them might not ever come back again. The thoughts burned in a painful lump in her throat.

The commanders assembled at the table outside the cottage, bringing in torches to review the map on the table. The warriors were deadly serious and focused their attention on Alex. They would follow his command and waited anxiously for his orders.

Alex paced, considering the information the scouts brought back to camp. Robert and Iain were still in

London and wouldn't be back until the morning. So that only left him Gideon, Daniel, Evan, and William to lead an attack since he'd decided he wouldn't lead a battle unless he absolutely had to.

His brothers were already assembled. Daniel was his first choice but not his best choice. "All right, gentlemen. Are there any suggestions?" He always invited the commanders into the discussions.

William suggested, "I say we execute an overnight raid on the Prince's camp in a first attack and then a second attack when they start pursuit. Don't give the Prince the advantage of meeting us in our camp."

Daniel nodded approval.

Alex issued his orders. "William will command the overnight raid. Take a hundred warriors with you. Daniel and Evan will be prepared with the second strike of seventy-five warriors and disable the Prince's warriors as they start pursuit. A third phase attack led by Gideon with a small group of twenty-five warriors will guard Daniel and Evan's retreat. William, once you have completed your raid, retreat, and attack again as Gideon's warriors make their exit from the glen."

William boldly challenged Alex and issued another order in Gaelic. "Daniel and Evan—on your retreat, split your forces into two groups. Take one group east into the glen and the other along the ridge. On my retreat, Gideon can rejoin my warriors, and we will split. Daniel and Evan can turn back, and we will have them caught between us. Once we split their forces, we get double points because we will fight with two different commanders and then a triple point advantage when Gideon rejoins us at the glen."

Melissa followed the discussion by watching the drawing that William did in the dirt. It seemed they were discussing attacking and counter-attacking.

Alex raised an eyebrow as he considered the tactic. "I like it. Tomorrow morning I will lead a small group of warriors to guard your retreat, gentlemen. Prepare for battle."

The camp that had just a little while ago been light-hearted with musicians and dancing became serious with men shouting orders to their commanders and horses being saddled. Overnight provisions were prepared and wrapped for their saddlebags.

William had ascended to a commander position during the past week, and his warriors waited for his word to depart. The camp was buzzing with excitement. The current plan would be a decisive victory for the Laird, even if he didn't personally command the attack.

The warriors who had just returned from patrol would have a chance to rest before they joined Alex to guard the final retreat in the morning.

William was ready to depart. The white Andalusian stallion Alex had given him for his birthday pranced sideways with excitement. William had grown up on horseback and could outride them all. He was young and agile with a streak of recklessness that often got him into trouble. The stallion had taken to him right away and William had complete control of the fearless horse.

Alex was proud of him. Iain, Evan, and William were more like sons to him than brothers. In truth, Alex thought, it was like seeing your son become a man.

William had grown up this summer and accepted responsibility. Alex had to wonder if William's affection for Melissa had caused the radical change. William had become a warrior who could challenge the Prince.

Alex and William were so much alike it was frightening at times. Alex could see himself in his brother's strengths and abilities but also his weaknesses. His reverie was disturbed by the gentle love of his lady putting her arm around him.

Melissa's love had allowed him to see the world in a very different way. Alex also had a summer he would never forget. William nodded to Alex and departed the camp. The warriors moved into position behind him. Alex and Melissa waved them on to victory. From the camp, they heard the argument begin.

"That kiss was meant for me…"

"Och! Ye're as ugly as a horse's arse…"

Melissa waited until they were out of hearing range. "Alex, I can't believe you're not going with them. This is an important battle."

Alex felt a slight twinge of regret. He hadn't missed a battle in thirty-five years, but then he looked down and her beautiful smile touched his heart with her magic. He let out a long sigh.

Alex kissed her temple and smiled. He had made his choice and would never regret the decision. He loved her more than he wanted to play in the game. His brothers had all expressed concern that Alex's heart wasn't in the game this year, and they were correct in their assumption that he would rather be in bed with Melissa than on a horse in the rain with them.

For Alex, the game had always been a responsibility and not the excitement they found. The mantle of command weighed heavily at times, and he rarely got to have fun.

Alex and Melissa walked slowly back to the cottage. "I know tha' kiss was meant for me." He ginned smugly and took her to bed.

***

Alex had the few remaining warriors up before dawn and ready to ride out. He was anxious about the battle. If everything went as planned, William would take the lead for points, and he wanted his youngest brother to win the game.

He had done everything in his power to put William in the winner's saddle and was certain he would be a strong leader. Now, everything Alex had worked for was about to come together. He hadn't been able to sleep during the night. So much depended on what happened today that he found himself getting nervous. Alex had never been worried about a battle and paced the cottage through the night while Melissa slept.

The warriors had come in to speak to him during the night, and Alex hadn't worried about waking her. Once she was asleep, she didn't flutter an eyelash as the thundering warriors stomped through the cottage and gave their reports during the night. Alex was informed that William's raid was executed without a flaw, Daniel and Evan were also in position, and Gideon and his men were making their way to guard the retreat.

Laird MacKenna and his warriors departed before the first light of day had reached the crest of Loch Voil. They moved quietly and rode quickly up the side of the hills. It was a path they had taken often.

The ancient sword at his side was about to be handed over to his youngest brother, he thought wistfully. Alex had always cherished the ancient sword of Baron Jolbert and the heritage that went with it. He knew William would be a Laird they would all be proud of and would lead them on to victory.

It would be his final battle as their Laird, he thought with mixed emotions. His life would be very different with his lady at his side, but he was more than ready to retire his leadership to his brother.

***

William moved silently on foot to the edge of the Prince's camp. It was shortly before dawn, and he knew it wouldn't be much longer before the warriors woke and went about their duties. His scouts had told him the Prince was asleep in the cottage. They had been steadily watching the camp for the past few days, certain the Prince had some new plan up his sleeve. So far, he hadn't noticed anything different.

Men slept on the hillside, covered in their tartans. William signaled his men, and they advanced over the ridge. Twenty warriors made their way up to him. They heard the signal from their men informing them Daniel and Evan were in position. Bloodthirsty anticipation drove them on to victory. This battle would decide the winner in the game. Adrenaline flowed in their veins as they moved as a shadow of ancient warriors.

It was at this moment that William felt the thrill of adventure. Time stood still, and he was certain the ghosts of his ancestors stood beside him. The hair on his arms stood up, and his breath frosted in billowed clouds. He finally understood what his brothers felt when they went into battle. It was a challenge, yet something much stronger — something he struggled to identify.

And then he knew. It was his destiny.

William signaled the warriors to stop, and they looked at him with confusion on their faces. He looked around him, sensing something was missing. In an instant, he knew — they were walking into a trap. The men who were sleeping on the ground didn't make any noise. All was too quiet.

William signaled for them to retreat and regroup.

"It's a trap," Evan said quietly to Daniel who also noticed William making a hasty retreat.

William ran back to his horse and rode swiftly back to Daniel and Evan. His warriors followed.

"Alex!" William shouted as he rode past at a gallop, Daniel and Evan understood and mustered their warriors to follow. William signaled to break into three sections with Daniel and Evan leading the other two forces. They had left Alex undefended, and he would be vulnerable with only twenty warriors with him.

So this was the Prince's plan, William thought. The man was being even more clever than usual. They had underestimated him.

The warriors galloped back toward the Laird's cottage. Gideon's men stayed the advance of the Prince's men who had been left at their camp and then rode hard and fast to catch up to the warriors that protected their Laird, and ultimately, Melissa.

***

Robert and Iain returned just before the first light of dawn. The horses were stabled near their launch pad. The two of them had partied through the night in London and were ready for a little rest. They rode quietly in the predawn hour.

The guards at the gate to the camp were missing. Something was wrong. Robert reached over and grabbed hold of Iain to get his attention and then signaled for him to ride up to the cottage to see if Alex and Melissa were still there.

They could make out a band of warriors coming over the ridge toward them and had already guessed their army was out in the hills. The camp was almost completely deserted, except for a few men in the hospital tent that roused quickly and informed Robert of the battle plans for the day. Robert and Iain silently rode up to the cottage.

Chapter Nineteen

Melissa was sound asleep when a hand covered her mouth, and she wildly struggled in the dark. It took a few moments for her to understand it was Iain who had a hand over her mouth, and he was whispering for her to be quiet. They were under attack and had only a few moments to get her to safety before the Prince's men would descend on the camp and take her hostage. Iain put a finger to his lips to quiet her and handed her a wrapper to cover her naked body.

Melissa was terrified. Iain turned around to look out the window while she put the wrapper on. "Where are you taking me?"

"To safety," Iain whispered, pulling her into the water closet where he opened the window, lifted her into his arms, and out to Robert who waited with their horses. Iain had just eased through the window to join them when they heard the first sounds of warriors in the camp. Robert tossed Melissa onto a horse and instructed Iain to take her to the other cottage by the glen.

Iain reached around her to take the reins. Robert remained at the camp to direct a defense. He was hungover and in a dark mood when the Prince's men advanced into the camp.

Iain and Melissa rode through the woods. They moved slowly, uncertain if they would find any more of the Prince's men and stayed in the shadows as much as possible. The cottage was being watched with a scout on the ridge, Iain pointed out for Melissa, and they moved silently along the edge of the woods.

The trees were thick and brush hid them from view, but from out of the darkness, the hilt of a sword crashed against Iain's temple. He didn't see it coming and crumbled unconscious against Melissa.

Melissa felt him sag against her back and then noticed there were two men in the woods who tried to reach out and grab the reins of the horse. She screamed and kicked the horse into moving away from the men, while she held onto Iain.

He was dead weight against her back, and she nearly lost him when the horse bolted into a run. The dawn finally glowed pink on the horizon, and she could see where they were going—just as she could see the pursuit of the two men who had knocked Iain out.

Melissa kicked the horse harder, and let it run while she held on to Iain. The robe fell off one shoulder. She heard Iain groan and yelled at him to hold on to her. His arms circled her waist and held on while she directed the horse.

Iain was dazed and couldn't get his eyes to focus. He held onto Melissa and then noticed they were being chased. "I canna tell if there are two men or four riding after us. I'm seeing double of everything, and I'm going tae puke!"

His hand was wrapped around the hilt of his sword, and she pried it away, holding onto it one hand and the reins with the other.

The warriors galloped alongside them, and Melissa brought the sword down against the warrior's blade. It was just enough of a shock to him that he dropped back.

"Hold on," Melissa called out and kicked the horse harder. They gained some distance from the warriors, but it wouldn't take them long to catch up. She struggled to direct the horse that rapidly tired with both their weight.

They reached the edge of a ridge, and Iain began to slide over the side of the horse. Melissa didn't have the strength to hold on for him, and he wasn't letting go of her. She dropped the sword as they fell to the ground and rolled over the edge of the cliff.

His dead weight pulled them down, and they slid ten feet to a rocky ledge before they finally came to a stop. Melissa landed on top of Iain who had been knocked out cold when they fell. He took the brunt of the fall against his shoulder.

Their horse had continued on, and Melissa hoped the Prince's men wouldn't come looking for them. She tugged Iain back against the overhang so they couldn't be spotted from the ridge and covered him with her body. The gray wool wrapper she wore made them appear like a shadow.

She heard the men ride past them and breathed a sigh of relief. It wasn't long before the sound of their return was muted by the thunder of an army moving past on the ridge. Melissa didn't know if it was Alex's warriors or the Prince's, so she decided to play it safe and wait until she could get Iain awake before trying to climb up the cliff.

She worried about the cut on his forehead and couldn't seem to wake him, no matter how hard she slapped his face. She could tell he had been out drinking for the aroma of beer clung to his shirt. She didn't know if he had passed out from the beer or from the injury to his head.

Melissa moved away from Iain and sat up on the ledge to get her bearings and then wished she hadn't. How they had managed to find the only ledge within twenty feet in both directions was beyond her comprehension. It was a miracle they hadn't fallen down into the valley below. Her fear of heights overwhelmed her, and her head spun when she looked down. It was a long drop to the rocky bottom of the cliff.

Iain groaned, and blood oozed out of the side of his mouth. He was seriously injured and needed immediate medical attention. She tried again to wake him, knowing she would need his help to get them off the cliff, but he didn't respond to her touch.

She wished she had any means of communication with Alex or any one of his warriors. She scanned the side of the cliff, seeing there wasn't any way that she could climb up and over the ledge. They were stuck until someone came along who could pull them out.

Every moment she waited for the sound of passing horses became an eternity. Melissa worried about Iain, who didn't move and what would happen if the Prince's men caught her with nothing on but a wrapper? She was terrified and angry. There was no way she could help either one of them.

***

William, Daniel, Evan, and two hundred warriors descended on the Valley of Tears. They had named that valley as such when their father had a lethal heart attack there eighteen years ago. It was a suitable setting to meet the Prince's warriors. They weren't expecting to find the entire Laird's camp coming over the ridge to meet them with the Prince's men scattered out of formation.

William directed Daniel to take the right flank and Evan to take the left. The two groups split off and met the Prince's warriors in the middle of the valley. The Prince's men had Alex and his small band of twenty warriors surrounded. At the heart of it stood Alex and Prince George locked in furious sword slinging, arm crunching, steel clanging battle. Neither one of them would back down. Alex was relieved to see William. The troops quickly had the battle under control.

Prince George stepped back to catch his breath. "How about we agree to a secondary challenge? If we can catch the Laird — the game is finally won?" He ran his hand over his brow and waited for the answer to his challenge.

Alex gave him a moment to recover and considered the challenge. It would certainly put an end to the game that year if they could catch the Laird. The thought rolled around in his head and then Daniel's many lectures came to mind.

"Your challenge," Alex restated for him. "Is, if ye can catch the Laird, ye win the game?" He was a stickler for details.

The Prince nodded, still gasping for breath. "What's the timeline?"

"Ye must catch the Laird before the final battle."

The Prince agreed and conceded the battle.

They were completely surrounded by the Laird's forces. The Prince's warriors were already calling surrender and moved back to the ridge. Prince George mounted his horse.

"I agree tae the challenge," Laird Alex G. MacKenna, proclaimed and then grinned. "Ye won't catch the Laird, George."

Prince George smiled in return. "We'll see." He rode back to the ridge with his men and then disappeared down into the valley below.

Gideon and his band of twenty warriors had raided the Prince's camp before departing. They engaged the Prince's retreating men on their way to the Valley of Tears and won fifty points. Their mild mannered doctor had just kicked a warrior down when they noticed Robert riding up at a furious pace.

Robert stopped beside Alex and quickly explained the raid from the Prince's men.

"I secured the camp. Iain escaped with Melissa. The horse they were riding returned, and I tracked them to the ridge," Robert said in a worried voice. "The Prince's men who attacked them said they knocked Iain out, and the horse took off at a run. They couldn't catch up to Iain and Melissa so didn't know they had been lost."

Alex ran to his horse with the warriors following. It was short ride to the ridge but every moment seemed like an eternity for Alex. "Spread out," he yelled.

A little way down from where Alex was standing someone yelled they found fresh blood and a sword on the rocks.

Melissa had heard the horses and decided to yell, even if it was the Prince's men. They needed help for Iain right away. She screamed as loudly as she could, "help!"

"Melissa," Alex yelled back, standing at the edge where they had gone over. He could see her on the ledge.

Daniel and Evan brought ropes and tied one end to a tree to rappel down the side of the cliff.

"Alex! Iain got hurt. We need Gideon right away."

"He's here," Alex called.

Alex and Gideon went over the side of the cliff and moments later were standing on the ledge with Melissa. She quickly hugged Alex but then rushed to tell them Iain was injured and had blood coming out of his mouth.

"Has he been able to speak at all?" Gideon asked and checked Iain's head.

"He moaned several times but hasn't said anything. He took the brunt of the fall against his shoulder, and I fell on top of him."

Alex looked over the side of the cliff and was relieved they had managed to stop on the ledge. The fall to the bottom of the cliff would have been perhaps mortal injury to either one of them. Melissa appeared shaken but unharmed — unlike his brother.

Alex made up his mind that he wouldn't put her through another night like this one. She had been dragged out of bed in the middle of the night, tossed on a horse to escape capture, and then fell over a cliff.

He held her close when the warriors pulled them up. She had refused to leave Iain, but Gideon convinced her they needed the space to get Iain off the ledge.

"He's got a broken rib." Gideon tried not to upset her further. It had been a trying night for her, too. He listened to Iain's breathing to find out if the rib had punctured his lung. Gideon and Daniel brought him up carefully. Robert had ridden on to prepare the helicopter for launch, and Iain would be checked out at hospital.

Melissa stood next to Alex and watched them haul Iain up the cliff. She ran over to him, and he looked up at her and managed a weak smile. "You're going to be all right, Iain," she said and kissed his cheek. "Gideon will take care of you now."

Iain groaned, still seeing double. "Would both of you please kiss me again?"

They were ready to put him on the back of Gideon's horse. Melissa leaned down and gave Iain a quick kiss on the lips. "Take care of him, Gideon," she said softly, brushing a dark curl from Iain's forehead.

He had a gin, even with a pounding headache.

"We'll have him back in the saddle before ye know it," Gideon promised.

She didn't realize all the warriors were watching her every move and suddenly felt very self-conscious about standing there in Alex's wrapper.

William, Evan, and the warriors were taking note. They admired and respected the wee lass who didn't think about her safety or comfort and insisted they take care of Iain. She was distraught, thinking Iain had been seriously injured. They had all had a concussion or two in the past few years and were a little envious of the kiss Iain got.

James and Jonathan, their Marine cousins, were standing beside Evan.

"We're going tae have tae quit fighting so well," Jonathan noted.

"So we can be injured," James said wistfully.

"Don't worry," Evan said. "We can give ye a broken leg. Now that ought tae get ye a hug and a kiss."

Alex shook his head and laughed softly. "Now, see what you've started," he gently reprimanded his lovely lady and hugged her tightly to his side.

"I wonder what I could get for a missing leg," Jonathan asked Evan seriously. They debated the issue all the way back to the camp and had decided they would have to stick with concussions. A missing body part wasn't the preferred method of getting the lady's attention. However, in dire circumstances, it could be held out as an emergency option.

Melissa didn't hear a word of the conversation. Evan had lifted her up to Alex's lap, and she put her arm around him, pressing her cheek against his warm chest. She could hear his heartbeat, and the sound was a soothing relief.

"How did the battle go today?" she asked Alex.

William rode behind them and spoke up. "We won!"

Alex smiled. "William earned the right to brag. It was his fast thinking that saved the battle and protected me from capture. The Prince almost had me, too. We were outnumbered, but William figured out it was a trap and they rode back in time to turn the battle back on the Prince."

Melissa smiled up at him and tightened her grip on Alex's waist. She didn't want to break down and cry in front of the warriors and struggled to gain control of the emotional riptide that suddenly had tears stinging her eyes. Alex held her tightly in his arms to still her tremble, and she felt safe, for the moment.

***

Robert dropped Gideon, Iain, and Daniel off at hospital and picked up a guest of his own. Agotha was waiting for him and took a seat in the helicopter. He smiled and picked up her hand to give her fingertips a kiss. Moments later, the helicopter was air born and they headed for the glen where they could have a few hours of privacy. He had personally repaired that cottage and prepared for a long lovely afternoon there with his lady.

Agotha put on a headset so they could talk while they flew. "Robert, I talked to Rebecca. Who is the woman with Alex?"

Robert smiled a flash of straight white teeth. "She's an American tourist who stumbled into the opening battle. Alex took one look at her and fell in love."

Agotha wasn't about to give up on this subject. "Is this Yank in love with Alex?" She had promised Rebecca she would find out what she could from Robert.

Robert landed outside the tiny cottage and shut the helicopter down. He walked around and lifted Agotha into his arms.

"Yes, my darling. Ye can tell Rebecca that Melissa is a verra fine lady and very much in love with Alex. You'd like her, Agotha. She cares about all of us, and there is a light in her eyes when she looks at Alex." He knew Agotha and Rebecca were close friends.

Robert wrapped his arms around his beautiful Agotha. She had been on his mind a lot lately, and he missed her during the past few weeks. Her dark brown hair filtered through his fingers. He loved to touch her. She was very loving when she wasn't kicking his arse in battle.

He grinned and ran his hands over her back. She was agile and strong enough to hold a sword against a man, yet a lady in every respect when they spent precious intimate hours together.

They had discovered a raging passion between them one day when she had given him a private lesson. She had knocked him down to the ground, and he had kissed her playfully. One thing had led to another, and they had spent their first night together making love under the stars at the glen.

Their love play could get a little boisterous, not that he was complaining. He had never known anyone like her, and he couldn't get enough of her.

"So this is the cottage you repaired." Agotha walked through the door.

Robert stood in the doorway and watched her reaction to the cottage with its new floors. He had brought in a few provisions for an afternoon delight and even put sheets on the bed, a blanket, and pillows—a fact Agotha noticed right away.

Raising one eyebrow, she studied him. Robert's long straight hair was loose and hung well past his shoulders.

He was magnificent to look at with a tanned, honed physique that drew her hands like a magnet. She loved to touch her warrior lover. She walked over to the doorway and slowly pulled him inside.

Robert kicked the door shut. He reached out and gathered her into his arms. His darlin' Agotha was an eager lover. The touch of her fingers sliding over his muscled chest reminded him he hadn't seen her for weeks.

He picked her up and brought her over to the bed, sitting down on the edge with Agotha on his lap straddling his hips. His lips crushed hers in an agony of desire. He wanted her now. Waiting another minute was not an option.

She wiggled just a little as he slid her jeans off and he shrugged his shirt off. She felt good in his arms, and he loved to kiss her pretty red lips. Robert pulled her t-shirt off and threw it across the room. He kissed a trail over her shoulder as a bra strap fell to her elbow and then left a trail of sizzling kisses along the curve of her throat.

He managed the clasp with one hand and their clothing quickly became a pile on the floor. Her breath was warm and fast on his cheek, and he lifted her, touching his lips to her full pink breast.

Agotha almost cried. He teased her body with his warm tongue sliding over her breast before she slid down the length of his body, allowing him to fill her completely. She cried out his name again and again as the ecstasy nearly drove her to madness.

Her teeth on his earlobe got his attention, and he grabbed a handful of her hair and captured her tempting lips. His tongue slid into her hot mouth and retreated, teasing her, caressing her, until she groaned in the back of her throat, pushed him down on the bed, and rode him hard and fast.

Robert slid his hands over her luscious body and cupped her heavy breast in his hand while his thumb brushed the hardened nipple to taunt peaks. He flipped her over on her stomach and returned to the heat of her with his legs straddling her hips. His hands caressed her back and the curves of her lovely body until she called out to him to have mercy on her.

Robert could wait no longer and held her hips in his hands, filling her again and again until the quiver of ecstasy overwhelmed them both, and he collapsed on top of her, panting and fulfilled.

He kissed her shoulder, moved beside her, and pulled her into his arms.

"I think you have missed me," Agotha said softly, brushing her fingertips over his warm chest.

"That," he gasped, still catching his breath, "is an understatement! Agotha, me darlin', I missed ye and thought about ye all day -- every day."

She smiled, her green eyes sparkling sexily. "I missed ye too, Robert. From what we heard on the news, the Prince is winning this game. Is it true?"

Robert laughed and stroked her waist long sable hair. "Aye, it was true for a time, but Alex will change that fast enough. He's going tae resign as Laird," Robert knew he could trust her. Agotha trained their warriors. She was their Master Swordswoman and knew all of the warriors and their capabilities very well. Her mouth dropped open when he gave her the news.

"Ye're joking!" She said aghast. "But he can't resign! He's the Laird of the Game. The game will be forfeit!"

"Alex won't forfeit the game," Robert said softly. "He is resigning and naming William as his successor and Laird. He is going tae retire with Melissa. She's a beautiful woman and loves him deeply."

Agotha felt a slight tinge of jealousy. "Well, she must if Alex would resign for her. She obviously has all of ye wrapped around her finger." Agotha didn't want to hear him tell her how beautiful Melissa was or that because of Melissa, the game could possibly be forfeited.

Her friend, Rebecca, was broken hearted, and Agotha could understand her pain. There was just too much at stake for everyone involved. The monetary losses would count in the millions of pounds, and there was also their honor at stake. She trained the winning team and wouldn't accept their defeat.

Robert opened one eye and peered at her with a frown. He didn't like to hear the harsh edge of jealousy in her voice, but Robert was also certain Melissa deserved defending. She had dropped into their world and loved Alex beyond reason.

"Agotha, I'll not have ye talking poorly about Melissa. She's in love with Alex, and he's in love with her. There's no need tae be jealous of her."

"So why then are ye defending her?" Agotha was suddenly very irritated. "If there's nothing tae worry about, why would ye make such a point of protecting her?" She rolled from the bed and quickly found her clothing and dressed. She was irritated that Robert seemed a little too protective of Melissa, and Agotha didn't like the flare of jealousy.

"Agotha, don't do this," Robert said, anger seeping into his voice. "Ye have tae meet her tae understand. There just isn't a sweeter, more loving woman on earth."

"Have ye forgotten one verra important fact, Robert? Alex is married! Rebecca was madly in love with him for years waiting for him tae divorce Catherine. And now ye tell me Melissa shows up from out of the blue, snags him right out from under Rebecca, and Melissa's the most wonderful woman on earth! She's a Yank!" Agotha threw his tartan at him and walked outside.

It just seemed that no matter what he said, it only made her angrier. Robert got dressed and met her at the helicopter. "Ye already know Daniel was in love with Rebecca and that Alex never did have any romantic feelings for her. Alex knew Daniel had a crush on her years ago, and Daniel hoped she would get over her crush on Alex." Agotha turned to walk away, and Robert was furious. "We're goin' tae discuss this, Agotha."

"No, we're not. Take me home. Now, Robert!" She was insanely jealous at the moment and not acting like herself at all. What was Alex thinking taking a tourist into the game? If the game forfeited, or Alex resigned because of this...Yank...Agotha knew the press would blame the failure on Alex. They had all worked hard for the game to be a complete success. Many long hours were devoted to the warriors and preparing them for the battles. Melissa had obviously gained all of their loyalty and affection from the look on Robert's face. She wanted to shove that ridiculous smile of his into the side of his helicopter. She got in and put her seat belt on. Robert didn't say anything and they took off moments later.

Robert had a few minutes to cool his temper and then couldn't help but smile. Agotha had never been jealous of any other woman before now. He looked over and gave her his most brilliant smile. He had just figured out she was in love with him, even if she would never admit it.

She just frowned at him and watched the ground. When they touched down, she took off running without another word, got into her car, and drove off before he could shut down the helicopter.

Daniel walked out to the launch pad. "Was that Agotha?" He asked, already knowing it was their VixenBlade.

"Must be the sun in your eyes," Robert answered. "Ye're getting old and probably need glasses."

Daniel chuckled. "From the look on her face, ye had an interesting afternoon."

Robert grinned. "She's in love with me."

Daniel scoffed. "Ye ugly bastard. Why would she fall for ye?"

"I'm damn good in bed."

"Ye'd better get us back to the game. I have a feeling the Prince has a few more surprises in store for us."

Robert took off, and Daniel's mind wandered. Iain had a concussion and a cracked rib but would recover in a few days. Iain had informed him he wanted to marry his beloved, Bonnie, and wouldn't put it off another day.

They would be married at the Kirk before the celebration party began.

Daniel's frown began to disappear. It gave him an idea and a resolution to a problem he'd been trying to solve. He scratched his whiskered chin. He'd been away from civilization too long and was beginning to think and feel like a Celtic warrior.

"We need tae make one stop," Daniel said to Robert and gave him the direction. "Set down in the parking lot, and I will get this piece of business taken care of quickly."

Daniel had Iain's Power of Attorney in hand when he walked in to the Registrar's office and got a marriage license. He could take care of all his problems at once. Iain would finally have only one woman in his life and would be a happy man to have his Bonnie. Alex would be delighted, and the arrangements were already made.

Daniel returned to the game grinning like a bobcat with his tail on fire.

Chapter Twenty

The Prince pulled off an amazing upset in the MacKenna camp and now has the lead with a one hundred and fifty-point advantage over the Laird. It is rumored that the youngest MacKenna has been leading more challenges than the Laird this year. It's my guess the Laird's just too busy with his lady to pay attention. The Prince is going to win if the MacKenna boys don't have an amazing upset of their own to retaliate.

On the Streets, with Rosabel

It was long after dark had settled on the tiny village that one dark figure moved silently to the hospital door and walked into the MacKenna wing at the hospital. Her small body was covered in a black velvet cloak lined in white satin. The full-length cape touched the tops of her toes, and the hood pulled low concealed her identity. She made her way past the nurse's station and down the hall to his room. She already knew where to find him and eased the door open to peer inside the darkened room.

The nurse just raised her eyes heavenward and went back to filling in her charts. Iain had already told her that he was getting company late that night and then wouldn't want to be disturbed until morning.

Bonnie draped the velvet cloak over the chair and quietly eased into bed next to Iain. He was asleep when she walked in, but the warmth of her body woke him. He reached out and pulled her into his arms. She had on a black lace teddy under the cape, and the soft body that snuggled up to Iain was already flushed with excitement. He had called her the moment his brothers had left the room, and Bonnie drove from London to join him for the night. Her scent of wild roses surrounded him, and he brushed her soft, tempting mouth with his lips.

He groaned when he moved his head. "Hello, Bonnie, my love." Iain lay back on the pillow and closed his eyes but the spinning only got worse. "The world slides away from me if I move my head, lass."

Bonnie was in tears. "Iain, you're really hurt!" She kissed his cheeks and eyes and then gently kissed his lips. Long golden-brown hair spilled over his arm as she reached for the nurse's call button. "You need a doctor."

Iain caught her hand as she reached over him and brought her fingers to his lips. "Later, my darling. Right now the only cure I need is right here beside me. I'd be delighted if ye'd kiss me again," he said dreamily. "My sweet Bonnie lass, I want tae marry ye. Will ye have me for your husband?"

Bonnie couldn't believe what she had just heard. Iain had many women falling all over him. She smiled and kissed him happily. There were tears streaming down her cheeks and blended into the kiss. "I will marry you, Iain, and I'll love you all the days of my life."

Iain reached under the pillow beside his head and took out a ring box. "Good thing ye want tae marry me," he said softly against her ear and took out the three carat pink diamond solitaire, slipping the ring on her finger. "Daniel is taking care of the license for me, but you'll have tae stop and sign the papers. We're getting married at the Kirk right before the party."

"We are?" Bonnie brushed the hair from his face and kissed him everywhere she could reach. "Why marry me now, Iain? Is it for the bairn?"

"No lass, it's not for the child, although I am delighted. I'm in love with ye. Melissa helped me see how much I wanted ye in my life. She's such a fine lady."

"Should I worry about this fine lady?" Bonnie bit her lip, already worried.

"No' unless ye are in love with Alex, too, lass. I want a life with our family. I offer ye my heart and soul, love."

Bonnie bent down to kiss his lips, and her warm body covered his. "Then I will have you forever and always, my handsome love."

It didn't matter how much he hurt. Iain wanted to make love to her and ease the agony in his body. She kissed his closed eyelids. He whimpered slightly, just enough to get her attention. He was enjoying her attention and couldn't think of a better way to spend the night in the hospital. In fact, he was feeling better by the moment.

His Bonnie loved him gently, and he was grateful. Iain couldn't open his eyes when she collapsed on him, exhausted from pleasing him. He wrapped his arms around her and fell asleep instantly.

Bonnie adjusted the covers around them and thought she would put her head down on his warm chest just for a few moments. Her eyes closed sleepily, and it was the last thing she remembered.

***

Gideon found Iain and Bonnie wrapped around each other the next morning. They were both sound asleep, and a black lace teddy was hung over his intravenous stand next to the bed.

The nurse called on the room intercom. "Dr. MacKenna, are you in the room with Iain?"

"Yes I am," he said softly so not to jolt Iain and Bonnie awake.

"There's a Rosabel here inquiring about Iain's injuries. We thought you might want to answer her questions while I take care of matters in the room."

Gideon understood exactly what she was talking about. They had to get Bonnie out of the room before Rosabel spotted her, and Bonnie ended up on the front page of the tabloid.

Gideon walked out to the hall, just as the nurse passed him and went into the room. He stood in front of Rosabel, blocking her view of the room.

"It's good to see you again Dr. MacKenna," Rosabel said and was amazed her voice sounded clear. When he stood so close to her, she couldn't stop a slight tremble in her hands as she reached for her notebook.

Gideon smiled but said nothing. He towered over the beautiful Malaysian woman. Her long black hair was straight and hung down to her waist. Her eyes were dark pools of simmering liquid ink that sparkled when he got near her. The desire she felt for him was obvious, but so was the fact that she refused to follow the reaction to his bed. He wanted to feel the warmth of her naked body against his, and the thoughts nearly caused a groan.

Rosabel noticed something peculiar. "Mind telling me why you have Iain MacKenna on the ObGyn floor? I thought he had a concussion not a baby."

"I don't mind telling you. Iain donated this wing of the hospital."

"From what I've heard, he needs an entire wing of a hospital to deliver all the babies he's fathered this year. Is that correct? The rumors are astounding. He must be a Celtic God to have four paternity law suits at once."

The door to the hospital room opened, and a cloaked figure walked out with the nurse. She took the lady out the side door, and Rosabel couldn't help but smile. "This must be a full-service hospital?"

"Only the best," Gideon said quietly. "Will you have a cup of coffee with me, Rosabel?"

"Coffee?" He wanted to sleep with her. It glimmered in his gray-green eyes. He towered over her, and she was a little apprehensive, especially since she had walked out on him at dinner.

Gideon took her arm and led her to the elevators. They waited until they had their coffee and sat down at a table in the outside courtyard where it was quiet. Her exotic beauty and dark eyes had haunted his nights since they had dinner together before. The lush scent of lilies wafted over him and reminded him again how much he wanted to make love to her.

Rosabel felt the heat of his ardent stare. His gaze devoured her, caressed her, and made love to her without a blink of his eyes. His tall, sexy body was within a few inches, and her knee brushed against his leg. She felt warm all over and desired. It had a heady affect on her senses, and she wanted to reach out and touch his cheek. His presence made her blush, knowing he wanted to make love to her and also that she desired him. She envisioned him lounging on a bed after making passionate love for hours, and the heat rushed to her cheeks.

Her imagination raced to what it must be like to be touched by a man so powerful and intimate. He was, from all the years of reporting the MacKenna playboys, one of the quieter men in their family. His brothers, Robert and Iain, were infamous with several lusty affairs, some with married women, but Gideon's love life was very secretive. He didn't kiss and tell or parade the notches on his bedpost in public.

"I'd like tae kiss ye," he said quietly to Rosabel. "But, I'm going tae wait until ye kiss me." His face was set in a dead-serious look that made her blush even more.

"What incredible arrogance!" Rosabel stood to leave and dropped her notebook on the terrace stone floor.

"Nevertheless," Gideon replied. "Ye want me tae kiss ye, so you can tell yourself it wasn't your decision. Ye will kiss me, Rosabel. And then I will make love with ye until ye fall asleep in my arms, exhausted and smiling."

Her eyes closed just thinking about his muscled body naked and pleasing her. She opened her eyes, and he was gone. His movements were silent and dangerous, like a prowling cat that had just spotted his prey. Rosabel suddenly felt very self-conscious. She couldn't let herself get involved. The memory of him caused a jerk in her belly, and she wanted to caress that lean body.

Rosabel suddenly realized he had managed to avoid even one question. "The bastard!" She took her coffee to leave. The distraction of his sexy body had completely unnerved her, and she forgot to do her job. Now, she had no idea if Iain MacKenna had a concussion or not. One thing was certain; she wasn't going to end up a momentary diversion for Dr. Gideon MacKenna. The disappointment was almost unbearable.

***

Their scouts raised an alarm. Alex was on his feet a moment later, shouted commands, and the warriors scrambled to find their swords.

They were under attack from what Melissa could understand of the shouting men around her.

William had his scouting party ready to ride out when the alarm sent the camp into battle preparations.

Evan ran to the stables and brought out Alex's stallion. The horse was saddled moments later and reared up in the excitement. He took the reins and led the horse out to Alex.

Melissa stood silently in the center of the maelstrom and watched the enemy ride over the ridge. The sight of the Prince and his army was enough terror to get a scream out of her.

Daniel stood beside Alex. "It's a good day for a fight."

"It's always a good day for a fight," Alex agreed.

"Melissa?" Daniel asked.

Alex looked down. Melissa was firmly attached to him with her arms around his waist. He put his arm around her to protect and comfort her. "Don't worry, sweetheart."

Evan brought the stallion up to the clearing and then took a defensive position beside William. Alex eased into the saddle, and Daniel lifted Melissa up with two hands on her waist.

Melissa held on tightly to Alex. "You're very relaxed for a man who just got ambushed," she said testily. The Prince's men were fighting their way into camp.

"I'm taking her back tae the Manor House, Daniel."

"I'll send her things along." Daniel smiled and casually dropped one of the Prince's men with a kick.

William met the oncoming warriors at the edge of their camp and landed the first blow of sword against shield that knocked the Prince off his horse.

"Daniel doesn't have a sword," Melissa said frantically to Alex as they rode away.

"He doesn't need one," Alex answered. He rode to the top of the Western ridge and turned back to watch the battle.

William had already turned the Prince around and now had the offense. Alex felt a twinge of pride. He had taught William everything he knew about how to gain an advantage in a battle. The lad had learned how to turn a battle and gain victory even in a surprise attack. It was as if he were looking at himself, eighteen years ago, as William commanded the warriors, and they obeyed without question. Alex felt content that he had made the right decision.

William met the Prince on foot, and the warriors were pressed back beyond the edge of the camp. The Prince conceded the battle and rode back to the opposite ridge on the eastern side of the loch to watch the battle. Gideon had also joined the fight and stood next to William to fend off any rear attacks.

The Prince's men didn't fight for long. They departed the camp without a fight. The surprise attack gained the Prince's warriors an additional one hundred points, and the spirit in the MacKenna camp was getting dangerously low. If William could pull off a victory now, he would have earned his right to be Laird.

Alex paused on the ridge. The Prince raised his sword and yelled in Gaelic. Alex smiled at Melissa and turned his horse back toward the Manor House.

"Why didn't you fight?" Melissa held on to him.

"I quit fighting the day you told me it upset you," Alex said, lazily caressing her back.

"You quit for me?" Melissa couldn't believe it.

Alex nodded. "You can show me later how much you're going tae love having me all tae yourself." His smile was charming.

"Aren't you worried about the battle?" She couldn't think straight when he looked at her with that smile.

"The battle was over before we left. William had them on the run." He urged the horse on faster. They had a few precious hours to themselves, and he didn't want to waste a minute of their time together. Melissa soon fell asleep in his arms, and he enjoyed the moments he could look at her beautiful face.

They arrived at the house at dusk, and her things had already arrived with Daniel and were put in Alex's chamber. Robert brought Daniel in the helicopter. Daniel hated to ride a horse, when faster means of transportation were always available. Daniel's first love was a MC12 Mozaratti that he took out on the Autobahn.

224

"You're an amazing man, Daniel." Melissa woke when they arrived. "It takes me hours to pack, and you do it in minutes."

"I am amazing," Daniel agreed and helped her down from the horse, holding her until she could feel her legs again. Alex jumped down next to Melissa. Daniel took the reins and said he would take care of bedding the stallion down for the night. Robert would then take Yorath back to the cottage as the preparations were being made for the final battle.

Melissa looked at Alex, and they both had the same thought. "Hot water!" They both turned to go upstairs for a hot bath. The bath at the cottage had grown cold. They hadn't seen Robert for most of the day, and when he did return, he looked exhausted, but happy and slept most of the day in a hammock by the loch.

Chapter Twenty-One

The Laird's team has been plagued with injuries and misinformation. George is as charming as ever and has promised he will return to London for a while before he goes abroad. Niki was unavailable for a comment on where they will winter this year.

On the Streets with Rosabel

Amber received the report from the Embassy and telephoned Sarah. She dropped her law books on the dining room table. Her last summer school finals had been that morning, and Amber was exhausted from long hours of study before the exams.

"I don't believe this report for a minute. Has anyone heard from her yet?"

"No," Sarah confirmed.

"I'm going to Scotland to rescue my sister," Amber said finally. "Something is wrong."

"I'm going, too. I've got us booked on flights where we connect in New York for the flight to Glasgow. Amber, you won't believe what I found on their web site."

"You cracked their codes?"

"Of course," Sarah gloated. "There are over five hundred names of warriors on this site. I'll tell you all about 'the game' and Laird Alexander G. MacKenna when I meet you in New York."

"Is Chad coming with you?" Amber asked. Sarah's new boyfriend didn't like traveling, especially so far from home.

"No, he's staying here. He said someone has to feed our fish."

Amber laughed. "I'll meet you in New York, and you can tell me all about the game."

***

The hot water was just the earthly side of heaven for Melissa. Alex was detained taking care of business, and she was already soaked with her head under the water and soap bubbles dripping down her face when he joined her.

It was good to be back in civilization again. The hot water was heaven. She could hear him chuckle and opened her eyes.

"Ye have the sweetest smile on your lips." He bent down to kiss her and got his head wet in the process. She looked blissfully happy with the soap rinsing from her hair.

Alex had stopped in the kitchens to meet with Cynthia, their Party Planner who was getting the celebration ready. Alex wanted their supper tonight to be private in his chamber. He wasn't ready to share Melissa with anyone else. This was their night together, and he had every intention of spending those precious moments with Melissa in his arms.

He bent down to kiss the swell of her breast. Tonight, he would tell her everything.

"Hmmm." Melissa reached out and put her arms around him. The hot water splashed down between them and washed the soap away. She was already done with her bath and took the soap from him to start on his chest.

He kissed the side of her neck while she worked her way down his flat stomach. His groan and ardent interest became amazingly apparent as the soap slid down the curly chest hair into the vee on his belly.

Melissa had her hands full of soap when she caressed him clean all the way to his toes. His eyes closed, working for concentration, as her soft hands slid over his hips.

She touched him with such gentleness, and Alex lost all thoughts of being patient. His arms hugged her tightly to him, and his mouth touched hers in a torment of desire. He wanted to feel the heat of her again. He ravished her tender lips, and his tongue delved into her sweet sanctuary. Melissa moaned softly in the back of her throat as his desire pressed against her belly.

Conversation was overrated, he thought. He could bear the torment no longer. He pulled her out of the bath with him and dried her with a sheet.

He laid her across the bed and couldn't wait a moment longer to feel the heat of her surround him. Alex groaned, lost in the warm, slippery haven. He cupped her breast and rubbed his thumb across her nipple. Melissa's breath caught, and she moaned softly against his lips. He held heaven in his arms. The feel of her lips on his, the heat of her body surrounding him, and the touch of her hands on his back and shoulders was all the torment he could endure. He loved her with his heart and soul in those few moments of bliss until she cried out his name, panting and fulfilled.

Her arms held him close, and they rested — the rage of passion abated for the moment.

A knock on their door delivered their supper on a tray from the house staff.

Alex chucked at the blush on her cheeks. He waited until the door was shut and got up to tempt her with supper. She still wasn't willing to eat much, and he was getting concerned. The aroma of garlic filled the room. Melissa's head popped up off the pillow. She was delighted to find chicken on the plate. Alex wrapped his kilt around his hips and handed her the wrapper. The food was so divine, Melissa didn't stop to talk.

"Now I know all your secrets, sweetheart." Alex laughed and handed her glass of wine. He pulled her to his lap, and her head fell back against his shoulder. "Why didn't ye tell me ye didn't like mutton?"

Melissa thought again about the enormous amount of cost it would take to feed so many warriors, and they all seemed to enjoy the aroma. "What makes you think I don't like mutton, my love?" She kissed his ear lobe, trying to distract him.

Alex breathed out slowly to find some concentration. The touch of her lips against his neck was a severe temptation. The warmth of her tongue against his lips made him forget the question. And when she started squirming on his lap, he forgot to speak at all.

The wrapper fell open, and her warm body beckoned his touch. His hand moved over her velvet skin to the curve of her breast. She straddled his hips, and the pressure of her body against his pushed him back against the overstuffed chair.

The room was cool and dim now that the sun had gone down, and the candlelight shimmered reflections from the mirrored bureau. Melissa pulled the tuck out of his tartan, and the heat of her body surrounded him.

His arms went around her, holding her tightly. He had wanted to talk to her; he had so much yet to say before the dawn arrived and he was captured. Alex pulled back to tell her he had to speak to her, but she pressed forward, her sweet lips finding his, and desire overwhelmed any need to speak.

She loved him with her soft body moving against his, and her tender lips beckoned him to forget everything but the magic between them. She whimpered against his tongue which explored her luscious mouth. His hands slid to her hips and pulled her down to fill her completely.

"Alex," Melissa cried out as he took her to ecstasy. His strong arms held her tight as a deep quiver built in her belly. She put her head down on his shoulder, dizzy from the heady feelings.

His hand wound into her hair and pulled her lips back to his. His breathing was ragged against her cheek, and the trembling in her belly began all over again as he passionately claimed her body. And she surrendered her heart to him completely.

"Say it, Melissa," he demanded of her in a low growl. Alex was terrified he would lose her, and with the dawn, his worst fears would be realized. He had to hear it one last time, had to know her heart belonged to him.

"I love you, Alex!" she gasped and clung to him.

He closed his eyes to shut out everything but the feel of her beautiful body joined with his. It was an act of desperation that he claimed her hungrily, demanding that sweet innocence.

Tears stung his eyes; he couldn't bear the thought of never touching her again. The torment was nearly destroying him. Alex couldn't go through another day of his life not knowing she would stay with him and love him for the rest of his days.

The grief and agony of many long years of frustration fell down his cheek in a tear. He inhaled the scent of her, trying to remember every detail of her before she would walk away from him. Their moments together were precious, but now he was out of time and would have to tell her everything.

She called out to him again, and he couldn't hold back any longer. His release brought her with him into ecstasy. Melissa collapsed in his arms, and her eyes were closed. Moments later, his sweet love was sound asleep with her head tucked on his shoulder, her arms around his neck.

Alex held her awhile longer, savoring the feel of her and kissing her gently so not to wake her. She did look tired lately, and the changes in her body were so subtle she probably didn't notice. But he knew there was something very different. There were dark circles under her eyes, and he knew she was exhausted.

The harsh lifestyle had been too much for his lovely lady. She could use a long holiday on the beach, and with that thought, he smiled and set his worst fears aside. He thought about growing old with her, having children, building a home and a life together, and wondered if he would ever get over the horrible fear of losing her.

She clung to him, and he couldn't let go of her. They were destined to love, and he would never give her up without one hell of a fight. No matter what it took, his resolve was set. Alex would find a way and do whatever it took to keep her.

He moved out of the chair, holding her in his arms. She was sound asleep by the time he covered her with flannel sheets and pulled the blanket up around her shoulders. Alex hoped the final battle would be over before she woke in the morning, and he could tell her then about all his demons and the past that haunted him.

He leaned down to kiss her lips one last time and brushed the hair from her face. "I love you, Melissa. More than I ever thought possible. Forgive me, my love."

Alex took a quick bath and found clean clothing in his wardrobe. Melissa slept peacefully and never heard him leave. Daniel was already waiting for him in the Drawing Room.

Gideon, Robert, Iain, Evan, and William made their way through the dark house to the soft glow of the Drawing Room where Daniel and Alex waited. There were papers stacked on the table waiting for signature. Daniel and Alex were seated at the table waiting for their arrival. There was a stand off of wills going on between Daniel and Alex, and the family took a seat at the table to find out what the hell was so important they were dragged back to the house in the middle of the night.

"Where's Melissa?" Gideon asked quietly.

"Sleeping," Alex answered.

Daniel had to ask one last time. "Alex, are ye sure this is what ye want tae do? There has tae be another way."

"I'm certain. This is my choice."

"What will ye do if she will not forgive ye? What if she goes back tae the States?" Daniel had already asked from every possible angle but needed to confirm that Alex was committed to the end result, no matter what path his future took.

"Then I will follow her," Alex said plainly. "I will beg if I have tae, but she will forgive me, and we will have a life together. She is my *Anam Cara,* and I would be lost without her. You have all supported me through the years with your hearts and your loyalty. I couldn't have made it through those years without your love. Now it's time tae step down and support the new Laird of the Celtic Warrior Game."

Alex looked down the row of faces to his youngest brother. "William, you have been named my successor. I am formally resigning as Laird."

William was momentarily speechless. His brothers seemed to know all about this decision because no one argued. They looked at him, waiting for him to figure out that with the stroke of the pen, William would become one of the most powerful men in Europe, and he had just turned eighteen. "*Och,*" he finally uttered and leaned back against his chair to stare at the ceiling.

William's thoughts spun with the possibility. He hadn't planned on devoting all of his life to their business interests as Alex had. He hadn't planned on spending his life in service to anyone but himself. He had planned to study music, not balance sheets and stock markets.

He suddenly realized how comfortable it had always been to be the youngest with six older brothers who had always shouldered the burdens.

"Ye won't be alone, William." Daniel put the papers in front of Alex and handed him a pen. They were signed a moment later. "We will all support ye with the same affection we supported Alex."

"May God help ye," Alex said and laughed. "Aye, there are lots of good memories. Ye took care of me, and now I will help take care of ye, William."

"Alex." William finally found his voice. "What if I don't want the honor?"

Alex smiled. "This wasn't easy for me, William. First of all, ye think of this as an honor not a horrible mistake. Each one of us has a special talent that together we are invincible. I thought long and hard about this before I made my decision. Ye don't get this honor by default. We all thought about the choice tae be made. Ye proved ye're a man this summer and will make a formidable Laird."

"But why not Evan and Iain," William argued. "They are almost finished with law school and would be able tae assume the responsibilities without too much trouble. I haven't started University yet."

"We all agreed ye are the best choice." Daniel stated with authority.

"Aye," Evan agreed. "Ye won't be alone, William. Alex has earned the right tae a little happiness. My future is already set tae support your business interests."

Iain jumped in as well. "And my future, too, is already in your hands, William. Be gentle with me."

That comment got William to laugh a little.

"Don't worry William. Ye will be a good Laird." Alex gave him a pat on the shoulder. "I have faith in your abilities, and ye will do what I did and find a way. Learn from my mistakes and follow your own heart. Duty and honor nearly destroyed my life. Now I have a second chance and a willing angel. I'm not going tae lose it. If ye do not accept this honor, William, no one else will. Ye have all sworn allegiance tae me, and now we all swear allegiance to ye."

Alex took out the sword he had carried every year for his adult life. The ancient runes were still there, and the inlaid gold and gemstones still held the same mystique. The sword had been passed down for every generation since Baron Jolbert brought it to Scotland, and it was now William's turn to lead the battles.

William stood up. Alex handed him the sword. William saw past the older brother who had kept him out of trouble for his entire life. The look in Alex's eyes was one of love. It almost made William step back a few paces. He had always known he was loved but had never really seen it in Alex's eyes until now. William's hand closed over the hilt, and he drew the sword, testing the weight in his hand. The ancient Claymore was still beautifully polished. He sheathed the sword and set it down on the table.

Alex gave him nod of approval. "Ye will do well, William."

Daniel put the paperwork back in his briefcase and sat on the edge of the table. "In a few short years, Iain and Evan will take over my work for the family holdings, and I will also be able tae follow in Alex's footsteps and retire tae a life of debauchery and lust."

Robert said simply, "We believe ye are a man of honor, William. We're all very proud of ye. All of our expertise will be at your disposal. Ye won't be alone."

Gideon opened a bottle of champagne and poured a glass for everyone, except Alex who drank mineral water.

Melissa appeared in the doorway and walked over to the table. She looked like she had just rolled out of bed and could barely keep her eyes open. The last thing in the world she expected was to run in to anyone at this late hour.

"What is the occasion?" she asked sleepily. "Is William in trouble again?"

Chapter Twenty-Two

"I'm crushed." William feigned a painful look. "I'm never in trouble."

"Oh, champagne." Melissa took a sip and set the glass down.

"We were just going tae toast William," Alex said honestly. "Here's tae William."

They lifted their glasses and said, "To William."

"Why?" Melissa asked again.

"Because…" Gideon couldn't lie any longer.

Alex leaned down and kissed her lips. "Because."

"Because," Daniel agreed.

"You're not going to tell me, are you, Alex?" Melissa gave him a frown. "Some day perhaps I'll be accepted by this family beyond your bedroom door. Excuse me, gentleman. Enjoy your celebration."

"Melissa." Alex's voice cracked.

She turned and left the room before Alex could stop her. She had hoped Alex wanted something more. He hadn't in all their time together said anything about marriage or a family.

It was time she accepted the truth. The holiday was beyond her wildest dreams. It was going to be a nightmare to walk out that door and never see Alex and his brothers again. By the time she reached the front doors, the floodgate opened, and tears poured out. Such an intense feeling of sadness came over her. In truth, she knew that one word had said far more than a thousand words; it was because they didn't trust her enough to tell her anything.

Melissa stepped out into the cool night air, needing a walk to clear her jangled nerves. Lately, every little thing was getting to her. She couldn't just cry at the drop of a hat before she had met and loved the most perfect man in the world, but lately, it seemed she could cry in an instant without much provocation.

She needed some time to think, but it wasn't easy trying to put two coherent thoughts together when Alex was around. He could melt any defense she had by looking at her. And when he smiled, her backbone turned into blithering mush.

She walked toward a ridge and noticed the incredible moonlight that lit up the area. She got to the crest and couldn't help but gasp at the beauty. It was as if the Ancient Celtic Gods had opened their pallet and painted a moonscape of breathtaking beauty.

Emerald green and gold reflected in the misty dew and reflected a million diamonds. It was the moon that stunned her. *La Bella Luna*, she thought and reached out her hand to touch it and claim its magic. It had to be the size of Scotland it was so huge. The Hills in the distance were etched into the horizon with a fog settling in on the lowlands.

She stood there, completely mesmerized by the sheer beauty of a country that had completely claimed her heart. The Scotland in all the books she read had fascinated her with its colorful history, and now that she had met so many wonderful and interesting people, she had no idea how she could ever leave. The faint, haunting sound of a bagpipe filled her head, and she knew there was a powerful magic in the air around her.

"I will have a word with you, Alex" William said when his brothers stood and left the room.

Daniel, Gideon, Iain, Evan and Robert walked through the dining room and noticed the front doors were left ajar.

"Hell," Daniel growled. "We are so close tae resolving all of this." They walked out the doors, found her shadow moving in the moonlight, and followed her to watch over her.

The vision stopped them in their tracks. From their viewpoint, she reached out and touched the face of the moon. They felt the magic that surrounded her and her joy. She stood in the midst of a fairy treasure of emeralds and diamonds. The nightgown cast a silvery mist around her, and the shawl fell off one shoulder. She looked sexy and also innocent in the enchantment that wrapped around her.

Mist swirled around her feet. Her golden hair glowed in a halo and fell down her back in shimmering waves. The gentle curves of her body were set in relief against brilliant moonlight.

"I don't think I've ever seen anything that beautiful," Gideon said out loud the thought they all shared. They could feel her tears when her body trembled slightly and her hand dropped to her side. Her head bowed. The defeat in her profile wrenched at their hearts.

Alex slowly walked up behind her. His hands were clasped behind his back, and he stood quietly behind her. The silent tears tore out his heart. "Forgive me, *A Grá*."

Melissa thought for a moment and then asked. "What does that mean?"

"It means my love."

"You hurt me, Alex." The sting was still very fresh in her mind. "Please don't touch me yet." Her mind was made up and had to say what she felt in her heart. "I don't want to be just a toy to be taken out to play with when you desire my body. I want it all. You don't give me a chance to love you or your brothers, and yet, you all cater to my every whim. You think this thing called love means I will sit back and be adored. I don't want a life where I don't get to participate fully in all of the wonder of being alive. You don't need me except in your bedroom. You and your brothers have a bond from spending your lives together, and I have felt like an outsider long enough. I have never mistrusted any of you because I have no reason to — but none of you trust me."

"We all need ye, Melissa. More than ye will ever know." Alex breathed a sigh of agony and realized he had hurt her badly, but he needed only one more day.

Melissa took a deep breath to calm her ragged heart. "I want it all, Alex. I want to be here the day William goes to University to study music, and we get to hear him sing and play for us. And because Robert is so very talented, I want him to know that he has the most beautiful hands in the world. Evan has the heart of a Bard and has so many more stories yet to tell. And because Iain is going to graduate from law school and will — some day — become a judge. And because Gideon is going to be a doctor and, damn it, someone needs to tell him he has a heart of gold. And because someone needs to tell Daniel it's all right to hurt some time. I want to be there the day he finds someone that can see beyond that steel exterior and will love him half as much as I love you. I am going to be there to hug them and tell them they are loved and cherished for the wonderful persons they have become. I want to be their shoulder to cry on when they hurt and someone who will always laugh at their jokes."

"But most of all, I want them to feel they can trust me. I want them to know in their heart that I would die before I would betray them. I love them, but I love you most of all. What you offer me is half of a life. You want me to share your bed but not the joy and sorrow of your life. I don't want the kind of love that isn't filled with all the treasured memories that makes life worth living. The relationship I have with my sisters and my cousins is real. We laugh and cry together. We hurt for each other. We appreciate the gift of love from each other and the honesty and respect that bonds us all tightly together. You are all so perfect…."

Alex put his arms around her. Her head tucked under his chin. "Only in your eyes, my dearest Angel, are we perfect. We're all very human and make mistakes. You are my *A Store*, my darling," he translated. "I ask only for your patience for another day while I put the world back in order. I promise you that by the end of the day things will be very different." She turned in his arms, and his head bent until he tasted the salt on her lips.

"Trust me," he said against her lips.

She had a feeling she had heard him say that once before but thought it was from a dream.

Alex kissed her hard for a moment and then crushed her against his heart. How could he let her go even for a few hours? The path was already laid at his feet. He had only to complete the journey.

His brothers heard it all.

William had tears in his eyes when he heard that she knew he wanted to study music. He had never told anyone. He loved her now in a way that staggered his heart. He would never tell her a lie again, he vowed. He wanted her to know how much he trusted her. They all had a part to play that day, and William stepped into the mantle of Laird and Chief. "Hell," he choked out and turned back to the stables.

Robert would never be able to look at his hands in the same way again. She had said he was a maker of worlds and he wanted to put his arms around her and tell her he loved her and how beautiful their world had become since she became a part of their lives. "Damn." He spun on his heel and followed William.

Evan put his head down and walked away. Not once had any of them had a woman take an interest in their lives, let alone one who had come to love them all. He was stunned to think she knew his heart so well. He had never told anyone about his dream to become an actor and a writer. There were tears in his eyes, and it hurt to breathe. Only once before in his life had he ever cried and that was for a broken leg when he was seven. Now, it took all of his strength to finish what they had started. He tromped toward the stables.

Iain followed Evan to the stables. He stumbled on the path, unable to see past the mist in his eyes. They all knew there would be a price to be paid but had no idea the she would bear the brunt of it all. His heart raged because she was so loving and beautiful. The deception was cruel.

Daniel was the last to leave. "If we hadn't been there for Alex so many years ago when Catherine left him, I couldn't have done what he asked from us," he said to Gideon.

Gideon let out a long, shaky sigh. "I can't do this any more, Daniel. I won't ever lie tae her again."

"Today," Daniel said with conviction. "It all comes together today."

"This is going tae be one hell of a day," Gideon said and braced himself.

Daniel stopped and talked to his courier who waited on the steps for the paperwork that had to be filed in London. The briefcase was handed over, and then Daniel followed his brothers to the stables to play his part in the final battle.

William had Daniel's horse already saddled and waiting. His brothers were in a wicked mood and ready for the battle ahead of them. They all felt the strain of the past few weeks.

The horses moved quietly with their hooves clad in rags to muffle any sound. Moonlight gave them the advantage. Ian had thought of that fact, and William mentally reminded himself to tell Iain how clever he was. The warriors had been moving out during the night, a few at a time so not to draw any attention. Their plan was already in motion. He had only to play his part in the game.

Daniel wouldn't allow his heart to feel anything yet. There were still so many things that could go wrong. He raised his eyes to the heavens, hoping for a miracle.

The sound of thunder closed in around them. Alex held Melissa tightly for a moment, kissed her forehead, and then released her and pushed her into Gideon's arms. "Get her out of here," he growled.

Gideon swept her up into his arms and carried her down the hill. Moments later, Alex was surrounded by his enemy. The Prince's warriors had captured Alex at last. They taunted and jeered at him. Alex watched Gideon disappear down the side of the hill and then waited patiently for the warriors to bind his hands.

"Let it all be finished today," Alex said softly. He was put on a horse and taken away.

He could hear Melissa scream his name, and the sound of hysteria in her voice. He had wanted to prepare her for this day, but he had run out of time.

Melissa screamed for Alex to come back. She was sobbing hysterically by the time Gideon had made it down the hill to take her back to the house. Melissa, he found, could wiggle her way out of just about any hold he had on her. She was desperate to run after Alex to help him. She begged him to help her, and Gideon was furious. Melissa should have been in bed sleeping, not going through this ordeal. He was angry with Alex for not seeing her back to bed immediately instead of hurting her tender heart and making her a witness to his capture.

He couldn't give her a sedative. She needed to be told the truth about their game and what would happen to Alex. She was terrified Alex would be tortured. Gideon's nerves were frayed beyond comprehension.

He hauled her back into the house and took her to the Drawing Room. Cynthia had been awakened by a screaming woman and walked into the room. Gideon asked her to make some tea.

"Why won't you go after him?" Melissa screamed hysterically at Gideon. She was alternately furious with all of them for disappearing just when she needed them all the most and their cavalier attitudes about the capture.

"Where are the warriors? I'll go myself if you won't help me!" Melissa pounded on Gideon's chest, trying to rouse him to save Alex. "Find them Gideon. Get him back. Please? I want him back! Don't let them hurt him!" Her last cry was barely as whisper as pins and needles prinked her eyelids, and breathing became labored and shallow.

With a final sob, Melissa fainted.

Gideon sat down on the couch next to her. She was flushed, and dark circles were etched against her ivory complexion. Cynthia brought in the tea and left to calm the staff that had also been awakened.

"I need a brandy," Gideon growled and poured a glass full. He gulped the fiery amber liquid and let out a long sigh.

Alex had met Cynthia in the kitchen when the catering staff arrived earlier that day and had told her all about the lovely woman that had stumbled into the game. At the moment, Gideon would throttle Alex for scaring Melissa.

He covered her still form on the divan with a tartan blanket. Gideon also took out his medical bag and his stethoscope found her strong, rapid heartbeat which relieved him.

He met Cynthia in the hallway and told her the plans for the day. She cried with joy. "Will your aunt, uncle, and grandfather also be here for the wedding?"

"They are arriving shortly," he answered. "It's going tae be one hell of a day, Cynthia." Gideon followed her into the kitchen. Since the staff was wide-awake, she put them to work preparing for the festivities.

"That's an understatement! I wouldn't miss this party, and I will take care of everything."

"I love ye, darlin'." Gideon gave her a kiss on her lips, and Cynthia shoved him back, laughing.

"You MacKenna boys are going to drive me crazy with your *snogs*. Get out of my kitchen!"

Chapter Twenty-Three

The game of the season is nail-biting close with counter-measures taken on both sides. The Prince is ahead by over 100 points. The race is on to the finish, but who will be the Laird at the end of the game?

On the Streets, with Rosabel

Gideon had time to check in with his office before they rode out to meet William. Daniel's computer booted quickly. He logged in to get his email and sat back to read through the information sent from his office.

Gideon couldn't help breaking out in laughter. He logged off his email just as Daniel walked into the Drawing Room.

Daniel had returned to the house and kissed Cynthia on his way through to the Drawing Room so he could also check his email and waited for the courier to arrive. His cell phone beeped as he walked into the Drawing Room, and his courier arrived via helicopter. Daniel let out a long sigh of relief.

An hour later, Gideon went back to the parlor and woke Melissa, telling her to be dressed and ready to ride out with him in ten minutes. She ran up the stairs and said she would be ready on time. Her cheeks were still pale, but he hoped with something to eat and some fresh air, she would feel better.

The horses were waiting outside, and Gideon had a portable breakfast ready to go for her. Daniel had to stay at the house to finish up some business so he would miss the final battle.

Melissa was eager to see that Alex was unharmed. Now that they knew she could ride a horse on her own, she was given her own horse and saddle. Gideon set a slow pace so she could eat something, but when she finished, he urged them on at a gallop. They rode for nearly ten minutes before Gideon finally slowed the horses down to cool them off. He kept them near the trees and their approach was signaled to William.

Melissa rode beside Gideon through a stand of trees.

"This is where we stop," Gideon explained.

They had a clear view of the valley below, and she noted the Prince and his men were circled around Alex. Alex was bound to a pole in the center of the clearing. Ropes tied his hands together and held him to a ring on the post. He looked relaxed and unharmed. Melissa was grateful. She wasn't sure what she would do if something had happened to him. For the moment, she had to wait out the battle.

"Oh, my God!" Melissa exclaimed. "That's the Prince?" It was the same guy who had visited with her at the Kirk. "I had no idea. When he said he was your cousin, I thought he was fighting with you, not against you. He's a very handsome man."

Gideon smiled. "George is well liked by the ladies." He should know. They had partied together on countless occasions, and George never went home alone.

William had all the pieces in place. Iain and Evan had thought of every detail, and it was now just a matter of timing. They had waited for Gideon to arrive and noticed he was safely tucked into the tree line while Melissa waited on horseback. William signaled to Alex, informing him that Gideon had arrived.

The Prince stood in front of Alex, and the warriors quieted down. "So I have captured the Laird at last. The game is finally won, and I will be the Laird. We have already called London and informed the Bookies of my victory this year. The upset will cost you millions."

"Not exactly," Alex commented. "Your challenge was victory if you captured the Laird. I'm not the Laird. I resigned last night. Daniel filed the papers in London this morning, and William was named my successor." Alex gave the signal. He didn't want to drag this out a moment longer. Melissa was frantic when he left her, and he was worried about her.

Prince George and his army were completely surrounded. They made the mistake of thinking only of their victory, and that left them vulnerable. Iain and Evan were right when they had predicted every turn of events.

William rode at the head of his army and closed the circle around the Prince. William had learned to draw from the strength of his warriors, and they respected his command.

William no longer needed protection, Alex thought. He had stepped into the role of Laird, and Alex felt a wave of gratitude for his youngest brother. Alex was free.

William rode up to the Prince, flanked by Iain and Evan. "You are surrounded, George. Admit defeat."

The Prince drew his sword. "I will not accept defeat, and I challenge the Laird for the title."

William expected he would and drew his sword. It was the sword Alex had given him, the one his ancestor had carried. And William held it with pride, nodding to Alex before taking his position.

Evan rode up and cut the rope holding Alex to the pole.

The battle between William and George began with a clang of swords. Alex kept his distance and waited for the outcome. He watched every move his brother made and silently praised his skill. William was younger, faster, and stronger than George.

William attacked with a fury to keep his opponent on the defense. He landed shattering blows that reverberated in the air around them. He pushed the Prince back until George was panting and finally went down on one knee.

William's army roared their approval.

Evan pulled Alex up behind him and rode to where Gideon and Melissa waited.

William would be remembered for this day for a long time to come. He was hardly winded, and George was panting heavily.

Melissa got down off her horse and waited for Alex. Gideon joined the warriors, and Evan brought Alex to her. Evan left them alone and joined the army. It was an important moment for William and the Bard in Evan didn't want to miss a thing.

Alex took her into his arms and breathed a sigh of relief. He inhaled the scent of her, and his fears calmed. The day wasn't over yet, his mind warned. Alex could feel her tremble.

Melissa's eyes told him how grateful she was that he wasn't harmed. "Gideon told me that you resigned, and William is now the Laird." She could feel him tense up, and she smiled. "I was terrified you were going to be hurt. I can't believe you gave up fighting for me."

His mouth curled in a smile. "William will take over all of my duties. I am proud of him. He will make a formidable Laird, and I will be here tae support him."

Alex bent down to kiss her. The feel of her warm lips against his left him breathless. He tasted and caressed her lovely mouth until he heard her moan softly. Her gaze for him today was brilliant blue-violet, and he couldn't look away.

Melissa loved the way he looked at her. There was always a sparkle of mischief in his soft jade eyes that she knew was just barely under control. He flirted shamelessly with his gaze focused on her.

That quirky smile of his sent her pulse into hyper-drive. Her cheeks had to be hot pink by now, and she felt like she was glowing from head to toe. Her arms were around his neck. She needed to touch him and kiss him again.

"I know ye want me. But ye can't have me yet." Melissa teased.

Alex laughed.

"You need to get out there and help William." She pulled back from his embrace.

Alex looked at her with shock. "I thought ye didn't want me tae fight?"

"Not when I thought someone would kill you every day. That was horrible to live with that worry. Now get

251

out there and help William send the Prince back to England with a complete victory."

He hesitated, unable to move; he couldn't believe she wanted him to fight.

Melissa gave him a smile. "I know you want to get out there and jump into that battle. I'll bet it's taking every ounce of your self-control to stay here with me while men are hacking away at each other just behind you." She handed him the reins to her horse. "Here take this one. Just don't forget where you left me."

His smile almost made her weep with joy. It showed in his flash of white teeth and the light that came into his eyes. She sensed that Alex was no longer in mortal danger and wanted him to help support William. She could tell by the look in his eyes he didn't want to miss the battle.

Alex leaned down and kissed her quick. "I love ye, darlin'."

Alex found a scimitar sword already tied to her saddle. He drew the sword out and turned to enter the battle. No longer their Laird, he was going to have fun for the first time in eighteen years.

The battle had already begun with William and the Prince at the heart of it. Surrounding them Gideon, Robert, Evan, and Iain, held defensive positions around their Laird, protecting his flanks while William battled the Prince. Alex soon joined them, and the roar of approval from the warriors became deafening. Together, as brothers, they quickly turned the battle back on the Prince and had him surrounded. The Prince threw his sword aside and lunged at William.

William sidestepped George and knocked him to the ground. "Ye're getting slow, old man."

The Prince knocked William down with a boot to his mid section. Alex reached down and pulled William up with one hand while defending a blow from a warrior with the other. William spun and dropped the Prince with one kick to his gut, and George went down one last time.

William had a sword at his throat when the Prince looked up. "Admit your defeat, Prince George."

The warriors all raised their swords, and their war cry became their roar of victory. They were warriors and had survived the game one more year.

The army descended upon Melissa with William, the conquering hero, at their lead. William's smile was glorious. He had defeated the Prince and had proven to himself and everyone present, that he was a warrior worthy to lead their army.

Alex pulled Melissa up behind him for the ride back to the Manor House. She wrapped her arms around his waist and laughed with them as they told of William's victory. It was a man's world, and she shook her head in wonder. They all seemed so pleased at the outcome.

Alex, Gideon, Iain, Evan, and Robert rode behind William, their new champion. The warriors rode circles around them, shrieking and screaming in victory.

They had won! Now, the final scores would be tallied, and their new Laird would be announced. Since Alex hadn't participated in many of the battles, they knew someone else held the high score. There were several other possible candidates, including one of the twins who might have won.

They laughed and enjoyed their victory all the way back to the house. Melissa was delighted that Alex was unharmed, and William was now their hero.

Alex helped Melissa down and took a moment to give William a hug.

William looked stunned at the affection. "Ye've been my hero and the only father I've ever known, Alex. Thank ye for kicking me in the arse and forcing me tae sober up."

Alex shoved him hard. "It's hard tae think of ye as my little brother. When they handed ye tae me, a newborn child, hell, I didn't know how tae change a nappy. I'm very proud of ye today."

Gideon stabled his horse and put William in a headlock on their way back to the house. "Don't think for a moment that ye can order us around, little brother."

William slipped out of the headlock and punched Gideon. "Damned right I can. And you will obey me, or I'll have ye mucking out the stables for disobedience."

Gideon rubbed his jaw. "Stables?"

***

Amber and Sarah arrived at the Manor House and demanded to speak to Alexander G. MacKenna. They were escorted into the Drawing Room and told to have a seat and wait. They had a copy of every tabloid they could find that depicted their sister naked in the arms of that barbarian.

"I can't believe Melissa would be involved with a bunch of huge hairy men who run around in skirts and probably ripped the leg off a cow to eat for breakfast," Amber said frostily.

Daniel leaned his head against the doorframe of the Drawing Room and groaned. "Yanks!"

"You can't make out his face, but her smile is absolutely radiant. It just can't be true." Amber was outraged. They couldn't get to Scotland fast enough. "No one is going to destroy Melissa's reputation and get away with it."

Alex and Melissa walked through the front door and had no idea all hell was about to break loose.

Melissa's mouth dropped open when two women stood up from the couch. It wasn't possible to see her sisters standing in the same room with her, was it?

Alex had turned pale with Gideon, Robert, Iain, Evan, and William all standing behind him.

She looked back at Alex who suddenly appeared very nervous "Alex, what's wrong?" For a moment, Melissa was terrified! She stood at the threshold between both worlds and reached a hand out to him to steady the spinning room. "Alex!" she screamed, panicked.

A sob wracked her tight throat. She knew he would disappear in a few moments, and she would be trapped in the future without him. She couldn't bear the thought of losing him.

Melissa's face was white with fear and shock. Alex took the few steps between them to put his arm around her to steady her. "It's all right, love. I'm here," he soothed her with his voice pitched low and soft against her hair.

She held on to the front of his shirt with white knuckles. When her chin tipped up, she had tears streaming down her cheeks. "Don't let go of me," she begged, terrified he would evaporate into the mist.

"Last night I tried tae tell ye something," he began in earnest. "I go' distracted and didn't tell ye everything."

Daniel stood silently watching the ladies. Alex looked at him then. He would remember that look for the rest of his life. Daniel had never seen Alex plead for anything in his life, but he was pleading now for an answer. Daniel nodded. The realization and relief staggered Alex.

He gulped down air as a spasm of fear gripped the back of his neck with icy tentacles. "I didn't tell you that you are not in the year 1745. This is a Celtic Warrior game that we play every year. You just happened to stumble into the midst of our opening battle."

Melissa received the answer with wide-eyed wonder, and he wanted to kick himself for not telling her the truth last night when he had the chance.

"I thought you really were a Celtic God," she chocked out, uncertain if she was angry. "I thought the mist would steal me away from you, and I'd never see you again." She was rambling from weeks of anxiety. "Do you know how scared I was every day? I thought that you would ride off, and I'd never be able to find you. I wondered why no one was ever killed, but I thought it was perhaps part of your magic."

"I'm so sorry, Melissa." Alex felt like a monster.

"You're not Celtic Gods?"

"Only in your eyes, love. We are merely humans."

"Speak for yourself," Evan interjected and found he was the focus of the room frowning at him. He wanted to crawl under the rug and hide.

"Are you sure I'm not in the past? Your game is very realistic." She matched his frown.

"I know, but I didn't want you to leave," Alex said so softly she had to strain to hear him speak.

She looked down at her feet. "I must have looked like an idiot to all of you."

"No!" his brothers said loudly and in unison.

Melissa's sisters had heard enough and pushed their way to stand next to their sister in a protective manner.

"Alex, I'd like you to meet my sisters."

"Oh, we'd like to meet you, too." Amber smiled too sweetly. "Wouldn't we, Sarah?"

Daniel waited for the fireworks to start. Amber was a very tall woman. She was probably what most men would call a statuesque blonde who stood at least six feet tall, thin but shapely, and gorgeous beyond belief. Her smile almost blinded him from across the room.

Sarah was stunningly beautiful with auburn hair, but it was also the fact that her eye color matched her hair color that could drop a man to his knees. He sensed that she was the shy, feisty one.

"Alex, it looks like ye got the runt of the litter." Daniel put on his best lawyer face and stepped into the melee. Melissa was all of five foot two inches tall.

The tension in the room became strained. Amber stared at Alex. The boys, as Melissa loved to call them, all stared at her sisters. Alex stared at Melissa, and she was getting uneasy.

"Melissa, he probably also forgot to mention he's married." Amber looked directly at Alex and made the statement of fact.

Alex flinched, but Melissa also saw sadness in his eyes. Angry, Melissa looked at her sister. "That can't be true. He would have told me." She turned her head to look at Alex and then knew.

He hadn't denied it. Her heart dropped to the floor.

It had finally registered in Melissa's stunned mind that she was still in the present day. She had spent a month running around the hills of Scotland with a married man, convinced she was trapped in the past.

"Ye'd better tell her the truth," Daniel insisted.

Alex watched his world end. He couldn't will his feet to move an inch. He had envisioned taking her in his arms and telling her the entire truth long before now. He had just been so happy. He cleared his throat and exhaled. "Six years ago, I married Catherine." He waited for Daniel to fill in the blanks.

"There's more to tell," Sarah interjected. "I cracked the codes on your Internet site."

"She cracked the codes." Iain sounded horrified. "That isn't possible!"

Alex wouldn't look away from Melissa. The shock and then anger in her eyes was worse than if she had yelled and screamed. Her face had gone completely pale, and she was trembling.

She knew they were all waiting for her to do something, but she didn't care at the moment what anyone wanted. She looked at their faces set in a grim frown and their eyes. So this was the reason for the haunted look in Alex's eyes. The room was spinning around her. It had suddenly become stifling hot inside the hall. Her world had just completely ended.

The memories of him flooded her mind and devastated her senses. How could they withhold such an important detail from her? Was she just a summer fling and now that the game was over he would send her home and return to his wife?

It was ironic that the first man she really, truly loved heart and soul was already married. She took a step back and wanted to run until the pain didn't engulf her heart and feel like it tore her into tiny little pieces of agony.

Evan nudged Gideon with his elbow. "She's going tae faint," he whispered but Gideon's attention was on Alex who looked like he was going to kill someone.

And then it all hit Melissa at once. "You all lied to me, didn't you? You all knew I thought I was in the past. Alex is married and not one of you would tell me the truth." The betrayal crushed her last hope, and a single tear slid down her pale cheek.

"I loved and trusted you all."

Chapter Twenty-Four

The room exploded in shouting people around her. William yelled at Alex, Gideon yelled at William, and Amber yelled at Daniel. When Daniel asked why she was yelling at him, she unleashed the warrior princess and verbally flayed Alex and his brothers alive. Her furious tirade didn't stop for nearly five minutes though Alex and Daniel tried to calm her down.

Melissa felt mercifully numb. She couldn't bear to look at any of them and felt the life drain from her body as tiny pin pricks of black dots clouded her vision. The room was so stifling hot she couldn't get a breath, and her stomach fluttered.

Her knees started to buckle. This had to be just a nightmare. She would wake up in his arms, she was certain, and he would tell her he would never leave her.

Daniel gave in and yelled louder than all of them. "Alex is now legally divorced. Give him a chance tae make it right with your sister."

"He had no right to ruin her reputation with this tabloid trash!" Amber yelled back.

Evan stepped into position and caught Melissa as she fainted. "I'm getting damned good at this," he stated, proud of himself. It was time he took matters into his own hands, literally. He walked out of the room, with Melissa firmly tucked into his arms. He walked out of the house as she started coming around and he had just enough time to put her on the back of a horse and ride off before they knew he was even gone.

Alex saw Evan leave the room with Melissa in his arms. He was suddenly terrified she would never come back. Amber yelled at him, and he truly hated to be rude to her, but he had to go to Melissa and explain. He ran for the door. Evan had just crossed over the ridge. Yorath hadn't been unsaddled yet, and Alex mounted and headed for the ridge.

The entire camp heard the argument, and the warriors decided to take matters into their own hands. The Laird's entire camp was saddled and ready to ride in minutes. They had trained for a quick response, and they weren't about to let her get lost now.

Gideon, Iain, William, and Robert were also saddled and followed Alex. Daniel was left alone with Amber who was now completely furious with them for leaving and wanted to know where they were taking her sister now.

Melissa had her arms around Evan's waist, and her head rested on his shoulder. He could feel her anger through his body. In truth, he hoped she would scream or cry. The silence was unnerving. He still hoped there would be a happy beginning for them all. She had so much to forgive.

They finally came to a stop, and she got off the horse and walked to the shore.

She couldn't speak to Evan or anyone else for that matter. Her thoughts were torn between betrayal and the horrible fear she would never see them again. She stood on the shore, hugging her arms around herself for comfort. Her heart was breaking. They couldn't understand what she felt. Her trust was complete in them, and they didn't trust her with the truth.

Evan stood beside her, helpless.

Melissa began to tremble and walked out into the waves. Her hands covered her face. "No, please not this. Oh, God, I can't bear the thought of losing them all." She dropped to her knees and sobbed hysterically into her hands. The waves crashed against her, soaking her dress, but she was numb to the cold water and her own heart. The pain was unbearable.

Evan picked her up out of the water and brought her back to the shore. "Listen to me, Melissa," he shouted at her to get through her hysteria. Laying her down on the ground, he began to pace, angry it had come to this day at last.

"There is one person in this world that loves you more than life itself. That's my idiot brother, Alex. He doesn't deserve you, and we made sure we told him that every day. If there was any one of us who really objected to the relationship, it was me. I wanted Alex to send you back to your hotel. I didn't want to go through this day and see you hurt or have our world turned upside down by a woman. But you brought something with you we hadn't counted on. In your sweet innocence, you brought love back into our lives. We know you love us, too, so don't give up on all of us because he's a moron. We've had to learn to live with his eccentricities and hoped you would learn to love him enough to see past the Celtic God and know he loved you."

Evan stopped pacing knowing Alex was standing behind him. "Give him a chance tae explain, Melissa." With his arms clasped behind his back, he strolled away with a scowl on his face.

Alex's heart said what he could not find words to say to her.

I stand naked before you
   here in this one moment in time,
I have lost you
   my love come softly now
I must find you
   Can you hear me my dear
    Can you see me so near
Desire
Burns
Forever
Through the mists of time
I will not give up what is meant to be mine
   The wind whispers in your ear
   Is it love that you truly fear?
A dragon's heart will beat forever
   Lost in a reign of fire

Chapter Twenty-Five

Evan's eyes narrowed, and his forehead wrinkled as he stood next to his brother. "Not once did she ask anything from us. She just loved us all. You're not the only one who loses something today, Alex." He walked away before Alex could respond.

Alex reached down to pull her up against him.

Melissa screamed back at him. "No, you don't get to touch me again! You lost that right when your silence made choices for me, and you lied to me." She walked along the shore. "I'm going home now. I won't need a ride so don't bother to lie to me about that, too! I'm just furious enough to walk all the way back to Glasgow."

It broke his heart to think she would leave him. He wanted to protect her from this terrible hurt and knew he was guilty as charged. He ran after her. "Melissa, don't leave me. Let me explain."

She was furious and turned to face him one last time. Tears streaked her face, and she swung at him. "I said you don't get to touch me again, Alex." He ducked and caught her hand. "I was so in love with you. You must have thought I was so stupid and gullible, that I would believe anything you told me. You humiliated me!"

Alex held on to her hand. "No, Melissa. Ye love in ways a *mon* can only hope tae find once in a lifetime. Please, luv, give me a chance tae explain."

Melissa didn't see the warrior's line up on the ridge behind her. The moved quietly and every man dismounted beside his horse. She turned to walk away and noticed warriors surrounded them. Alex's brothers were at the front of the army that faced her, and they went down on one knee.

"We are willing tae make any sacrifice ye want, Melissa. If ye want us tae throw Alex into the ocean, we're more than willing tae accommodate ye. Whatever ye command, your orders will be carried out without question. Tell her the truth, Alex—all of it!"

Alex wanted to crumble into dust. He looked at her angry face and gulped against a dry throat. "You already know we're human."

"And you're about to find out I'm no Angel! Why the hell did you all lie to me?"

Alexander said with reservation. "The warriors train for a year to play for a month, and the rules state that once the game begins, we canna leave until it's over, or we forfeit to the Prince. So once you were in our realm, you had to stay, or we would automatically lose. One of the warriors was called home on an emergency, so we put you in as his replacement."

Melissa's mouth dropped open. "Is that what I meant to all of you? I was just a game token to toss aside once the game is over? I'll spare you effort!"

"No! Don't leave." Alex grabbed hold of her arm and turned her back to face him. Please, luv. Stay."

The warriors were prepared to torture Alex, certain that a few blood curdling screams was appropriate for his actions.

Gideon watched her, and there was so much hope in his eyes she felt a twinge of regret.

Iain looked just plain guilty as hell, and she could tell he felt responsible for his part of the deception.

William looked furious and anxious. She wanted to hug him and tell him she still loved him.

Robert looked like he was lost and near tears. It was Robert's lost puppy look in his eyes that broke her resistance down, and she exhaled loudly. No one had moved a muscle while she considered the options.

Melissa turned to look at Alex. She knew her face must reflect the agony she felt in her heart. She thought about losing him forever and the lifetime of pain that would fill the empty years of her life without him. The dreams of holding his children in her arms and loving him every day of her life were so powerful, she could never let go.

"Melissa, please stay with me," Alex implored her. He got down on one knee in front of the army. "I'm asking ye tae marry me, lass, now that I'm a free man. I would be honored if ye would be my wife."

There was so much hope in his eyes she just couldn't stay angry at him for very long. She turned back to the warriors. "I command you to," she took a deep breath, "return to the house."

They hesitated only a moment, and then William ordered them to follow their orders as commanded. They were ready to do whatever she wanted, short of murdering their brother.

Melissa stood quietly watching the warriors move out. They would have done anything she asked, and she couldn't hurt anyone, no matter how much her heart was breaking. She hoped Alex had one hell of an explanation for his deception.

She could feel him behind her long before his arms reached around her to hold her. Melissa waited until the last warrior had left the area before she turned around. The cold, wet dress clung to her body, making her shiver and his warmth surrounded her.

"You're cold," he said huskily and sat down on the shore holding her close to his heart. He couldn't believe how close to losing her he had been. It was his worst nightmare coming to life, and he couldn't bear the thought of hurting her.

"Melissa, please listen tae me," he pleaded, gently caressing her. "Ye have every right tae hate me. I don't even know where tae begin." He paused to take shaky breath. "When we first met and I looked into your eyes, I wanted ye so badly I couldn't think about anything else. That was lust. You were so sweet and innocent. I knew what I was doing. I didn't think about hurting ye because I couldn't feel anything. And when I did find ou' that first night just how innocent and beautiful ye are, I knew then that I would do whatever it took tae keep ye. Ye brought something wonderful tae my world. I had found hope again."

His voice cracked from the strain of the emotions, all clamoring for relief at the same time. "It is my doing that my brothers became involved. In their defense, ye should know they were furious with me, but I was desperate. I asked them for help. Because they love me, they sacrificed their honor, too. It was a horrible thing tae ask them tae do. The blame belongs tae me. Please forgive them. They love ye, too, lass, and want ye tae be happy."

Alex stroked her hair and rocked her gently. "I love ye so much. But it was a greedy love that didn't care who got hurt. Ye were so innocent, and I wanted that innocence tae restore my broken heart. It wasn't fair tae ye because ye trusted me. The thought of being alone again frightened me worse than facing a hundred warriors. I thought I was only hurting myself because I couldn't live in my dreary world without ye. I am so sorry." He squeezed her to him.

"My marriage to Catherine was arranged as a business deal. She had a title, and I had money. I married her, but I didn't love her. She soon left. Two months later, I ran into a friend of hers at a party and asked about Catherine. She'd been staying at a flat in London, so my brothers and I went tae see her."

"Catherine laughed at me and told me she didn't plan to ever return. She didn't care abou' me nor did she have any intention of returning to the marriage. It was just a business deal to her."

"Daniel told me several years later that I just stood up and walked out. I never saw her or mentioned her name again. It didn't matter tae me. I went through the motions every day but didn't feel alive. Not until an Angel dropped into my world. I held in the palm of my hand, everything I could hope for — but at a terrible price of hurting your tender heart."

"I couldn't tell ye I was already married because in my mind, it was over so long ago, it no longer mattered. Daniel reminded me of the legalities and then forced me tae acknowledge the truth of the matter and make an end of it. Daniel just go' the divorce settled, and I am now a free *mon*. He moved heaven and earth tae get my divorce filed before I would have tae tell ye the truth." Alex couldn't speak for a while and bent to kiss the top of her head. "My *Anam Cara*. I will no' give up what is meant tae be mine. If ye leave me, I will follow ye. Forgive me."

"I love you, Alex, not the Celtic God."

His gaze turned upward, and he knew there was still hope. "Evan was right." Alex continued. "You never asked us for anything and loved us all. I didn't realize how emotionally numb we had all become until ye loved us. For the first time in years, I could finally start tae feel again, and my heart felt safe, even though my head kept telling it this day would come and ye would leave me. When ye held me in your arms, I could put all my demons tae rest. Please luv, stay with me. I am so lost without ye."

"William said you have the most perfect heart he had ever known, and he wanted tae marry ye tae save ye from any dishonor my actions had caused. It was a humbling experience tae have my little brother tell me I had screwed this up."

She tipped her head up to look at him, and his heart started hammering in his chest. She smiled, and his iron control broke down completely as a tear rolled down her cheek. "I couldn't marry William! He's like a little brother to me, and I'm so much in love with you."

"You were the strength for your entire family, Alex. They look up to you and respect you because you do make sacrifices for those you love. I knew you were haunted by something. It showed in my painting, and I didn't ask you what hurt you because I didn't want my own perfect dream to end. I would have to risk losing you because I wasn't an Angel after all, just a silly girl who fell madly in love from the first moment I looked into your eyes. I didn't want the magical dream to end, and I didn't want to lose you, or your brothers. I want your heart to heal and you to feel the strength of my love. Ignoring someone can hurt worse than a direct confrontation. It eats at your hope until you have none left and then leaves you numb. In Catherine's world, you didn't matter. In my world, you are all that does matter."

"Please forgive me, my love." Melissa said softly and looked down at her lap. "If I truly loved you, I should have asked you what haunted you."

"I want ye beyond anything I have ever thought possible. I will love ye forever and always. Melissa, will ye marry me?"

She sat up and brushed a tear from his face. "Yes, Alex. I will marry you—the mortal man—not the Celtic God." The words had bubbled out of her mouth, and she laughed at how wonderful it felt to reveal her fears and be honest with him. "Although, I do have to admit, you do kiss like one of the Gods."

He was laughing and crying at the same time when he pulled her to his lips. She was warm and salty from tears. She kissed him with her heart and fears clearly defined, and he responded tenderly and lovingly.

His voice trembled. "Ye said yes?"

"Yes," she repeated.

Alex laughed and pulled her to her feet. He hugged her and turned in a circle laughing and yelling, "She said yes! We're getting married today," he shouted before carefully setting her back on her feet.

"Daniel has made all the arrangements—just in case ye said yes—and we can be married before dinner."

"Today? Alex, I don't even have a dress."

"Yes, ye do. Ye have your tartan, which is a proper Celtic wedding dress. I won't wait a moment longer, Melissa. If ye want a big church wedding, ye can have it, but I want the marriage tae take place today. I just canna go through this horrible fear of losing ye for one more day, or I'll have a breakdown!"

She laughed at the thought. Her warrior was very human, and it was a great relief to know he could feel love and loss. It made him even more real in her eyes, and she was grateful he really wasn't a Celtic God, after all. Being human meant he was capable of making mistakes, and she felt the strain of the past few weeks drain slowly away.

His brilliant smile and the soft glow in his jade eyes almost made her heart break again. She had almost walked out and left, and now they found they could face the worst of their problems and still love each other.

Alex whistled for his stallion and pulled her up into his lap. He urged the horse onward at a walk as neither one of them was willing to give up their moments of privacy. Both their hearts and fears had been wide open. Now, together they could find peace and contentment. It was at this moment that their hearts beat as one in love.

He bent down to kiss her again. He just couldn't believe she'd said yes. Her mouth was soft and warm. The scent of fresh air and heather filled his breath. She was his Scotland, his love, and soon to be his wife.

He would never forget their first kiss, or how every kiss and touch of her gentle hands brought him a moment of heaven. Alex couldn't erase those years of pain and agony, but finally had hope for a future with a wife who cared about him. It was her loving heart that had brought him to life, and now he would have a home and a future with her.

"Alex, I do have to wonder if the man can make love half as well as you did as a Celtic God."

He grinned. "We will have to find out, luv. We are leaving tomorrow for our honeymoon," he said against her lips. "I realized I had forgotten tae mention that I planned tae take ye tae The *Isle of Mor* in the Caribbean."

"But how can we afford that? Alex, from what I've seen, the entire clan doesn't have the kind of money that a honeymoon in the Caribbean would cost."

"I think I forgot to mention that you would also be mistress of several houses."

"Several? So you're not dirt poor?"

"No. What made you think we were poor?"

"You never ate anything you didn't steal."

"That's part of the Celtic Warrior Game. We get points for thieving. We just didn't know ye didn't like mutton, or we would have found something else for ye tae eat. We were half crazy trying tae get ye tae eat anything, lass."

272

The rode on for a few moments, and then he said softly in her ear, "tell me again. I need tae hear it one more time."

"You're very demanding for a man I have just agreed to marry. Perhaps I should think about this just a wee bit longer?"

"You've got ten seconds." He smiled in a delightfully wicked way.

"Yes," she said softly. He nuzzled her ear and held the sensitive ear lobe between his teeth. She was wrapped up in his tartan, and he warmed her against his muscled body.

"Yes," she said again, and he chuckled softly and slid his tongue over her soft lips.

"Oh God, yes," she groaned. "That's cheating!"

"No, *A Grá*, that's effective."

Chapter Twenty-Six

I have an official invitation to the Victory celebration from the Laird of the Game. Prince George remains the favorite till the end. This is going to be an exciting evening when the winner is announced. The note I received also said there were still a few surprises in store for their guests so I'm ready for anything.

On the Streets, with Rosabel

Daniel let out a low growl and knew he needed to finish his task. They were all waiting to find out what would happen. "Now let's presume," he began in his best lawyer voice. "My brother has managed to pull off a miracle, and she will agree tae marry him."

Amber sat at the table. Her legs were crossed and she was looking very bored. She quickly caught on to where Daniel was going. "I presume you're talking about a pre-nuptial agreement?"

"Yes." He blinked at her.

"Then I can speak for her on this." Amber sauntered up to the bar and selected her favorite tequila. "Nice." She also took out a bowl of limes and collected salt and two shot glasses.

Her smile dazzled Daniel when she set the bottle down in the middle of the table. She placed a shot glass in front of him. "The rules are simple. Every time we agree on an item, we get a shot of tequila."

Daniel's eyes sparkled with the challenge.

Amber huffed. "I just can't argue with a man in a skirt. Do you mind putting on a pair of pants?"

"It's a Kilt," Daniel corrected, equally huffed. "It's appropriate attire for the Highlands of Scotland." The burr in his voice became evident when he was riled, and Daniel was ready to fight.

"Perhaps it is," Amber yelled inches from his face. "But I can't stop myself from wondering what you have on under it!"

***

"It's abou' time." Robert was completely out of patience. The stallion walked slowly toward the house, and they strained for any indication of the outcome. Iain went inside to get Daniel and Amber. They hadn't stopped shouting at each other, and if Iain hadn't stepped between them, they wouldn't have heard him.

William felt as if there were steel talons on his heart. If Alex could resolve the relationship with Melissa, she was lost to him forever. If Alex couldn't, they would both be heartbroken. There was a price to be paid either way, and William hoped he could console her broken heart.

Daniel and Amber took a seat next to Evan. It seemed to take forever for Alex and Melissa to finally arrive.

Robert stepped forward and held on to the stallion's halter while Alex jumped down and helped Melissa to the ground. Alex held her a moment longer so she could feel her legs again.

"I am the luckiest man alive. She said yes!" Alex kissed her again.

The group behind them broke out in cheers, tears, and laughter. There was lots of hugging and kissing. Melissa got hugged by all of Alex's brothers.

"I'm going tae like having sisters." Alex guffawed. "We have a wedding in fifteen minutes." He took Melissa's hand in his and tugged her up the stairs.

"The priest is waiting at the Kirk." Daniel had personally seen to all the details. "Ye'd better hurry, Alex!" Daniel reminded him of the time.

Aunt Marianne and Uncle Adrian arrived by helicopter along with their esteemed Grandfather Sean MacKenna. Daniel walked up to meet the family members that had been given short notice of the upcoming weddings.

A beautiful young lady with sparkling dark eyes walked out of the house. She met Iain on the stairs, and he reached his hand out to her. Iain's smile could dazzle the morning sun. She wore a strapless white satin wedding dress with pale pink ribbons laced to crisscross up the bodice. Small pale pink silk rose buds were scattered over the satin skirt that hung loosely to her ankles.

"Hello, sweetheart," Iain said and reached out to take her hand. "Ye look beautiful, darling. We'll do formal introductions later since we're about tae have a wedding. Everyone, may I introduce my lovely Bonnie and her friend, Emily, who will be standing up for her."

"Hello, Bonnie and Emily," Amber said, walking down the stairs with Daniel. But she stopped in her tracks as a drop-dead gorgeous man walked up to them, and Daniel greeted him casually.

"George, you're just in time. Alex and Melissa are getting married, too." Daniel couldn't help but notice Amber's reaction to his cousin or his cousin's reaction to Amber. They looked star struck at each other, and he was about to issue drooling rags when he cleared his throat and took Amber's arm. He nearly had to drag her away from George, who suddenly looked very lonely.

"It's a ploy," Daniel said testily. "George hasn't been lonely for a single day in his entire life."

"I can see why," Amber said dreamily. "Wow. That guy is hot."

Daniel rolled his eyes. They had heard it all. Normally, Daniel didn't have any trouble getting a woman to notice him, but Amber didn't seem to remember she was walking on the path with him.

Alex gave Melissa five minutes to get ready. He put on a clean shirt and kilt while she changed into her dress and brushed her hair.

They walked to the Kirk together, relieved the day had turned out to be sunny and dry. Melissa was introduced to their aunt and uncle, Adrian and Marianne, and their infamous grandfather who had made a fortune gambling on the outcome of the game.

Rebecca, Agotha, Rosabel, Bridget, and Niki walked in just before Iain and Bonnie said their vows. Niki sat beside George, and he put his arm around her. Agotha sat beside Robert who took her hand in his and kissed her fingertips.

Rosabel had arrived at the house in time to hear the news of the weddings and joined the group walking to the Kirk. Bridget looked calm now that she was sedated, and they all wanted to meet the infamous Melissa!

Rosabel could only imagine the sparks that would be flying that evening. It was obvious Rebecca was preoccupied and deep in thought about something. Bridget was also in love with Alexander and wasn't about to concede their long-term association to a Yank.

Rosabel introduced herself. While Bridget smiled, Rebecca looked terrified, but Rosabel quickly assured her she had a personal invitation from Gideon. It was only a slight exaggeration.

Rosabel's curiosity was piqued when she arrived and there was a wedding cake that would feed an army being delivered in a helicopter along with Russian caviar and a shipment of champagne.

Chapter Twenty-Seven
A time for forever…

The Priest began with Iain and Bonnie.

The vows were beautiful, and Sarah filmed the event, including the stunning men who played the bagpipes. The warriors lined the path with their swords held aloft, greeting the happy couple.

The Priest addressed the witnesses in the Kirk. "I ask all of you to support and encourage this couple in keeping their commitment, promises, and vows. If you so agree, I ask that you repeat after me and say, Aye."

"Aye," was said loudly enough to shake the rafters.

Iain looked deliriously happy and slipped a gold band on Bonnie's finger.

She reached up to touch his cheek. The love she held for him sparkled in her tear filled eyes. Her bouquet of rose buds tied with pale pink ribbons was handed to Emily who stood beside her.

Daniel stood up for Iain and got a little misty eyed when he handed the ring over to Iain.

The happy couple was introduced to the family as Mr. and Mrs. Iain MacKenna, and Bonnie's mother and father greeted the groom. Alex shook Iain's hand and gave him a hearty congratulation.

Melissa hugged Iain and said to Bonnie, "We are going to be the best of friends."

Bonnie brushed a tear aside and hugged Melissa back. "Oh, we have so much to talk about."

"Traitor," Bridget said quietly under her breath, and Rebecca nudged her with an elbow.

Melissa would always remember the warm glow of stained glass windows and the brilliant smile on Alex's face while the Priest read their vows. In his eyes, she could see their children and days of love and laughter. She could hold him forever, and the joy overflowed in her heart. There were no doubts in her mind they would be happy. There was no hesitation when she said, "I will, forever and always."

Amber, who stood up for her sister, handed her a ring for Alex. A little taken aback at the appearance of a ring, Melissa slipped the gold band onto Alex's finger. Gideon then handed Alex a ring for Melissa.

Alex took her hand in his, and the ring slid perfectly onto her finger. He then tenderly kissed her fingertips.

I love you so much it hurts. Though she thought the words, she knew they showed in her eyes. The Priest asked again if their family would support Alex and Melissa's commitment, promises, and vows.

"Aye," was repeated loud enough to drown out Bridget's antagonistic "nay".

They took such good care of her and had gotten all of the details right. The gold band fit her, and she had to wonder how they did it considering she didn't wear any rings. They were amazing men.

The Priest gave them a blessing and introduced them as, "Mr. and Mrs. Alexander Girard MacKenna."

Alex breathed a sigh of relief. He felt a little shaky, considering everything they had planned was executed to perfection. His love, his wife, was now safely tucked into his arms. The sparkle of love reflected in her eyes as he bent to kiss her.

"*Go deo, a grá,*" he whispered and touched the warmth of her lips with his. His eyes closed, and he felt true contentment. The abyss in his heart had begun to heal; she brought such joy into all their lives. The warmth of her mouth was his safe haven. He loved her with his kiss, with his heart, and his soul.

There were tears streaming down her cheeks when she looked up at her handsome warrior. "Forever and always, my love," she whispered back. Melissa was overwhelmed with emotion and wrapped her arms around his neck, sobbing onto his clean shirt.

Evan looked sad for a moment. "Bloody Hell, I'd cry, too, if I had tae marry him."

Amber looked at Evan, shocked at his statement and then thought about what he had said. It was Amber who started laughing first they would all recall when the details of that day were remembered. She started with a body-rocking laughter that soon got everyone else laughing, too. It broke the enormous amount of tension they had been under.

The group departed the Kirk.

Daniel held out his arm for Rebecca, and she walked away with him. They chatted on about the game with George and Niki.

Gideon was delighted to find Rosabel and offered to escort her to the party. Rosabel didn't apologize for crashing the wedding, and hoped she'd get the exclusive story on the weddings of the decade.

Marianne and Adrian walked with the younger boys back to the party. There were lots of hugs and kisses for their beautiful Aunt Marianne and hearty shoves for their uncle, Adrian.

Their grandfather walked with Bridget. William was last in line to congratulate his brothers and just happened to be available to escort Emily to the party. The pretty, young lady blushed and placed her hand in his.

Alex and Melissa were given a few minutes of privacy before the party would begin.

Alex leaned back against the pew and held her close. She couldn't quit crying and had soaked the front of his shirt. It was a small price to pay, he thought.

Somehow, they had just pulled off a miracle. Daniel had gone to the ends of the world to give him this gift.

"I don't want tae let go of ye," he said softly when she began to quiet.

"I love you, Alex. Don't ever stop loving me." She pulled back a little and looked up at him. "I am the happiest woman alive!"

"And the most beautiful." His voice was a husky growl. "We will have a happy life together. Ye are my *Anam Cara*, Melissa. I never knew what it meant tae be happy. I had work tae do, and problems tae solve, but never knew this euphoria called love."

"Love is beautiful and terrifying," she agreed.

"You're going tae have tae wait until later tae be properly bedded," he teased.

"Oh, and what would you call what we've been doing for the past four weeks?" She looked aghast. "If that wasn't proper bedding, perhaps I should call one of your brothers back here and try them out first."

"They wouldn't dare touch ye now." He gave her a mock glare which was tinged with smugness.

"Perhaps they wouldn't," she teased softly.

"*Och*, ye wouldn't dare." Alex frowned, the cockiness erased from his face by a fierce frown.

Melissa turned, smiled at him, reached out, and took his hand. They walked out into the sunshine and paused to pay their respects at the stone Angel that guarded his ancestors.

"I think that I love ye as much as the Baron loved his Lisette," Alex said fondly. "They sacrificed so much for their love and knew a rare kind of happiness. It's been said that they died in each other's arms, but no' before they grew old together. I have that kind of love with ye, lass, and I'm certain we will live a long a happy life."

"I feel as if I know them." Melissa hugged her husband close to her.

Alex had finally found the kind of love his parents had shared.

***

Melissa found her luggage had arrived and changed her clothing for the party. Alex met her at the bottom of the stairs.

She wore a pearl beaded white tank top and a drape short skirt with a side tie that was made of plaid georgette and rayon that swished and swayed when she walked. Her shoes were ankle wrap high heels, and her hair was piled up on her head with a wild abandon of curls hanging down to her neck.

"God, ye are sexy." Alex kissed her fingertips. "Ye take my breath away."

She realized she hadn't seen Alex in anything but his Kilt, and tonight he wore black slacks and a black shirt. "Wow! You are one handsome man, Alex MacKenna."

She pulled his head down for a kiss. He kissed her tenderly, lovingly. They walked out of the house on to the lawn that was prepared for the party.

Melissa met up with her sisters at the bar and got a glass of champagne for a toast. "Here's to the men in our lives. May they be warm, willing, and wonderful."

She had barely swallowed a sip when Evan sauntered by. He gave her a hug, took the glass from her hand, gulped it down, and gave her a big kiss and an empty glass.

Amber laughed. "I can't believe these guys. They aren't the barbarians we thought they were."

"They are all charming." Melissa twirled the glass in her hands.

Alex and George met and shook hands. "It was a good game."

George smiled. "I was certain we'd win this year."

Melissa joined Alex, and he draped his arm around her. "I'd like tae introduce you tae my wife. Melissa, this is my cousin, George."

"We have met." Melissa smiled. "You're the wandering art critic."

"That was a sneaky move, cousin." There was a hint of displeasure in Alex's voice.

"This was my final season," George announced. "I am also retiring. My brother, Richard, will be taking over my duties. He should be here shortly." The object of George's affection arrived and turned the heads of a hundred warriors. "I'd like to introduce Melissa to my love. Niki, this is Melissa."

Melissa was instantly jealous of her long legs. Niki wasn't that tall, but in high heels, she looked elegant. She walked like she was on a runway, and Niki's blue eyes, dark hair, and flawless ivory complexion could make any woman beg for her secrets. She didn't just walk, she caressed the earth with long strides and a sway to her hips that stunned all who watched her.

"It's very nice to meet you, Melissa." Niki absently draped her hand through the crook of George's arm. "It's good to see you again, Laird MacKenna. Congratulations on your victory."

Alex took Melissa's hand in his. "It is a glorious day, indeed!"

Chapter Twenty-Eight

The ceremony began, and Alex stepped forward to announce William, his successor. "Many of ye already know I resigned my office and named my youngest brother, William, as Laird until a winner could be announced today."

There was a lot of cheering, and William raised a mug of ale. "I was the Laird for a day."

"We still don't have the final scores for the game," Alex announced. There was a heated debate going on at the Judge's table, and the warriors waited with anxiety as the final points were tallied.

Evan and Prince George were called to the Judge's table to review the points.

Alex joined Gideon and Melissa while they waited for the outcome.

"It's too close to call," Gideon said quietly.

The tension was thick in the air. You could hear a child cough from the hill it was so quiet. The argument was raging, and Evan was meticulous with his notes.

"What's wrong?" Melissa was worried.

"I didn't fight verra much this year," Alex said softly. He knew the warriors were waiting for the outcome. There was so much at stake.

"Aye, and it's a good thing ye have such a verra courageous wumman tae protect ye," Iain grinned.

Gideon snapped his fingers, as if he had just remembered something important, and ran over to speak to Evan. From what they could see, Evan brought out his journal, and they entered the information. Gideon and Evan were satisfied and stood talking to George for a few minutes before returning.

Gideon stood beside Melissa and introduced Rosabel. The Malaysian woman held out her hand and greeted Melissa with a smile. "I have written so much about you already it is nice to meet you at last. I hope you won't hold the comments against me? I have readers to please, and they love the hot gossip about the MacKennas."

Melissa could tell what attracted Gideon. Her exotic beauty and long, straight black hair and ruby lipstick could make any man crumble to his knees. Rosabel's eyes were dark and a sparkle indicated there was much more going on than Gideon was willing to tell.

"I am delighted to meet you, Rosabel." Melissa could see Gideon slowly exhale.

Gideon smiled at Melissa and nodded in an unspoken understanding that he would explain the odd comments at a later time. He had troubled over their meeting for some time, knowing Melissa may eventually read what Rosabel had written about her.

Amber and the MacKennas' grandfather were in a heated debate about international politics at the punch bowl, and for a brief moment, Melissa worried if Sean could withstand Amber's fierce temper.

Sarah was busy getting the entire day on film and being introduced to so many warriors she couldn't keep track.

Alexander was called to the judge's table and given the envelope to announce the winners.

The party hushed as hundreds of warriors waited for the announcement.

"Alex has won eighteen years in a row. The winner accepts the responsibility of Laird of the Game," Gideon explained.

Alex swaggered across the stage, comfortable in his role as Laird for so many years. "We do have some verra important business before the winners are announced. Where is VixenBlade?" he asked the crowd.

"Where's Robert?" One warrior called out from the crowd, and Alex smiled. It was obvious they were a hot item. They couldn't keep their hands off each other.

Cynthia ran up to the stage and handed a microphone to Alex so every one of the twenty-five hundred guests would hear him.

Agotha walked on the stage, and Alex took her hand. "May I introduce the lovely VixenBlade. Agotha trains the warriors' Florentine style fighting with scimitar swords. She is ruthless, relentless, and will kick your arse if ye don't defend yourself."

There was a lot of whistling and cheering as Agotha walked across the stage. She looked beautiful in a long black silk evening gown with spaghetti straps across her back and a deep plunging vee neckline that was held in place by a criss-cross row of rubies on her chest. No one would ever guess they had seen her sweaty and dirty from fighting and her hair in a ponytail instead of the delicate *coiffure*.

Agotha was asked to say a few words to the warriors, and she walked to the edge of the stage. "Next year," she began in earnest. "I won't be so nice tae ye. I'm going tae kick your arse, ye miserable excuses for warriors. Don't think for a minute ye get tae rest on your bums. We will work even harder!"

Robert walked on stage with them. He had already warned Alex about his plans, so Alex stepped back.

Robert took her hand in his. "Marry me."

Agotha looked at him in shock. "Are ye out of yer blithering mind, Robert? We're in front of a crowd!"

He ignored the comment. "Marry me, my sweet Agotha."

"*Och*," she said and pushed him back hard. "Ye've been out in the sun too long."

"I'm crazy about ye, luv, and I'm not giving up till ye say yes."

"Robert ye've gone daft," she proclaimed.

"I am, lass, crazy in love with ye. Marry me and put me out of my misery."

"All right!" she yelled the words, and Robert stood to kiss her soundly on her ruby lips.

Agotha handed the microphone back to Alex. She said quietly so that only he could hear her. "Next year I will be in the battle, or ye can find a new trainer." She walked off the stage with Robert, and they got a rousing cheer from the warriors.

"We have another person tae thank for our success," Alex continued. "Where is Rebel?"

Daniel and Rebecca were walking toward the stage when Alex made the announcement.

Rebecca wore a beautiful evening gown of long blue silk that had a lace overlay that touched the tops of her high heels. With a shawl over her arms and her red hair in long ringlets, she was a stunning sight to behold and received lots of whistles and cheers from the warriors.

Alex handed her the microphone, and she turned to address the warriors. "Next year, ye will beg for mercy," she said with conviction, "because I will be here tae kick your arse every day." She handed the microphone back to Alex and glared at him.

"Weel then, we have a change in the program for next year. It seems our most beautiful and prominent trainers will be joining us for the game."

The reactions ranged from stunned to cheers. Eventually the cheers overwhelmed the groans. Agotha and Rebecca had earned the right to fight in the game.

"Are they going tae strip nekked and jump into the Lock with us?" One warrior yelled.

"We can only pray," William yelled back.

"At least we'll know where tae find Robert," another warrior shouted.

"Yeah, in the hospital after Agotha gets through with him," another responded, and whoops of laughter echoed through the crowd.

The winners were announced starting with third place. Evan and Iain jointly won that award for outstanding battle tactics, and together swaggered forward to claim the statue of a bronze warrior.

George and his brother, Richard, moved to the side of the stage in preparation for the announcement of George's retirement and replacement.

"Ye canna be serious!" Rebecca whispered to Cheri, but the anger in her voice was unmistakable. "Richard is a Sassenach! He is the enemy. Ye canna do this tae me, Cheri. You're my best friend in the world!"

Cheri was determined to meet the new Prince. "He is absolutely beautiful," she whispered back to Rebecca. "Why would I care if he's English? I'm from New York, and it doesn't matter to me where he comes from."

"How can ye say ye're my friend and then run off with—him?"

"You are holding an ancient grudge," Cheri said, and rolled her eyes. "This is the twenty-first century not ancient Scotland. He's tall and handsome."

"He's blonde and English!" Rebecca felt the sting of betrayal. "How could ye not honor my wishes?"

Cheri had already decided she was going to meet Richard after the introduction. Rebecca wouldn't understand her interest in Richard, but no matter what it took, she was going to meet him.

"Second place goes to Prince George for extraordinary battle tactics," Alex announced.

George accepted the award and bowed. Alex handed him the microphone, and George made his announcement.

"This is the last year I will be Prince of the Game. I have many fond memories over the past twenty years to take with me into retirement. My lovely, Niki, and I thank you for the years of loyalty and support. My brother, Richard, will now take my place."

Richard waved from the crowd in response.

Alex put his arms behind his back and stood with his feet braced apart. They waited for the final envelope to announce the winner of the game. He winked at Melissa. The judges brought him the envelope, and Alex tore it open. The astonishment on his face was evident to the crowd.

"The winner and Laird of the Game — is William MacKenna! The Laird's team wins again this year!"

William accepted his award and the responsibility. There was a great deal of cheers as Alex stepped aside, and William stepped forward.

Alex bounded off the stage and wrapped Melissa in his arms! "You did it, lass! I didn't fight — but you did!"

"What are you talking about, Alex?" Melissa was equally astonished. "I didn't fight."

"Yes, you did," Evan and Gideon corrected her. "That night when you and Iain went frolicking around the countryside, you held a sword in your own hand, and you landed the blow that saved Iain from capture. The score was tied between the Laird's warriors and the Prince's army. Since you were listed as a warrior, you claimed the winning fifty points for the team! William had the highest-ranking points and won the Lairdship, but it's the Clan that wins the money! You just won £10,000 pounds for every member of the Clan!"

The warriors went mad with excitement and cheered their Angel! She had brought them to victory after all.

Alex took Melissa in his arms and leaned down to whisper in her ear. "I love you."

They were first in line to swear their fealty to their new Laird of the Game. Alex explained the custom, and she was enchanted. Alex told William he was proud of him, and Melissa kissed his cheek with tears in her eyes as she congratulated him.

William strolled through the crowd with his arms clasped behind his back. The swagger was every bit a MacKenna, Melissa thought.

The ceremony concluded, and the dance began. There were so many people packed into the area that Melissa hadn't seen her sisters for an hour.

Alex took Melissa outside to the garden. "Now I have all the time in the world." He captured her small hand and kissed her fingers. The ring slipped on her finger and fit perfectly. "There." He said. "You are properly engaged."

The diamond was stunning. She looked at the ring and gasped, "Alex! We could buy an entire house with that ring. Might I remind you that you that we are both unemployed at the moment."

He smiled. "Don't worry, love. We can afford it. I wanted tae give ye that ring last night but ye fell asleep on me."

"Oh Alex, I'm so happy." She kissed him soundly.

The warriors were all in high spirits. It was hysterical to see them get down and funky to sing about William's first defeat.

"He was in the right place, must have been the wrong time." William took the jest with a good-natured shrug.

Alex and Melissa found Amber and Sean, drinking tequila shots at the bar. Because the night was cool, Alex retrieved Melissa's shawl from the house to keep her warm. She was shivering in the short skirt and pearl beaded tank top.

Alex left Melissa's side for a few moments and met up with Iain at the bar.

"Are ye happy, Alex?" Iain asked the question but already knew the answer.

"Iain, I am ecstatic." Alex smiled again. "And ye look happy too, little brother. Where's Evan?" He leaned against the bar.

Iain pointed him out. Evan was having an argument with Beth, his girlfriend, and they saw her slap him.

"Ewww, that had tae hurt." Alex chuckled.

"I am happy, by the way," Iain responded. "Bonnie wants me tae finish school. We want tae build a home in Scotland."

"It's a good thing I bought that piece of property several years ago," Alex agreed. "We can build an entire village where the river runs under the trees and still have room for our children tae grow up."

Alex looked for Melissa. He found her leaning up against Daniel who had an arm around her and Rebecca. They laughed and hugged each other while Daniel introduced Rebecca.

Melissa hadn't stopped smiling for hours and was delighted to meet the woman she had heard so much about. "I am so delighted to meet you, Rebecca. I have heard so many wonderful tales about your training. Please consider training me to properly ride. I tried it once, and they laughed themselves sick."

"I thought ye did verra well," Daniel argued. "Ye saved Iain's life!"

"I don't know how to ride, Daniel. Not like you all do. Rebecca, I understand you are a graphic artist, too! I can't wait to get some time to talk to you."

Rebecca couldn't help but like Melissa a little. "I am an artist and would be happy tae teach ye how tae ride."

Melissa went in search of another glass of champagne and found Cynthia, the woman who planned the party and the banquet. Melissa congratulated her on the party. It was a smashing success and Cynthia was delighted to meet Alex's new wife.

Melissa reached out and took Cynthia's hand. "Please tell me that dinner won't include mutton."

Cynthia laughed. "I think every one of the MacKenna boys have warned me that if there is one ounce of mutton, you will be quite ill."

"Oh, thank you." Just the thought was enough to make Melissa queasy.

They also got a chance to cut their wedding cake, and Alex nibbled the icing from her lips. He was soon pulled away to settle an argument but he sent William to take care of the incident.

Alex found Melissa on her way to the bar and danced her out to the middle of the floor. There was a loving glow in his eyes. They played a slow song, and she wrapped her arms around his neck. He bent and lifted her up against him, nearly crushing her to him while her feet dangled a foot off the floor.

William took his position seriously, they all noted, when he asked for the music to stop and commanded their attention.

"As my first official announcement, I would like tae congratulate my brother, Iain, and the lovely Bonnie on their wedding day." There were lots of cheers for the groom and his lovely bride.

"And my second official announcement is to congratulate my brother, Alex, and the lovely Melissa on their wedding day." There were several groans from those who had hoped until the bitter end that she would become available. "There are hearts breaking all over the *Balquhidder* tonight," William said fondly.

Agotha appeared at Robert's side, and they intercepted Bridget at the champagne fountain.

"It's Bobby MacKenna!" Bridget was staggering.

"Ye've had enough tae drink, Bridget." Robert was amused. "Time tae call it a night, lass, and sleep it off."

William walked by and noticed Bridget was drunk. Melissa caught up to her sisters, and they headed for the house to find a bathroom.

"Nooooo!" Bridget held a glass of champagne in one hand and a bottle in the other. "Oh, please, Billy. Let me dunk Melissa's head in the champagne fountain just once? It will make me feel better," she pleaded with a smile. The beautiful blonde was broken-hearted.

Robert looked at William. "She's your Personal Assistant now William. Perhaps ye should put her tae sleep on the couch in the study? I canna hit a woman."

William shrugged "I canna do it either."

Bridget had other plans. She stumbled forward and tried to dump the glass of champagne down the front of Melissa's top. "He was mine!"

Melissa gasped and stepped back a pace. The champagne missed her by inches. "Not any more and I'm not a sharing type of lady. He's mine, ye ken?"

Robert and William were clearly impressed.

Amber punched Bridget on the chin, and she fell into William's arms.

"Ye go' a hell-of-a punch there, Amber darlin'. I'm verra impressed," Robert said casually, as if they had to knock out drunk and disorderly women every day.

William draped Bridget over his shoulder and addressed Robert. "She's going back tae London on the next chopper."

"Smart *mon*," Robert said. He wanted to get Agotha alone for a few minutes and remind her how much she loved him.

Grandfather dropped by to find out what the ruckus was about but only nodded as Bridget was hauled away.

He offered Amber the crook of his arm. "'Tis a pity we canna put ye into the game, lass. Tha' was a good punch! Ah well, it's time for champagne."

"I'm going with you," Amber insisted.

Melissa and Sarah picked their way through the crowd. There were well over two thousand people in the area. Torches were lit on the hills, and smaller groups were cloistered into family bands. Children ran through the crowd and played mock warrior games like their powerful fathers.

It was mayhem! There were warriors dancing to a wild Highland gig, and encampments sharing kegs of beer! Melissa and her sisters were introduced to groups as they made their way across the field.

Alex was getting worried that she had been gone too long. He found her talking to the wives and mothers of the warriors and reassuring them the warriors were absolute gentlemen during the game.

"Excuse me, ladies," Alex bowed low. "I'd like tae dance with my beautiful wife."

Melissa laughed. He could be so bloody charming when he wanted something.

Daniel and Amber made a special announcement. "We have a song just for Alex and Melissa."

Alex dipped her down and kissed the base of Melissa's throat. That got cheers from the party. The music was Carlos Santana and the song, The Game of Love. Melissa got her third thrill of the evening. Alex dipped her, spun her, and held her so close she could feel the muscles in his thighs against her legs. He could dance in the same powerful, seductive way he made love to her, and it was playing havoc on her senses.

"I want you to promise me something, Alex."

"Anything, *A Grá*." He caressed her back.

"Promise me that beautiful, wonderful things happen now. This is only the beginning and what happens next is truly amazing."

Alex could feel his throat tighten, and his eyes stung in unexpected emotion. She had repeated back to him what he had said to her their first night together. "I promise." He thought about trying to soothe her fears, but his voice was gone. He loved her more than he could ever comprehend.

Somewhere out beyond the fairy mounds, a bagpipe played a haunting melody; and on the ridge stood a loving couple that watched only a moment longer, and then disappeared into the magical mist of Scotland.

For a sneak preview of Laird of the Night, the sequel to Laird of the Game, please visit Lori's website at www.lorileigh.com.

Lori Leigh

Vintage Romance Publishing offers the finest in historical romance, inspirational, non-fiction, poetry, and books for children. Visit us on the web at www.vrpublishing.com for more history, more adventure and more titles.